The Phantom of Forest Lawn

Romance and Redemption in the City of the Dead

Also by
ROBERT BRIGHTON

Avenging Angel Detective Agency™ Mysteries

The Unsealing

A Murder in Ashwood

Current of Darkness

OTHER TITLES

The Buffalo Butcher

The Phantom of Forest Lawn

Romance and Redemption in the City of the Dead

ROBERT BRIGHTON

The Phantom of Forest Lawn:
Romance and Redemption in the City of the Dead

A Novel by Robert Brighton

Ashwood Press, the Ashwood Press colophon, Avenging Angel Detective
Agency, and the Angel colophon are trademarks of Copper Nickel, LLC

© 2024 Copper Nickel, LLC
All Rights Reserved

Cover and Interior Design by The Book Cover Whisperer

979-8-9891680-6-4 Paperback
979-8-9891680-5-7 Hardcover
979-8-9891680-7-1 eBook
979-8-9891680-8-8 Audiobook

Library of Congress Control Number: 2024930073

The story, all names, characters, and incidents portrayed in this book are
fictitious. No identifications with actual persons (living or deceased),
places, buildings, and products are intended or should be inferred.

Find out more at
RobertBrightonAuthor.com

FIRST EDITION

For GC

Who deserved better

CONTENTS

The Phantom of Forest Lawn

In this book, we travel to a different time than that in which my other books (thus far) have been set. I usually favor the period of 1895–1905, ten short years in which much of the foundation of our modern world was laid.

This time, though, we go back to 1867 and to a Buffalo, New York, that—while no longer the frontier outpost it had been before the Erie Canal was completed—was a much smaller and less sophisticated place than it would become only a few short decades later.

In this era, the city was still mostly made of wood—the buildings, of course, but even the sidewalks. There was no electricity, no automobiles, no sewers, and most of the land around the downtown core was rural—farm or woodland. There were trolleys (streetcars), but they were horse-drawn. The city's population was a little over one hundred thousand, and growing fast; in only twenty-five years it would quadruple.

Unlike the southern section of the country, in 1867, post–Civil War Buffalo was experiencing an economic boom. For all practical purposes, the economy of the former Confederacy had been wiped off the face of the map. And not unlike the post–World War II United States, whose economy benefited by being the only one left standing after the great conflict, the North—and Buffalo—enjoyed a substantial postwar growth spurt as a result.

As in my other novels, I have left costs in then-current terms. To understand them in our modern context, we need to apply a multiplier. For several decades after the Civil War, the US dollar *gained* purchasing power, before beginning its long inflationary decline (the erosion of purchasing power) into our present day. Thus to get the *rough* equivalent of 1867 money in today's dollars, multiply by twenty. Thus something that cost one dollar in 1867 would cost about twenty dollars today.

A note on pronunciation, as you will soon meet Christian (Christ) Schamber: the short version of his given name is pronounced with a short *i*—not a long *i*, as in "Christ Jesus."

One final thing. I try to hew as closely to historical dates as I can. In this book, however, I made one exception, which students of the finer points of Buffalo history (or cemetery aficionados) may notice. Namely, the exhumations that made room for the planned Buffalo City Hall happened fifteen years earlier than I place them here. It's a small adjustment, but I feel honor bound to mention it all the same.

I hope you enjoy *The Phantom of Forest Lawn*.

Robert Brighton

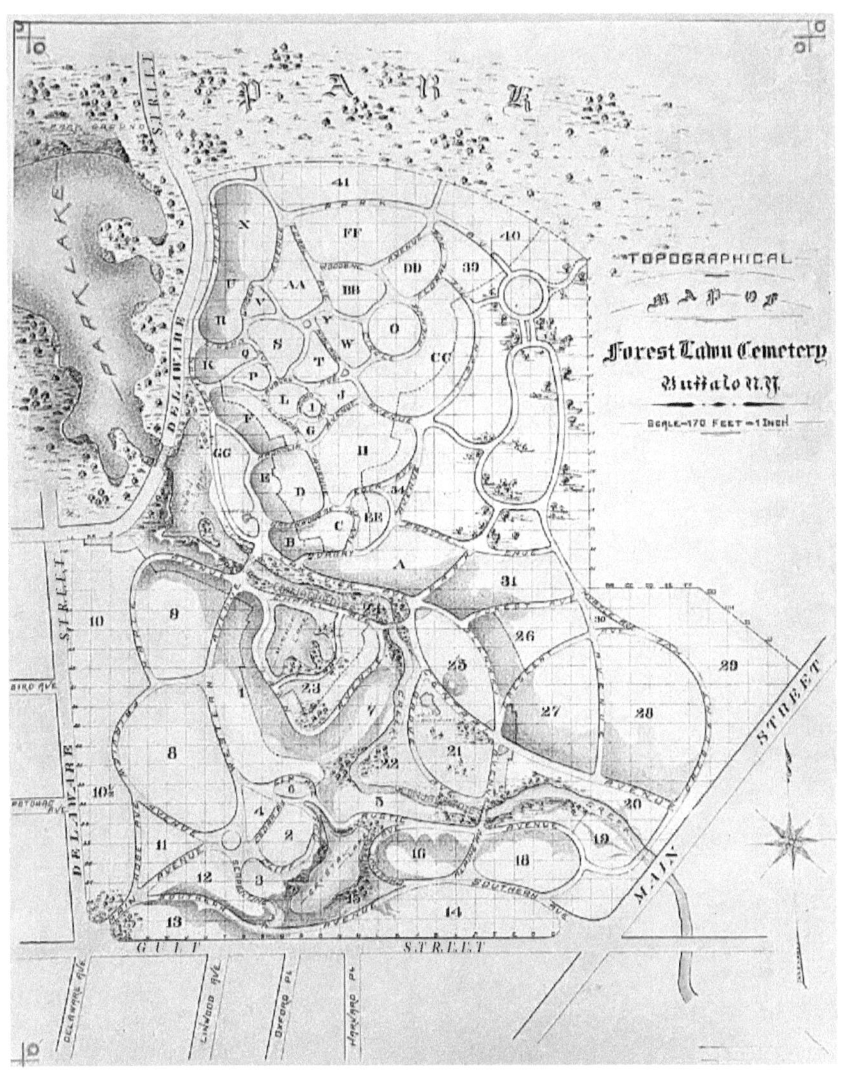

FOREST LAWN CEMETERY

BUFFALO, NEW YORK

Prologue

One Summer Long Ago

What time of day had it been? That he couldn't recall, only that it was late in the afternoon, and the grass was dry as straw and stiff as a flax hackle.

He had thought it might be best to leave her in peace, after all that had happened, but that resolution he found impossible to keep.

She lived nearby, just under the crest of a gentle hill. He walked slowly past the spot, trying to appear nonchalant. There was no sign of her, though; so he continued downhill, and tarried there a while, skipping stones across the bright stream at its bottom.

Then he tried again, and again. It was on his third, or perhaps fourth, mad circuit up and down the slope when he heard her call his name. *Calm, calm*, he reminded himself.

She came toward him at a trot, smiling that indescribable smile of hers, her golden hair glowing in the sunlight—so young, so beautiful, so impossibly full of possibility.

"When did you arrive?" she asked.

"A couple hours ago. I thought I'd stretch my legs a bit after the ride."

"Tell me about the war," she said, her crystal-blue eyes sparkling up at him.

He didn't know where to begin about that, all those long and difficult nights far away among enemies. So he asked instead about what she was reading and spoke of other things far less distressing than *war*, which he could never describe and she could never understand. "The South is a different world" was the best he could manage. "It could never be home."

They sat and talked in the sere grass for a long while, until their shadows stretched away downhill.

"Will you walk with me a little?" she asked at last.

That first ramble took them only as far as the creek, its familiar waters coursing by, always and never the same. He had the curious thought that they might both dive in and drift away to where it must, eventually, reach the sea; but this he kept to himself.

It wouldn't do for her to be out after twilight, and when the sun began to fail, with that same smile—beautiful yet somehow fey—she told him how wonderful it had been to see him again and went back up her hill, throwing a last look over her shoulder before disappearing.

As they parted, though, he dared to invite her on another walk the following day, as the weather again promised to be fine and warm and perfect. And she had agreed.

That would be the second of three days together, which began with the sun high in the sky and ended only when it touched the horizon. They were preposterously long walks, and all the while they talked about anything but the thing which kept them apart.

They meandered along the creek, under the shadows of the great oaks, and through the old orchards. Late on the second day, they climbed the sloping lee of a railroad cut. It was ankle deep in summer weeds, and grasshoppers with wings like Japanese fans fluttered away before them, clearing a path with their clatter. Near the top of the cut, they flopped down in the sun and the long grass, and she said to him, "I'll always remember this day"—and he said, "Will you, really?" to which she had no reply.

On the third day, they wandered into the shuttered precincts of the old school, which had around its recess ground a low stone wall. He handed her over it, both of them knowing why but neither saying a word. They sat, their heads out of sight, and eased lower.

There, in the cool shadow of the wall, they had fumbled toward a kiss—and when it was done they were quiet, perhaps suspecting that their brief connection had only widened the gulf between them.

As he walked her home that afternoon, they spoke at last of the future, as if to pretend that their parting wouldn't be forever, but only until he would again come strolling gravely down the hill, and she would again run smiling toward him.

He left her wearing his soldier's face, though he was secretly afraid to turn around and gaze on her one more time, for fear his heart might burst. And hers might have, too, but for the fact that a woman's heart can hold far more than a man's.

That was the most painful and beautiful day of his life; dream and nightmare wrapped in summer straw. And so it would always remain, like an insect trapped in ancient amber, perfect and awful, eternal life and eternal death in one glowing, golden, terrible August afternoon.

The City of the Dead

Compared to the living, the dead don't take up a great deal of space. But even when arranged in neat plots and rows, they still require a modest amount of elbow room. This was becoming something of a challenge to the booming city of Buffalo. Between a relatively high water table and the burgeoning commercial demand for every square foot of available real estate, there was almost no suitable burying ground that wasn't already stuffed to the gills with corpses.

Thanks to a few farsighted citizens who recognized that the coming legions of the dead had to be put *somewhere*, the problem was partially solved in 1849 by the establishment of Forest Lawn Cemetery—80 pristine rolling acres in what was still a rural tract in the northern outskirts of the city. The cemetery's new board of trustees' longer-term plan was to acquire additional parcels of land, one by one, and increase their holdings to 250 acres, or a little more. Such an expanse would provide more than sufficient room to house at least a quarter-million permanent residents—a veritable city of the dead.

But in the cemetery's earliest days, there had been only a relative handful of interments; and nature, it is said, abhors a vacuum.

Half forest and half lawn—and almost all still unoccupied—the green and pleasant cemetery quickly became the city's most popular picnicking ground. Each weekend, hordes of sometimes-rowdy visitors, eager to escape the heat and foul air of downtown Buffalo, spread out blankets, kindled fires, and even pitched tents. Soon any happy prospect the permanent residents had of resting in peace was soured.

Accordingly, the trustees of Forest Lawn devised a two-pronged solution: a board fence around the perimeter and a requirement that visitors possess an entrance ticket. The fence was straightforward—a whitewashed stockade of eight-foot-high planks, running up hill and down dale. It kept out most of the casual trespassers, though in time a few gaps appeared—the occasional loose board gone missing, like a knocked-out tooth—and these openings were used mostly by local boys sneaking in for a good scare on a full moon night.

Entrance tickets were free but granted only to those with a good reason for their visit: the interment of a friend or loved one, the business of purchasing a plot against their own inevitable dissolution, or such other excuse that the cemetery's business office on Main Street deemed legitimate. Picnicking was not among them.

SECTION TWO

The Poorhouse

January 1867

When the snow began to fly, which in Buffalo can be as early as October, the Erie County Poorhouse faced an annual wave of indigents who knew that, in winter, bunking there was the only way to keep body and soul together. This compounded the year-round problem of overcrowding, since not only the poor ended up in the poorhouse. Vagrants, prostitutes, brothel keepers, gamblers, other petty criminals, and the mentally ill—all were sent by cops, judges, or justices of the peace to the poorhouse, to serve terms of up to six months at hard labor.

Some of the labor *was* hard—farming on the poorhouse's 150 acres of tillable land, for example—but most of it was simple drudgery: monotonous work that not only helped pay the upkeep of the residents but also was thought to quiet the disturbed mind or to provide idle hands with something to occupy themselves instead of begging or pilfering. These repetitive tasks included picking oakum—unbraiding old ropes to recover their hemp—shredding rags into tiny bits of cotton that could be used to make fine paper or a hundred other things, and—everyone's favorite—hand sorting piles of gravel into the six different sizes useful for construction or paving.

Even for those unable or unwilling to work, though, the poorhouse wasn't easy duty. Between the nocturnal ravings of the insane, the frequent scuffles and brawls, and the screeching of infants, there was no escape from the pandemonium. And, as might be expected, sanitation varied from suspicious to simply horrendous. The water supply, in particular, was notoriously bad, pumped by hand through leather hoses from the muddy farm pond. In winter, at least, there weren't the outbreaks of typhoid fever that kept the grave-digging detail busy, but the cost of coal and wood kept the fires low, and hence the drafty building never seemed to warm up. Residents—unless serving out a sentence—tended to drift away in the spring, only to return again when the birds headed south.

Arthur Fermin and Bobby Dolan were regular visitors to the poorhouse. The two childhood friends had emigrated from Ireland about five years before and, perilously short of funds upon landing in New York City, immediately cast about for employment. They scrounged up two possibilities: hire on as crew aboard an Erie Canal boat or enlist for a stint in the Union army. The army paid better, but even on the far side of the Atlantic they had been warned about the carnage of the Civil War, so in the summer of 1862, the pair chose instead to drift leisurely west to Buffalo.

The city was pleasantly warm when they disembarked, the sky a deep shade of azure peculiar to the Niagara Frontier, and there was a gentle landward breeze wafting in from Lake Erie. And since they had been paid out, they had money to burn in the saloons and bordellos of Canal Street. As the name implied, Canal Street was both the terminus of the "Big Ditch" and the main thoroughfare of the city's lethal red-light district—a dozen crooked blocks known as The Hooks, so-called from the cargo hooks stevedores used to unload canal boats and lake steamers.

The Hooks was dangerous but cheap, and thus well-suited to those who had little or nothing to lose. In the fine part of the year—April through early October—a working man making a dollar a day could afford something resembling food, enough watery liquor to numb a sore back, and—at least half the time—a place to lay his head. When money ran short, the nights were warm enough to sleep rough in an alleyway or, if a fellow was lucky, atop a bale of cotton awaiting transshipment.

But when winter came in all its ferocity to collect summer's debt, Fermin and Dolan had never seen its like: four and five feet of snow falling in a single day, streets impassable for weeks on end, and no work for common laborers. They tried to hunker down in a cheap boarding house, husbanding their dwindling savings and shivering. This didn't do much to preserve their dignity, but at least it preserved their lives. *Next year will be better*, they reassured each other, trying to chase away their blues.

Yet the next year, and the next, and the next, had *not* been better. Indeed things grew considerably worse when, in 1865, regiments of men began marching home from the war. Their return swelled the ranks of the unemployed, and given the choice between hiring a returning veteran or a couple of scruffy Irishmen, businessmen would invariably select the former. This meant that even the occasional late-season work Fermin and Dolan could pick up now disappeared entirely with the first hard frost, as predictably as the local waterfowl, to return only with the spring thaw.

In a boomtown, one cannot survive for twelve months on eight months' pay, and so by Christmas, Arthur Fermin and Bobby Dolan had to throw in the towel and make their own migration, three miles north, to the poorhouse. And not unlike many other men of their ilk, they also visited at sundry other times throughout the year as guests of New York State, usually after having been sentenced to a week or two for disorderly conduct—in other words, public intoxication. A stint in the poorhouse was supposed to have a tutorial effect on such wayward men as Fermin and Dolan, but more often than not it had the opposite.

Once they had established a routine, Arthur and Bobby usually celebrated their arrival at the poorhouse with a fixed dice game or as many rounds of three-card monte as they could manage before either the marks' money ran out or one of the Men's Wing warders busted up the party. Then the pair would almost immediately spend their ill-gotten gains with one of the prostitutes confined to the Women's Wing. That was easy to accomplish, since the poorhouse's latrines were outdoors, twenty-five yards behind the rambling structure. The men's latrine was the place to go when something needed clearing out, and away from prying eyes.

A man who had the itch, and the money, would loiter behind the poorhouse proper—it never was too cold for a poke—and when one of the always-watchful belles glanced over, he'd give her the high sign, and off to the men's latrine the pair would go. No one seemed to bat an eye that one fellow might be hovering over his wooden hole, noisily evacuating his bowels, while right next door another man was grinding away for all he was worth on a bent-over hired girl. In fact, the free and arousing spectacle sometimes prompted adjacent shitters to give themselves a quick tug for moral support. No one seemed to mind; in the poorhouse, men worked, ate, slept, jerked off, and killed time, waiting for spring to arrive. If you were a good enough sort, and kept to yourself, the months passed well enough, and you would be welcomed back when the need arose.

By contrast, the two Irishmen soon established themselves among the least welcome guests at the poorhouse, mostly because they couldn't seem to keep their hands to themselves. Even some of the raving lunatics in the insane ward were more likeable; at least the insane had come by their madness honestly. But Arthur Fermin and Bobby Dolan were always getting up to something—none of it good, yet none of it quite so awful as to merit banishment. They had twice come close: once when the superintendent's gold watch had gone missing and Fermin had unwisely tried to sell its pawn ticket to another resident, and another time when the scrappy Dolan had picked a fight with an orderly. The superintendent then offered them a choice—leave and take your chances in the Buffalo winter, or expect graveyard duty whenever you darken this doorway.

No one wanted graveyard duty. Digging graves made farmwork look like loafing, and the poorhouse possessed no facilities for the storage of dead bodies, even temporarily. Besides, the coroner was certainly not wasting space in the already stuffed cemeteries downtown, nor even in the potter's field. That meant that when someone died at the poorhouse—and die they did, regularly, from causes as diverse as typhoid fever to throwing themselves out of windows in a fit of madness—their corpses had to be interred, pronto, and more or less where they had fallen. And in the winter, when all Fermin and Dolan wanted was a hot meal and a roof over their heads, their bad habits earned them the hardest labor of all: chipping away at the frozen ground, one painful shovel at a time.

A hole seven feet long, two and a half wide, and—worst of all— at least five feet deep requires the removal of a lot of frozen earth. It took the two of them half a day to dig the hole, and that was working steadily, if only to keep warm and not from any enthusiasm for the dread task. Then there were a few chattering peremptory words of valediction over the corpse, lowering it into the hard earth—if the chaplain had already scurried out of the cold, none too gently either—and then refilling the hole with the spoils.

As may be expected, winter was prime dying season, so Dolan and Fermin were kept rather busy. The grippe felled at least a half dozen in the period from November to March. Usually at least one of the asylum inmates would wander out into the cold and be found the next day, stiff as a board. Old age claimed five or ten. Invariably there were at least two suicides; one unclassifiable demise by misadventure; and another several deaths from tertiary syphilis—or "general paresis of the insane," as the medical euphemism would have it.

That meant that Dolan and Fermin's irrepressibly bad behavior would keep them outdoors for at least twenty full days during the hard season, and that was without a contagion.

"We might as well be digging our own damn graves," Fermin grumbled to Dolan one particularly frigid morning, as their shovels pried at the rock-hard clay. As cold as it was, they were both sweating profusely from their exertions.

"It's nobody's fault but ours," Dolan said, leaning on his shovel. "There's no two ways about it."

"Maybe. But I can tell you right now, I'm not sticking out another winter of this shite, just for a bowl of their slop twice a day."

"What else would we do?"

"I don't know, but a couple of strong young bucks like us could do a sight better than this."

"We'd better get back to it," Dolan hissed. "The super's giving us the eye."

Fermin grudgingly resumed the slow excavation of the grave.

Slow-Motion Magic

Near the northern limits of Buffalo, in a place called Buffalo Plains, stood Spring Abbey, a sprawling Tudor castle, two or three stories high, depending on which side one approached. The first of three Samuel Moffatts had built it in 1826, directly after making a fortune bossing gangs of men digging out the Erie Canal. After the canal job was finished, Sam the First had come up to this then-lonely patch of woodland to get away from people. His plans for rural solitude were soon dashed; he had scarcely begun clearing a spot for a home when one Jacob Granger began clearing the adjacent land to plant an orchard.

Fruit grows well on the Niagara Frontier, despite the short growing season. Warm days and cool nights make for juicy and sweet apples, pears, and stone fruits. And deep, cold winters kill off diseases and insects that plague fruit trees in more hospitable climates.

At first old Mr. Moffatt was not amused by his unexpected neighbor, but in time he found Mr. Granger to be an affable fellow who, as soon as his first harvest, was openhanded in sharing his bounty with the Moffatt family. The rest of his produce he trundled, one wagonload at a time, down to the Elk Street Market in Buffalo city. But after a ten-mile trip over rutted pathways hardly good enough to be called roads, half of the delicate cargo would be ruined. It was a dispiriting end to months of love and labor.

One autumn afternoon, Mr. Moffatt was smoking his pipe on the front portico of Spring Abbey. In the distance, he saw Jacob Granger's wagon creeping slowly back up Main Street, trailing a collapsing plume of dust. He waved, and his friend waved back, but without any of his usual bonhomie. When Granger's rig drew even with the iron gates of Spring Abbey, Moffatt walked out to meet it.

"You look like you've lost your best friend, Jake."

"Almost all my plums had turned to pulp by the time I got them to the market," Granger replied, nearly in tears. "Only a quarter of them survived. The rest I had to sell for hog feed."

"I'm sorry to hear that," Moffatt said, puffing thoughtfully on his pipe. "But since you brought it up—lately I've been giving your plums quite a bit of thought."

"Now why would that be?"

"Because you leave here with the best fruit in America, and you come back disheartened."

"What do you expect? I'm losing—"

"I know. I'm not rubbing it in. But I may have a solution. One that could make us both a lot of money, too."

"I'm game for anything at this point," Granger said. "What do you have in mind?"

"Jam."

"*Jam?*"

"That's right—jam. Preserves. Look, I know how to organize men and machines. You know how to grow fruit. So you grow the fruit, and I'll set up a factory to make preserves out of it. No more trips to Buffalo for you, and I have something to occupy my time."

Granger frowned. "What do you know about making jam?"

"Not a thing. So what? I can hire any two old farm widows from out east, and they'll teach us everything we need to know. They've been putting up preserves since they were girls."

Jacob Granger considered this a moment, scuffing his foot in the bottom of his wagon. "It could work," he said. "No more wasted fruit."

"Nary a one," Moffatt said. "And if you agree to sell your fruit only to me, I'll give you a share of the jam business, too."

"Why would you do that?"

"Because I don't love money. But I do hate waste."

Over the next decade, Samuel Moffatt and Jacob Granger made a small fortune in their joint venture, and then passed the business along to each of their sons, who grew it ever larger as Buffalo changed from a canal town to a booming industrial city. And those sons would have but one child each: Georgia Granger and Samuel "Sam" Moffatt III.

One day, Georgia and Sam III would become the sole heirs to an empire of jam.

MOST PEOPLE CONSIDERED GEORGIA Granger to be something of a tomboy. Fearless, athletic, and with a bumper crop of freckles across the bridge of her nose—very unladylike, her mother said—from spending so much time climbing the trees in her father's orchards, Georgia was always more comfortable with boys than with girls.

She had wavy sun-faded blonde hair and luminous blue eyes. "You're too pretty a girl to be playing at sports," her mother would say, and compel Georgia to sit and sew, while the girl looked longingly at the boys noisily playing shinny beneath her window. Whenever her mother would have to attend to other matters, Georgia would sneak out of the house to have a little fun—until she was discovered again.

Her sporting abilities were not the only thing admired by the boys, however. She *was* pretty, but she was also something far less common—even as an adolescent, Georgia was *alluring*. She had a bluff and unapologetic way of moving, a physical confidence that boys—and later, men—found intoxicating. Georgia held most of them off, having been taught from girlhood that—as sole heiress to the Granger Farm— only a select few young men could qualify for her hand. The best match of all, of course, would be young Samuel Moffatt III.

Both sets of parents assumed their children would eventually unite the two families, and Sam and Georgia inherited that assumption along with all the rest. Although there was never any particular spark between them, Sam was a decent fellow and Georgia a prize catch, and so as their adolescent years progressed, they grew accustomed to the notion that one day they would be husband and wife.

The only person who could be disappointed by such a propitious alliance was one Christian Schamber, who lived in one of the workers' homes on the Spring Abbey grounds. Christ was the son of immigrant Germans, who had come to the Moffatt works as jam cookers. He had three sisters, who annoyed him ceaselessly with their preening and affected manners, and his mother was too tired at the end of the day to pay him any mind. As a result, the only girl that mattered to Christian Schamber was Georgia Granger.

As children, Georgia and Christ romped in the Granger orchards, took long walks all the way to the lake, and played hide-and-seek in the woods north of Gulf Street. The whole time, though, young Christ was suffering the pangs of Cupid's arrow—while Georgia seemed cheerfully immune to any deeper feeling than a sincere affection for her likeminded playmate. In truth, the jam cooker's son never stood a chance. In 1862, when it became clear that Georgia would indeed marry Sam III, Christ became so despondent that he enlisted in the local Union regiment and marched away to war, hoping either to return to glory and Georgia's notice or, failing that, never to return at all.

Christ came back to Buffalo in 1865, three years and a lifetime older. He'd seen more than two hundred local boys from his regiment die, and many more crippled or maimed. He'd escaped the carnage with a flesh wound in the shin, a potentially serious problem had it become infected during one of the regiment's long marches in knee-deep mud and manure. To his surprise and dismay, though, it had healed perfectly, and Christ's last chance to make Georgia mourn his loss was gone. He dutifully marched home to find Georgia married to Sam III.

He thought about leaving the city for good, but he found that although seeing Georgia every day was like biting down hard on a toothache, it allowed him to retain some kind of connection to her. And so he stayed, loving and longing from afar.

There were a couple of times when rumors buzzed that Georgia was with child, and that soon there would be a fourth generation of Moffatts running the jam operation. But then, less than a year after Christ's return from the war, decent but dull Samuel Moffatt III contracted scarlet fever and in three short days was dead.

GEORGIA WAS STILL REELING from her young husband's demise when, two months later, her father died of apoplexy. Now she was in possession of both the Moffatt Jam Company and the Granger Farm. But another unpleasant surprise was in store for her. When her father's will was opened, the unthinkable had happened: convinced that the farming era in North Buffalo had passed, and knowing that Georgia had inherited Spring Abbey and its sixteen acres of grounds, Mr.

Granger had stipulated that the great majority of the Granger Farm was to be sold to the growing Forest Lawn Cemetery. The family orchards would be replanted with graves.

Georgia took the news hard. Although she was now a very wealthy young widow, with a factory to occupy her head, her heart had always been in the orchard. Since girlhood, she'd rambled over the rolling land, exploring its creeks and caves and rock outcroppings. She'd savored the slow ripening of fruit in the summer sunshine, the winey smell of harvest, even the smoke of the burning prunings in the barren sleep of winter. The Granger Farm had been nothing short of sixty-nine and three-quarters acres of slow-motion magic. Now, just beyond the back fence line of Spring Abbey lay not the graceful rise and fall of peach, plum, apple, and pear trees but jagged rows of headstones.

A MESS OF POTTAGE

The corridors of the poorhouse were long, narrow, slightly crooked lanes with impossibly tall ceilings—just why they were so tall defied easy explanation—and floored with slick varnished planking that resembled the deck of a sailing ship. The hallways were lined on either side with a neat row of doors, each of which had a hinged transom window over it for ventilation, just like any normal door. The poorhouse doors, though, were different in one important respect: each had a knob only on its outer face. Once the residents of the poorhouse were tucked into their rooms for the night, each and every door was locked from the outside by the warder. No one was getting out until it was time for breakfast.

Any overnight calls of nature were serviced by a plain glazed chamber pot under each bedstead. By morning, when the thunder mugs were emptied by the longsuffering staff, the smell was atrocious. A combination of poor food, intestinal parasites, and close quarters yielded up an eye-watering stench. And so it was not uncommon, even in winter, to keep the tall windows at either end of the crooked corridors wide open, to allow for a merciful cross draft, however frigid.

Each room was occupied by four inmates on two parallel sets of bunk beds. Arthur Fermin and Bobby Dolan shared one set, and across from them were a couple of itinerant German peddlers who had become stranded in Buffalo when the cold set in. The Irishmen and the Germans shared no language, so Arthur and Bobby amused themselves by lobbing over extravagant insults, which the Germans received with blank stares of incomprehension. This Fermin and Dolan found all the more hilarious.

"Bobby," Fermin said one evening, after the warder's key had rattled in the lock outside, "do you think the one on the bottom—across from me—looks like a fucking potato with arms and legs?"

Dolan leaned over from the top bunk to look at his friend, who was as usual lying fully clothed on top of his mattress, hands behind his head. In the silver moonlight Fermin looked very much like an effigy atop a Crusader tomb, if considerably less dignified. "More like a turnip," Dolan said, making them both laugh.

The Germans had some idea that they were being made fun of, but not enough to respond, so they lay there stolidly in their bunks.

"The other one looks as stupid as a bag of hair," Dolan went on. "Hey," he said to the German on the top bunk, "were you stupid back in Germany, too?"

The other man looked back at him blankly. "*Arschloch*," he said, which made the two Irishmen laugh.

Tired of their fun, Fermin and Dolan lay on their backs, waiting for sleep and thinking about breakfast.

Five minutes later, Dolan was almost in dreamland when Fermin's head popped up over the edge of the top bunk. "Bobby," his friend whispered, "I'm starving."

"Me too," the other man mumbled, his eyes still closed. "Just have to wait till breakfast."

"Fuck that. Let's go down to the kitchen and get ourselves

something to eat. They can't expect a man to dig graves on such skimpy rations. We're entitled to a full belly."

Dolan was now fully awake, and again aware of his rumbling stomach. "Go downstairs?"

"That's right."

"We're locked in, Artie."

"Maybe, but I have an idea. Come down from there."

Bobby Dolan swung his legs over the edge of the iron bunk bed and dropped quietly to the floor. The Germans seemed to be either fast asleep or ignoring their roommates.

"The transom," Fermin said softly. "We can wriggle out of there."

"It's way up in the air."

"Not if we push the bunks over under it," his friend said with a silver smile.

Dolan smiled back, and the two of them shoved the heavy bedstead against the door. It screeched into position, rousing the Germans, who began yammering away at them in their native tongue.

"Hush up, you," Fermin said, waving his hand. "Go back to sleep, you stupid fucks."

"Do you think anyone heard them?" Dolan asked, rethinking the plan.

"Nah. Let's go. There are only two warders for the whole place, and they spend most of the night in the insane wing."

Fermin climbed onto the top bunk with a long creak and opened the transom fully, assessing whether to go out head- or feetfirst. Wisely he chose the latter, and flipped onto his belly, easing his feet and then legs out the opening.

"Ah, mind this damn fool lock thing here, will you," he groused, looking down at his stomach. "It nearly tore off my ballsack just now."

Then he slid the rest of his torso out of the window, clung to its frame for a moment, and dropped into the corridor with a soft thud. Dolan, with the benefit of Fermin's painful experience, followed easily.

They stood for a moment, controlling their breath. Then Dolan started off toward the central staircase, but Fermin grabbed him by the collar. "Not that way, idiot," he said. "The service staircase, at the end."

"I don't like it when you call me names," his pal grumbled.

"Don't be so sensitive," Fermin said. "Come on."

Together they padded down the long corridor to the staircase at the end. The door was unlocked—as it always was at night, in case there would be a fire—and quiet as raindrops the pair tiptoed down the circular stone steps that led to the basement and the kitchen. There didn't seem to be a soul stirring anywhere in the vast building.

The kitchen was located at the far end of the basement corridor. The Irishmen were chuckling now, gleeful about the prospect of a full belly and, for a change, a decent night's sleep. When they opened the big door of the kitchen, they found the room in pitch darkness; the narrow clerestory windows under the ceiling were too small to admit even a ray of moonlight.

"It's dark as a dungeon in here," Dolan said. "I can't see a damn thing."

"We'll have to make do with matches." Fermin pulled a match safe out of his vest pocket and struck a lucifer. When it flared to life, a few rats scurried deeper into the gloom.

"Now that tells you all you need to know about the food in this shithole," Fermin said.

"Where do you think they keep the stewpot?"

"I know where it is. They set it into a little well kind of thing, to keep it cool."

The first match was scorching Fermin's fingers, so he waved it out and flamed off another. "Over here," he said to Dolan.

They walked across the silent kitchen, its giant copper pans hanging like trophies from the walls, and navigated around a long wooden table, where again they set off the *scritch* of rats escaping the light.

Set low into the far wall was indeed a brick-lined depression, and in it was sitting what looked like a small lidded bathtub.

"The stewpot!" Fermin said.

The pot was sitting in half a foot of water, which in the cold had turned to ice.

"It won't budge," Dolan said, pulling up on one of the bail handles of the stewpot. "It's frozen in place."

"Who cares? Pull off the lid, boy."

Dolan obliged, and the two found that the great pot was still half-full of cold stew.

"Beauty," Fermin said.

"We need to find a couple spoons," his friend said, looking around as the second match guttered out.

"Jesus, you can be a nancy sometimes," Fermin muttered, and as Dolan's eyes began to adjust to the darkness, he watched Arthur drop to his knees and dig a hand into the unfrozen center of the stewpot. He dredged up a congealed handful of greasy stew and stuffed it greedily into his mouth.

"It's not bad, actually," he mumbled, his face coated with cold stew. "I'd advise you to get some before I eat it all."

Dolan joined Fermin by the pot, and the two of them ate a remarkable quantity of the leftover stew. When at last they slowed down, Fermin patted his distended stomach.

"Now tell me this wasn't the best idea!"

"I don't believe I've ever been this full in my life," Dolan moaned. "I'm stuffed."

"That'll tide us over, and with no one the wiser, either." Fermin replaced the lid and, with some effort, scuffled to his feet on the stone floor. "And I can't wait until the middle of the night to take a big fat dump and give those Germans something to dream on."

"I have to smell it, too, you know," his friend protested.

Fermin chuckled. "We'd better be getting back to the room."

He flared off another match, though by now they could see almost as well as the grateful rats, who had resumed their foraging.

The pair heaved themselves up the circular stone staircase, and Fermin popped his head out of the door at the top. "No one in sight," he said over his shoulder. "Let's go."

They hastened down the long corridor again to their room, but in front of the door stopped dead in their tracks. Arthur let out a long sigh.

"Well now, if this isn't a fly in the ointment," he said under his breath.

His plan had neglected to consider that the door to their room was a good seven feet tall, and the bottom of the transom set another several inches above its frame. The bunk beds had made it easy to climb out, but now, absent a ladder, there was no prospect of getting back in.

Fermin scratched his head, looking up and down the corridor. "Well, fuck me."

"We could get a ladder from one of the storerooms downstairs," Dolan whispered. "Where they keep our tools."

"Yeah, and leave a ladder leaning against our door until morning? God, you can be thick sometimes."

"*Me* thick? You're the one that came up with this plan."

"Shut your hole, will you? I'm trying to think."

The two stood in front of their door, looking up at the transom window, which at its altitude looked impossibly small.

"What about the Germans?" Dolan said.

"What good are the Germans? There's no knob on the inside, and even if there was, we couldn't make those blockheads understand."

"Then what are we going to do, Artie?" Dolan said, with a rising note of panic.

Fermin's eyes narrowed in the moonlit hall. "Here's what we do," he said, and tugged on Dolan's sleeve. Back they went to the spiral stair at the end of the corridor.

On the top step, Fermin pulled out his match safe again and shook it. "We start a little fire," he said. "Then we sound the alarm. They'll have to unlock all the doors then."

"But won't they notice if we're not in our room?"

"Hell no. They'll be too busy putting out the fire to know a damn thing. We just get to the bottom of the main staircase and wait for everyone to come streaming down. They'll think we got out with everyone else."

"That's pretty sharp, Artie," Dolan said. "Now where do we set the fire?"

"Back down in the kitchen. There's heaps of stuff down there that'll burn."

They crept back to the kitchen and again navigated around the big wooden table. In a big basket near the water pump was a crumpled pile of used rags.

"These'll go up like tinder," Fermin said with a big grin, brandishing his match safe.

"You're sure we won't burn the whole place down?"

"It wouldn't be the worst thing if we did. They'd have to put us all up someplace decent then." He struck the match and dropped it into the basket of rags, which indeed did start blazing with surprising vigor. The two of them looked at the rising fire for a moment.

"Now we go out into the hallway and raise a ruckus," Fermin said.

The two turned, but had taken only a single step when they ran into the two big warders.

"*Christ almighty!*" Fermin blurted out, stunned.

One of the warders grabbed him by the collar and, in the flickering orange light of the rag bin, turned to Dolan. "Don't you think about going anywhere, either," the warder growled. "I know your face."

Meanwhile, the second warder hustled over to the water pump and filled a bucket, which he dumped on the blazing rags. It took a second bucket to reduce the fire to a soggy, smoldering mass of blackened cloth.

"You two are done for," the first warder said with an air of satisfaction. He was a formidable chap, with the flattened nose of a prizefighter and hands the size of small hams. "Let's go."

The second warder seized Dolan by the collar, and the two big men half dragged the Irishmen toward the basement corridor.

"Where are you taking us?" gasped out Fermin. "Can't we talk this out, boys?"

"We're going to wake up the superintendent," the first warder said. "And believe you me, he's not going to be happy with you lot when we do."

"Come on, fellows," Fermin pleaded. "We were just having a little lark."

"You'll shut up, if you know what's good for you," the second warder said.

The two firebugs begged and wheedled all the way to the first floor, where the superintendent's quarters were located, but the warders were having none of it.

The bigger one hammered on the superintendent's door. There was a minute's silence, and then the lock rattled, and the door swung open. Standing there holding a candle was the bleary-looking superintendent.

"What's the meaning of this?"

"We caught these two trying to burn the place down, sir," the second warder said. "They set fire to some rags in the kitchen."

"We weren't trying to burn anything *down*," Fermin protested. "We were just having a bit of fun."

"You two *again*?" the superintendent said. "You have a remarkable notion of 'fun.'"

"We're awful sorry," Dolan said. "It won't happen again."

The superintendent gave them a grim little smile. "No, it most certainly will not," he said, waggling his finger. "Because you two have earned yourself an eviction. Tomorrow morning, you'll be gone. For good, too."

"But, sir," Fermin said, "have a little mercy, would you? You wouldn't turn us poor lads out into the cold and snow, without anywhere to go and not a cent to our names?"

"Oh, but I would. And I shall, first thing. You have no one to blame but yourselves."

"Won't you just give—" Fermin spluttered.

"Warders," the superintendent said, "good work, both of you. Now if you please, take these two no-counts to the insane ward and put them into straitjackets for the night. Tell the morning shift to bring them to me, and I'll complete the paperwork."

"Have a heart, mister!" Dolan bleated. "We didn't hurt nobody!"

"Except for yourselves," the superintendent said. "See you in the morning, boys."

THE NEXT MORNING, THE poorhouse staff took their time about retrieving Dolan and Fermin, whose terrifying night in the insane ward had been almost enough to make them rethink the value of a bellyful of cold stew. At last, a couple of different, but still very large, warders arrived and worked the straps and buckles of the two men's straitjackets. The Irishmen stood with some effort, rubbing their stiff limbs.

"Let's go," one of the warders said, and they grabbed the pair by the elbows and escorted them downstairs. The superintendent was sitting placidly behind his desk, enjoying his second cup of coffee.

"Sleep well, boys?" he asked with a smirk.

"Har har har," Fermin said. "Very funny."

"Look, Mr. Superintendent, sir," Dolan said, "we didn't mean nothing by last night. Give us a second chance, won't you?"

The superintendent eyed the pair, still wearing his irritating smirk. Then he shook his head. "Sorry, boys, but not this time. I've given you second chances before. And third chances, and fourth ones. But setting a fire that could well have burned this place to the ground? And in *winter*? No, my friends, you've committed the unpardonable sin. But before you go, I have one little chore you have to do. Mr. Stroup from Forest Lawn is here to collect a body, and you're to load it for him."

"So if I understand right," Fermin said, "you're kicking us out, but you're still making us work."

The superintendent considered this. "Yes, I suppose that's about it."

"And what if we refuse?"

"Then I'll call the police and have you committed to the penitentiary for arson."

"*Artie*," Bobby whined, "let's just load the man's—"

"How about a little breakfast first, at least?" Fermin persisted. "I'm starving."

"After all that stew?" the superintendent said. "But yes, you may have breakfast . . . *after* you've finished loading Mr. Stroup's wagon." He looked over the two men's shoulders to the warders. "We're done here. Don't let them out of your sight, though. Not when they load the wagon, not when they eat. Not until they're safely off the grounds."

"Yes, sir," the warders said in unison.

The superintendent consulted his watch. "We mustn't keep Mr. Stroup waiting," he said. "So you'd better be on your way. Good luck to you, boys."

"*Good luck*, he says," Fermin muttered under his breath. "We'll be six feet under by this time next week."

"You'll have only yourselves to blame if you are," the superintendent said, and picked up his coffee again.

AS THE SAYING GOES, God makes the sun to shine equally on the just and the unjust, and Dolan and Fermin's errant ray of glorious sunshine would come only moments after leaving the superintendent's office.

As the man had said, Mr. George Stroup, the superintendent of Forest Lawn Cemetery, had come to collect a body that—quite to everyone's surprise—had been claimed by some sympathetic family members, who had felt an obligation to give the dear departed a decent burial in the consecrated ground of Forest Lawn.

Stroup was a somewhat nondescript fellow, dressed neatly in somber tones and radiating a palpable serenity. He was standing next to his cemetery wagon when the warders arrived with Fermin and Dolan in tow.

"Good morning, gentlemen," he said. "I was just now speaking with your superintendent, and he kindly offered your services in loading my wagon."

"So we understand," Fermin said, looking around. "Where is it? The body, I mean?"

"In the morgue room in the basement, I believe."

Unamused but without any other option, Fermin and Dolan—under the warders' watchful eyes—descended into the accursed basement again, retrieved the body in its pinewood box, and lugged it back up to the ground floor. They loaded it without a word, then turned, eager to return to the relative warmth of the poorhouse and their final meal before being sent packing.

"That all?" Fermin said, rubbing his hands.

"There is one other small thing," Stroup said. "In addition to arranging for the collection of my newest permanent resident, I had a little tête-à-tête with the superintendent about you two fellows."

"Aw, for the love of Christ," Fermin groaned.

"What's a 'tettatett'?" Dolan said, worried.

"It was about a little fire."

Fermin looked up at the grey sky. "The man's setting out to ruin us," he said. "One little—"

"No, no," Stroup said. "*Au contraire.* In fact, for reasons I can't quite fathom, he seems to want to do you men a good turn."

Fermin started. "Say what?"

Stroup chuckled. "I really do believe the man possesses a superabundance of Christian charity," he said. "He did tell me about the fire, as was only right for him to do. Yet he also suggested that I offer you an opportunity to recover your dignity and keep body and soul together."

"What does that mean?" Fermin said, breathing out a sarcastic cloud of steam in the cold air.

"It means that we won't die," Dolan replied.

"I know well enough what 'keeping body and soul together' means. Sweet Mother Mary, you're thick sometimes. I meant—what is the opportunity?"

"See here," Stroup said, "you two are young." He squinted at them. "And I'd guess reasonably healthy."

"You're full of compliments," Fermin said, almost to himself.

Stroup ignored him. "My cemetery is growing, but I'm perilously short of laborers. And so, after my talk with the superintendent, I'd like to offer you a situation."

"You mean a job?" Dolan said.

"What kind of situation?" Fermin asked, ignoring his friend.

"As it is here, your room and board would be provided," Stroup said. "We have recently erected a small but weathertight dormitory, which is currently unoccupied." He paused. "The big difference from *here*, though, is that, in addition, I will pay you wages of a dollar a day. *Each*. Year-round."

"Good night," Dolan said. "Artie, it's our lucky day."

"Don't mind my friend," Fermin said to Stroup. "As my mother used to say, if it seems too good to be true, it probably is."

Stroup shook his head. "Be that as it may, boys, it's what I have to offer you. But do make up your minds quickly. I'm freezing to death out here."

Fermin shot a glance at his friend, but he didn't need to. Dolan was already dreaming of free board and a dollar a day and a ticket out of this shithole.

"Fine, we'll take it," Fermin said.

"Good!" Stroup said with a little clap of the hands. "You've made the right decision. Why don't you meet me at the cemetery tomorrow in the forenoon? You may ask for me at the entrance gate. They'll show you in."

"Where are we supposed to sleep tonight?" Fermin said. "The super's turned us out into the street like so much garbage."

"The dormitory has to be readied," Stroup said. "And that won't be finished until tomorrow. But here"—he fished two silver dollars out of his pocket—"an advance on your first day's wage. This will buy you a decent place to sleep and omnibus fare, with a little bit to put away for a rainy day." He placed the cold coins in Fermin's outstretched palm.

"Thank you ever so much, sir," Dolan said, almost dancing for joy. "May I ask what we'll be doing at your fine establishment?"

Stroup smiled. "Of course you may, my boy. You'll be digging graves."

"Of course," Fermin muttered.

Mr. Stroup smiled again and mounted the driver's bench of his wagon. With a slight tip of his hat, he slapped the reins, and he and the lucky stiff lurched off toward eternity in the precincts of Forest Lawn.

As soon as he had rounded the corner and was out of sight, Dolan jumped up and clicked his heels. "Now what do you say about that?" he said to his friend. "It's always darkest before the dawn."

"Well, anything'll be better than this dump."

"You want that breakfast or not?" one of the warders said. "It's cold as hell out here."

"We won't be needing any more of your fine hospitality," Fermin said, rubbing the two coins together. Without dignifying his comment with a reply, the two warders turned and walked back into the poorhouse.

"Let's get out of here," Dolan said. "We'll take the omnibus downtown and find ourselves a proper hotel. Imagine it, Artie! Staying in a fine room on a soft mattress tonight."

"Not so fast," Fermin said. "We can walk downtown just as well. But instead of blowing all this good fortune on a fancy hotel, let's go behind the building and see if we can arrange a proper poke. One of these dollars will buy us both a real piece of pussy, too, not the usual hairy armpit shite. And we'll still have enough left over for a decent-enough bed and a couple meals."

Dolan seemed a little let down; he had never ridden in an omnibus or stayed in a fine hotel. But then again . . . he couldn't remember the last time he'd shot his load into an actual pussy.

"That sounds pretty good to me, Artie. You're always thinking."

"Your mother asked me to look after you when we left Ireland," Fermin said. "And so I shall."

SECTION FIVE

STROUP

George Washington Stroup had been superintendent of Forest Lawn since the cemetery had comprised only eighty acres. How he had won his position wasn't clear. It was said that he had come to Buffalo from one of the little canal towns near Rochester, and so his roots were elsewhere—a significant demerit in a somewhat clannish city like Buffalo. Nor was he a married man or a joiner, and was thus considered slightly defective, socially speaking. On the other hand, he certainly had the appropriate mien for a cemetery man: solemn, steady, dignified.

Whatever the reason, he had been given the job, and by all accounts Stroup had done yeoman's service. He had both administered the cemetery capably and also sniffed out and acquired, on the cheap, several attractive contiguous parcels of land.

His nose for bargains was aided by the simple fact that he was usually among the first to know when a nearby landholder had died, particularly if that landholder had been foresightful enough to secure a plot against the unknowable but unavoidable moment of death. In such cases, Mr. Stroup had little to do but wait for the family of the deceased to come and see him. In making arrangements for interment, he would casually inquire whether the family would be willing to trade a few unwanted acres against the cost of the burial, or sell outright.

If a nearby landowner died without having secured a plot, however, the resourceful George Stroup was not in the least dismayed. In that case, he would steer his buggy to the decedent's residence and present his case for interment in Forest Lawn. As he was not an undertaker, this visit was by no means an intrusion on any prior relationship the survivors might have had; instead, he would tell the family that he was merely a kind of real estate broker, selling land thirty-two square feet at a time—and, he didn't mind adding, always looking to acquire more.

In only a few years at the helm of Forest Lawn, this tactic had added a mind-boggling hundred and fifty acres to the original eighty. Stroup's biggest score—the entirely unexpected acquisition of the nearby Granger orchards, a whopping sixty-nine and three-quarters prime acres at a very reasonable $2,000 an acre—had earned him fulsome praise from the local potentates that comprised the board of trustees. That old Mr. Granger had been willing to sell his immaculately tended orchards at all, let alone to a cemetery, shocked everyone in town. Why, Mr. Granger's father had purchased the land from the Seneca Indians themselves, and not a soul expected that the Granger family would ever willingly let it go.

For all his accomplishments, however, all was not well between George Washington Stroup and his employer. For one, while most of the trustees would never deny that the man had done great things for their cause, in their cups they might just as well say that they found the superintendent priggish and unlikeable. And, perhaps even more to the point, Mr. Stroup was not of their ilk—the Buffalo Brahmins—and could never be; achievements notwithstanding, he would always remain some schoolmasterish upstart from out east someplace. He was useful, but he would never *belong*.

He had *tried* to belong, observing and aping the dress and manners of his betters and, more recently, enrolling in a variety of self-improvement courses in his off-hours. These refinements seemed only to amuse the trustees, which further wounded Stroup's already fragile pride. Yet even that indignity he could have let go by, if only one other inequity had been remedied: no matter how many plots he sold, no matter how many acres he annexed, his salary had refused to budge. He'd hinted at his dissatisfaction; he'd even cajoled a few friendly plot holders into writing letters on his behalf. But each new effort had been as futile and frustrating as the one before.

As 1867 broke cold and clear, Mr. Stroup had arisen to greet the New Year with one unshakeable resolution: to take the proverbial bull by the horns and see to it that he was paid what he was worth. One way or the other.

As AGREED, THE NEXT morning Mr. Stroup met Fermin and Dolan at the cemetery gatehouse, where Delaware and Gulf Streets intersected. He had them pick up shovels from the storeroom in the rear, and from there he led them up into Section 15. They came to a stop next to a large flat space of perhaps half an acre, standing about six inches deep in old, crusty snow.

"Your first excavation," Stroup said.

The two men looked over the snowy expanse. "Where?"

"Here."

"*Where* here?" Fermin asked, annoyed.

Stroup swept his hands over the entire field. "Everywhere. The whole thing."

"*What?*"

"Not all at once, mind you," the superintendent said. "But this parcel has been consecrated to the dead of Franklin Park Cemetery, downtown. In the spring, coffins will begin arriving, each one containing a decedent exhumed from the old cemetery. They'll be relocated and reinterred here. Franklin Park Cemetery has to be cleared to make way for the erection of the Buffalo City Hall."

"Whoever heard of a mad thing like that?" Fermin said.

"It's *tout à fait* common," Stroup replied.

"It's what?" Dolan said.

"It's a French expression. It means 'completely.'"

"Are you French?" Fermin asked.

"Very well you might think so!" Stroup replied. "But no. I am at present learning the language as a second tongue, under the tutelage of Monsieur Neuville of Main Street."

"*Merde*," said Dolan. "*Salope.*"

"Sir!"

"There were a whole bunch of French Canadians at the poorhouse," Dolan explained. "They taught us some curse words."

Stroup sniffed. "First of all, I'll thank you to refrain from using indecent language in my presence. And second, French Canadians are *not* French, regardless of any claims to the contrary. They are a different species entirely."

Dolan looked puzzled. "Don't mind him," Fermin said. "Now about this little project of yours. We can't very well dig a hole this big in frozen ground."

"Some things can be done as well as others," Stroup said, again mystifying both Irishmen. "It will be slow going, I'll admit, but steady as she goes and you'll get there. You may need a pick, but we have plenty of those. And I should add that your job here is made easier by the fact that the Franklin Park coffins will be laid side by side in rows, and then covered up all at once."

"Jesus Christ," Fermin said, "we had a sight less digging to do back at the poorhouse."

"Perhaps, but here you are paid a dollar a day, each, plus room and board, and as much coffee as you can drink. And I needn't tell you gentlemen that coffee is still very difficult to come by, so soon after the conclusion of the recent hostilities."

"I *do* like coffee, Artie," Dolan said to Fermin, who rolled his eyes.

"Fine then," Fermin said. "We'll do what we can."

Stroup smiled. "There's one other small piece of good news. Because of the age of most of the bodies, you will not have to dig down to the usual Forest Lawn standard of five and one-half feet. Having been in the ground for many years, most of the relocated bodies are well past the point of putrefaction. Thus you have no cause to fear roaming dogs and such."

"I thought it was supposed to be 'six feet under,'" Dolan said.

"That's a convenient figure of speech, Mr. Dolan. A shortcut. Imagine saying, 'Poor fellow, he was alive just yesterday and today is five and a half feet under.'"

Dolan shrugged. "I suppose that makes sense."

"Indeed it does. Now then, here you needn't go to five and a half feet. In this case your trench must be seven feet head to toe, as it were, but only three feet deep. This will still allow room for a good foot of earth atop each coffin, and you'll mound up the excess soil above that to allow for settling."

"How fast are these coffins going to come?" Fermin asked. "There's none but the two of us, you know."

"The gentleman who secured the contract to exhume the bodies has two years to accomplish the task, beginning this month. That said, he has to build a coffin manufactory first, before beginning to dig. I would expect to see our first permanent residents around the April thaw. Once that begins, you can expect about twelve new residents per week.

"Therefore, you are fortunate in that you have more than three months' head start. If you work steadily every day, by spring you will very likely have dug a sufficient trench for almost a full season's worth of relocations. But it will be well to make hay while the sun shines."

"Out of the frying pan, into the fire," Fermin muttered.

"*Bien dit*," Stroup observed. "I often find proverbs to be rather useful guides to action."

"What about 'another day, another dollar'?" Fermin asked. "How about we make that one 'another day, another dollar and a half,' instead?"

"You have a sharp wit, Mr. Fermin," Stroup said. "And as much as I'd like to enjoy more of it, I don't get paid enough to stand out here and freeze to death."

With that, the superintendent turned on his heel and began walking back to his office.

"Get a load of that, will you?" Fermin said to his friend. "*He* doesn't get paid enough? Look at the two of us broke dicks."

Dolan shrugged. "It's always that way, Artie. In Ireland or here."

SECTION SIX

LONGING

March

Christian Schamber usually stopped by Spring Abbey as soon as his morning chores were finished. Ostensibly, he dropped in to ask the widowed Mrs. Moffatt—Georgia—if there was anything needing doing that day. Christ could as easily have figured that out on his own, since he was much closer to the entire operation than was Georgia. But in the dead of winter, the jam factory was almost silent; its busy season came right after the harvest and continued through Christmas. After that, all of the fruit had been preserved and put up in jars, sold off, or squirreled away in the Moffatt warehouse to ensure that customers would have a steady supply until the next ripening.

Oddly, though, winter was a very active time in the orchards, or what was left of them since Mr. Granger's death. Early in the cold season, any trees past their prime were grubbed up and replanted. As the mercury dropped and the ground froze solid, the sleeping trees were pruned, so that they would flower extravagantly after their sap rose again. The heaps of cuttings were then burned in great Thanksgiving and Christmas bonfires, which attracted to Spring Abbey more than two hundred residents of Buffalo Plains.

Christ liked the cold, and so did Georgia. One local wag had said to her, soon after her father's death, that now that she had money, she could go anywhere she liked. Get out of Buffalo and go south, to her namesake state or, better, to the new wintering grounds of sunny Florida. She greeted this notion with obvious distaste. Buffalo Plains was her home, and while she hadn't much use for the booming city that was day by day creeping ever closer to her sanctuary, being near it did convey a sense of relevance, of belonging to something bigger than herself. *Florida?* The word held no attraction for her.

March was a strange month, though. The pruning was done, the bonfires long turned to ash, and now the sleeping land was readying itself for the short and spectacular growing season. Any maintenance in the jam factory had long been completed. Christ would therefore content himself with walks in the remaining orchards, and longer ones up to Forest Lawn Cemetery. Sometimes, if he could fabricate a good excuse—to see how things were going on the old Granger land, for example—he would ask Georgia to accompany him.

This might happen, at most, a few times in a winter, but those days were the sweetest of all. It might even be said that Christian Schamber lived for this shy week, when he would have Georgia all to himself, and far away from Spring Abbey and all its confining memories.

Because Forest Lawn owed a sizable chunk of its real estate to Mr. Granger's will, Georgia had free run of the property and never needed an entry ticket. When Christ was with her, neither did he, and one bright day in the early part of the month, the two strolled through the entrance gate at Delaware and Gulf Streets, waved to the guard, and entered what had only recently been Granger orchards.

"They do seem to be tending it well," Georgia said. "Though it doesn't look the same without the fruit trees."

"They've planted maples and oaks now," Christ replied, "and I saw two young beeches when we came through the gate. I sometimes wish I could live long enough to see them a hundred years from now."

"No thank you," Georgia said. "I don't want to live nearly so long. To fifty years of age, perhaps. That's enough."

"Fifty? Why, that would give you only twenty more years."

"Twenty-three, but thank you very much for the compliment."

"Sorry," he said. "I thought you were my age."

She laughed. "It's fine. How would you know?"

But Christ had feigned ignorance, if only to see her reaction. He knew everything about Georgia Granger Moffatt.

"I just thought since we played together as children, we were the same age."

"No. You were always almost three years older than I was, and you remain so."

He chuckled. "Do you ever think about our childhood days?"

Georgia exhaled steam in the frosty air. "Not too much. You?"

He wanted to say, *All the time*, but settled for, "Every once in a while, I suppose."

"What do you think about?"

Loving you, he thought, but kept silent again. "How much fun we used to have."

"We did have fun, didn't we?"

"Every day."

Georgia gave a small sigh. "Being grown up isn't nearly so fun, is it? There's always money and social things to consider, and business, and—well, lots of other things."

"Of course that's so," he said, "but I'd like to think that we're still young."

"I don't feel young anymore."

"You've been through a great deal."

"It's nothing compared to what you suffered through in the war. I haven't any right to complain about my lot in life."

They sat on a granite bench by a partially completed obelisk. "Yes, that was trying," he said. "Seeing so many promising young men die, though, made me want to live all the more."

"What does that mean, though?" she asked. "What does it mean to really *live*?"

Oh God, he thought. *Don't.* "I'd like to marry," he said, his heart thudding. "I'd like to have children, and have a nice little house—in Buffalo Plains, of course. That's my dream." He took a deep breath. "What about you?"

She smiled and looked off into the distance at the rolling land winding down to the Conjaquadies Creek.

"I'm sure you'll make some lucky young lady a very good husband."

"Thank you," he said, holding his tongue. He mustered up all of his courage. "Do you think that you would remarry—one day?"

Georgia looked over at him for a long heartbeat. "There's no requirement now," she said slowly. "I have enough money to be independent."

"That's certainly so. But don't you think there's more to marriage than that?"

"I wanted to have children, once, but—well, that didn't happen."

"It's not too late, Georgia."

"Will you look at the two of us?" she said, perking up. "Here we are, surrounded by dead people, and we're busily making ourselves miserable. Come on, let's cheer up and walk a little more." She scrambled to her feet and stuck out her hand as if to help the big man up.

Christ took her hand and stood. "Your poor hand—it's freezing," he said, rubbing it slowly. "Here, give me the other one." He clasped them in his and breathed on them.

"I think you've thawed them out," she said after a minute, and took them back.

They started down the gentle hill into the heart of Forest Lawn, Georgia looking up at the clear blue sky and Christ rubbing his hands, as if to conjure the feeling of hers in them again.

They had gone only a little way when they happened upon the Franklin Park pit. There they found Fermin and Dolan knee-deep in the frozen dirt; Fermin was leaning on a shovel, smoking, while Dolan swung a pickaxe.

"Good night," Georgia said. "What in the world are they doing? Look at the size of that pit."

"I heard about this," Christ replied. "This is where all the bodies from Franklin Park will go—for the new courthouse. They'll be digging until spring, I'd guess."

Georgia heaved a great steamy sigh into the bitter air. "Imagine—clearing out a cemetery. Doesn't *anything* last forever?"

Some things do, Christ thought. He looked over at her, wanting to plant a kiss on her rosy cheek. "I'm sorry, Georgia," he said. "I know how much this place means to you."

"I just don't think I'll ever understand how that Stroup talked my father into selling our land. I wanted it so badly that it makes me ache inside to know that it's gone forever."

"Maybe you could get it back somehow."

"No," she said. "I'd be a hypocrite if I made those poor people"—she inclined her head toward the pit—"move again."

"Maybe it will help to think that you gave up your forever for theirs," he said. She looked at him strangely. Then they turned away from the pit and walked slowly home.

RESURRECTION

April

The profession of the grave robber had changed a great deal since the Pharaohs had thought to protect their earthly possessions by building artificial mountains atop them. They knew that the hardworking ancient-Egyptian body snatcher didn't care about the king's mummy—it had no value, other than sentiment, and with few exceptions grave robbers are conspicuously lacking in that virtue. It was the gold and jewels, and the vast array of mortuary goods, that interested them. The backbreaking labor required to rifle the tombs was very well repaid in treasure.

That had all changed by 1867. Certainly any self-respecting corpse would be wearing a watch or necklace, wedding ring or tiepin, but those baubles were trifles. No one was about to spend a night digging, and risk a year in the Erie County Penitentiary, for a few dollars' worth of costume jewelry. What made the toil worthwhile would have stood the Pyramids on their heads—because nowadays it was the body itself that brought the big money.

Medicine was fast evolving from a motley collection of old wives' tales into something more like a profession. Where not too long before, doctors had learned their craft on the job, now medical colleges were springing up, credentials were being issued, and diplomas hung on office walls. And one of the fundamental elements of medical education was anatomy, and anatomy could be studied only so well from etchings in textbooks. A mastery of the structure of the human body required hands-on experience. And that, in turn, required dissection.

Since one couldn't very well dissect a living human being—although dogs, cats, and pigs were callously subjected to such vivisection—this new educational requirement created a swell of demand for corpses. And while people were dying every day, prevailing religious belief required that the body be preserved intact against the great day of Resurrection, when the dead would be reawakened and—this was the critical part—their mortal remains reunited with their departed spirit and transformed into a glorified being. Thus people guarded the bodies of their dead with the same jealousy that the Pharaohs had defended their treasure. Medical science would have to turn elsewhere to satisfy its ever-increasing appetite for flesh.

Enter the resurrectionist—the professional for-profit body snatcher, who would exhume a newly interred corpse and sell it to one of the medical colleges, or to one of the less professional schools of anatomy run by unscrupulous doctors. A freshly dug body—and freshness was crucial—fetched about twenty-five dollars. Since most working men made about a dollar a day, working six days a week, in a single night of hard digging an intrepid fellow could earn more than a month's wages. There was risk in it, but the rewards were irresistible to those interested in a quick buck.

The richest place for such prospecting was the potter's field, into whose soil went the bodies of the indigent, the unidentifiable, and the unclaimed. This burying ground—more properly known as Limestone

Hill Cemetery—was located just south of the city, atop the Ridge Road in Lackawanna. Its location made it convenient to wagon traffic, and yet it remained tucked discreetly under the crest of the hill, hidden from curious onlookers. Which was all by design: at Limestone Hill, city officials actively abetted the resurrection trade by issuing instructions to their gravediggers that a pauper's grave—in keeping with their modest circumstances—should be dug only two feet beneath the surface. This made the job of the resurrectionist much easier: two feet was a walk in the park compared to a recovery from almost six feet under, inside a cement vault, and in a properly sealed casket. *That* was hard duty. At the potter's field, a desultory dig and a crowbar inserted under the flimsy lid of the standard-issue pine box was more than sufficient effort.

Competition among the resurrectionists was accordingly fierce. Some chose to spend their days perched along Ridge Road, hoping to be the first to swoop down on a fresh body. Others paid a little earnest money to a cooperative contact in the Erie County Coroner's Office. Either way, the earthly remains of poor folk rarely remained unmolested until the final trump of the Lord sounded. They were lucky if they made it overnight.

None of this meant that the work of the body snatcher was a sinecure. It was gruesome, of course, but one did become inured to that after a while. Disinterring children, infants, and even fetuses could be emotionally distressing, but again, in time that became almost routine. The greatest risk, and a potentially lethal one, came from exposure to the very freshest bodies—always the most desirable—of those who had succumbed to a communicable disease, such as tuberculosis or syphilis. Left alone for a decent period, such a body would not normally transmit disease—but dig one up on the same day it had been interred, and all bets were off.

The resurrectionist's work abated in winter, when the ground was frozen and, for fear of discovery, it was unwise to risk a lengthy dig through even two feet of icy soil. Those unwanted souls unlucky enough to perish in the bleak season went instead mainly to Kraft's Dead House, on Huron Street, an enterprising offshoot of Mr. John Kraft's already lucrative coffin warehouse. The Dead House was no more than an unheated outbuilding, where the low temperatures would freeze the deceased solid and preserve them until the ground softened again in spring. Occasionally a body was spirited away from Kraft's place, but that was infrequent since toting a stiff through the streets of downtown was a far cry from conducting an isolated excavation in an unlit cemetery.

The medical academies, therefore, needed to stockpile dissectible specimens long before the bitter Buffalo winter set in. The solution to that little problem was the pickling vat. This was no more than an out-sized version of the pickle barrel found in every general store—a large wooden tub filled with a brine of vinegar and salt. The bodies would be dumped into the vat and could be kept fresh for as long as needed. And the pickling process had an additional advantage: it toughened the soft and spongy tissues into something more like the rubbery consistency of a pencil eraser, which was much easier to dissect.

Resurrection was a large and lucrative trade, and most of the better sort turned a blind eye to grave robbing, so long as the graves concerned were those of the indigent, who had—after all—sponged off of decent society long enough. It was high time for them to earn their keep. The dead of Forest Lawn, however, were a different ani-mal. Here a single plot, a simple burial, and a worthy granite marker could cost hundreds of dollars, and that kind of custom was difficult to come by in the cemetery game. So it was inconceivable that a common body snatcher would so much as dare to disinter one of Forest Lawn's fortunate dead.

And yet—as spring bloomed in Buffalo, that is precisely what was about to happen.

SECTION EIGHT

The Whore's Kiss

On the fifteenth day of April, Miss Mary Carkriff arrived in Buffalo aboard the Grand Trunk Railway from Brantford, Ontario. Rumor had it that there was work, and plenty of it, in the southern boomtown, and so with two changes of clothes, a parasol, a spare pair of shoes, and a pretty little silk reticule—a drawstring bag halfway between a handbag and a carryall—Mary had decided to take a chance. Certainly her prospects would be no worse than they were in Canada.

She stepped down from the train at the Erie Street Depot, in the heart of the perilous canal district. Fronting both bustling Erie Street and the stagnant, viscous canal was the slightly ramshackle Revere House, a large wooden hotel erected only ten years previously but which already seemed at risk of collapsing in upon itself. Since the establishment was built on pilings to keep it just above the fetid water of the canal—and was subject to the frequent storm surges off Lake Erie—the hotel's basement was forever awash in at least six inches of coffee-colored water, still as a millpond save for the wakes of swimming rats. Even the employees of the Revere House generally refused to visit the basement.

Nonetheless, Revere House had only recently changed hands, sold to one William Sheehan for the princely sum of $40,000, representing a neat profit to the original owners. How such a damp and ill-constructed pile could command $40,000 was something of a mystery. But it was widely bruited about that Sheehan, who had his finger in any number of criminal enterprises, had purchased the Revere because of its central location, deeming it a likely entrepôt for contraband smuggled in on the Great Lakes steamers—and aboard the Grand Trunk Railway itself.

Mary had telegraphed ahead for a room, expecting for a dollar a night she might enjoy a degree of luxury. But the deskman had taken her measure—a country girl in the big city—and assigned her to an unwanted first-floor room overlooking the canal. She dutifully trooped up one flight and tugged open the warped door, only to be assaulted by an overpowering reek. Horse manure mingled with coal smoke and the odor of the canal itself left a strange bitterness in the back of the throat, not unlike the aftertaste of vomit. Mary immediately shut all of her windows, but for April the day was unusually muggy, and soon her room was sweltering. She returned to the front desk to complain.

"Good afternoon, sir," she said, adopting what she hoped was a cheerful tone. "I'd like to request a different room."

The deskman looked up at her from his newspaper. "And you are?"

"Miss Carkriff. I registered only a half hour ago."

"Must have been with someone else than me," the man said, going back to the news.

"I don't believe so. But in any case, my room is not to my liking, and I wish to exchange it for another."

The man looked up again and smiled, showing a mouthful of tobacco-stained teeth. "All the rooms are the same. What's wrong— bed too hard for you?"

"The furnishings are quite adequate," Mary said. "But the loca- tion—overlooking the canal—is not to my preference."

"The rooms fronting the water are the best in the house."

"I'm sure they are, but to be quite plain about it, the smell is intolerable."

"Welcome to Buffalo. The whole city stinks. You're not in the country anymore, Miss."

Is it that obvious? she thought, stung. "I fully understand that, sir. Nevertheless, I'd like to request a room away from the water, if I may."

"Key," the man said, holding out a large palm. Mary placed her key gingerly in it, trying not to touch his skin. He closed his fist and turned to a grid of pigeonholes behind his desk. After a moment scanning the boxes—all of which seemed to have keys in them—he reached into one and handed over a new key. "First floor. Fronting on Erie Street. Not much of a view, but it's what we have left."

"I'm sure that will be very welcome," Mary said, taking the key. "Thank you for accommodating me."

"Happy to be of service," the deskman muttered, wiping a small dribble of tobacco juice from the corner of his mouth.

Mary smiled faintly at him and then turned away, almost bumping into a knot of men who had gathered behind her, apparently curious about her unusual request.

"What brings *you* to Buffalo, young lady?" one of the men asked with a sly leer. He was a sturdy character of middling size, wearing a slouch hat and needing a shave.

"Leave her be," the deskman said in a monotone, not looking up from his paper.

Mary ducked away and made for the staircase. Her new room smelled less of Erie Canal, but must have been located directly above the kitchen because the stale scent of frying onions and what may have been sausage seemed to have seeped into the damp wallpaper. Oh well, she thought, it will have to do. And he's right: I'm not in the country anymore.

She sat down on the mattress and examined the ticking for signs of bedbugs—small smears of victims' blood or, God forbid, one of the scuttling creatures themselves. There was nothing obvious, so she opened her reticule and fished around inside for her little porte-monnaie. She opened it and counted out her notes and coins. They amounted to two pounds, fourteen shillings Canadian—about ten dollars and eighty cents in American money, less any fees that she might be charged in currency exchange. She would have to be careful about that; although every Buffalo business happily accepted Canadian currency, one had to mind that an unscrupulous one didn't give short measure in exchange.

Ten dollars and eighty cents American, she thought. A dollar a day for the hotel, plus meals and transportation here and there—I have enough on hand to last a week or a little more, if I'm frugal. But after that . . .

She had thought to take a stroll around her new city but, in view of her financial limitations, decided it was more pressing to locate the proprietor and inquire about suitable employment for a young lady in Buffalo. Putting her money carefully away in the porte-monnaie, and replacing the little wallet in her reticule, she went quietly down the stairs again to the registration desk.

The deskman looked up warily. "Something wrong with this room, too?"

"Oh no," she replied, "the room is—quite suitable. I was wondering if I might speak with Mr. Sheehan."

The man squinted. "Sheehan? What do you want him for?"

"I should like to inquire about employment here in the city."

"You're not going to tell him you can't pay for your lodging, are you?"

"My heavens, no." She patted her reticule where it hung by her waist. "Neither you nor he need have any concern on that score, sir. I am well-supplied with specie, but as I am new in the city, I will need to find a suitable situation, all the same."

The deskman's face cleared a little. "All right, then. Wait here."

He disappeared into a back room and a moment later emerged with a burly man wearing a cap that seemed far too small for his large head.

"I'm Mr. Sheehan," the big man said, obviously liking what he saw before him. "I understand you are seeking employment."

"Yes, Mr. Sheehan, sir," Mary replied crisply, as she'd been taught. "It's a pleasure to make your acquaintance." She paused, but Sheehan didn't respond. "I'm new in the city, and while I have sufficient resources—"

"What kind of work are you looking for?"

"Sewing work, preferably. I have a great deal of experience—"

He took a half step back and examined her more closely. "You're very pretty," he said.

Mary blushed and looked down. "Why, sir, I . . ."

"There's nothing wrong with being pretty. Take it as a compliment."

"I do, of course," she said, flustered. "But as to sewing work, I wondered whether you might know of a dressmaker or a milliner in the city who is looking for a girl? I'm a very hard worker, and I'm good with the needle."

"I'm sure you are," Sheehan said with a yellow smile. "But you do know that sewing will ruin those beautiful eyes of yours."

"I—"

"And hunched over your work all day?" he continued. "You'll develop a hunchback. What likely fellow wants to marry a *hunchback*?"

Mary was at a loss as to how to respond—these city folk were certainly *very* unlike those back in little Brantford. Sheehan saved her the trouble.

"Tell you what," he said, rapping his knuckles sharply on the desk. "I've got an opening for a waitress in my hotel restaurant. It's *much* better work than sewing, and your room would be half-tariff, plus anything you'd like to eat in the restaurant for supper. Add to that any gratuities my guests may offer you, and you're easily making the equivalent of a dollar and a half a day. Maybe even two dollars."

Two dollars! Mary thought. Sewing's twenty-five to fifty cents a day, and it *is* punishing work.

"That's very kind, Mr. Sheehan," she said, "but in all candor, I don't know anything about being a waitress."

"Well, you're not all thumbs, are you? I don't expect you could be and make a living as a seamstress."

"No, sir, I'm not. It's just I don't know much about what a waitress *does*. I've never been to such a fine restaurant as I'm sure you have here."

"My dear *girl*," he said, showing off a partial set of stained teeth, "you leave all that to me. And by the saints, don't tell anyone else anything like that. People around here will take advantage of a girl without much experience of city life."

"You're quite right, Mr. Sheehan," Mary said, looking down again. "This is all new to me."

Sheehan stepped around the desk and, to her great surprise, put a big arm around her shoulders. "You know, you remind me of the daughter I never had," he said. "Or maybe a niece. Yes, more like a niece. Or a distant cousin. Tell you what—why don't you let Bill Sheehan take you under his wing? I can give you a very good start in this city."

Mary thought to wriggle free, but then considered that it might be rude, and that Americans might simply be more handsy than

Canadians. "You really are too kind, Mr. Sheehan," she said, trying not to smell his breath, which reminded her of the frying onions in her room. "I suppose I can give it a go. I'll do my best."

"A wise decision, Miss . . . ?"

"Carkriff," she said, at last finding a reason to duck out from under Sheehan's arm. She extended her hand demurely. "Mary Carkriff, from Brantford, Canada West."

Sheehan shook her hand with surprising gentleness. "Welcome to Buffalo, Mary Carkriff," he said. "I'm confident you'll like it here. Now, let's say you start tonight. Later this afternoon, drop by the restaurant and tell the steward about our conversation. He'll have a pretty little apron and cap for you to wear."

"I'll do it," she said, now feeling rather pleased about the prospects of waitressing. "Thank you again, Mr. Sheehan."

"It really is nothing, Miss Carkriff," he replied with a bow deep enough that it seemed it would dislodge his cap from its precarious perch. "I'm delighted that you're here. And I'll look forward to future intercourse with you."

"As will I, sir," Mary said.

Squinting and hunching over piecework was indeed difficult, but Mary hadn't counted on how strenuous it would be to carry heavy platters of food, mugs of beer, and God knows what else back and forth from the Revere House's kitchen to its tables. And sewing was quiet and contemplative, while the bustling restaurant was anything but. The patrons—mostly rough canallers and sailors—bellowed lustily to summon her, got up to loud and drunken quarrels, and kept the place continuously entertained with bawdy songs and shouted conversations.

By the time she climbed the stairs to her room, Mary was exhausted. She unfastened her shoes and sat down on her bed, halfway between numbness and tears. It's only my first day, she thought, trying to comfort herself. She stood up slowly and crossed the room to the washstand, thinking to sponge away the sweat and smoke coating her skin, but the washbasin was empty. That would mean putting her shoes on again and going all the way downstairs to the pump, which she was too tired to manage. Instead, she collapsed on her bed and fell into a dreamless sleep.

IT WAS STILL DARK when she awoke. She parted the thin curtain over her window and peered out over Erie Street. The roadway was twice as broad as a typical Buffalo street, and also served as a bridge over the canal—the canallers must have to duck for that one, she mused—to handle a day and night parade of heavy wagons, pulled by teams of horses or oxen. She couldn't tell what time it was, but the moon was still up, if faintly. A few wagon teams were already plodding toward the lakefront, to return laden soon after daybreak and begin shuttling goods into the city. Just across Erie Street was the depot for both the Grand Trunk Railway and the Niagara Falls Railroad, which conveyed tourists to and from the famous wonder thirty miles to the north. The station was glowing faintly from within, flickering like a jar filled with a hundred fireflies.

She thought of Canada. There hadn't been much for her there— her parents had been granted a rare and scandalous divorce after her father had blackened her mother's eyes one time too many. At first, she had lived with her father—who was as gentle with his daughter as he had been rough with his wife—in St. Mary's, but then her mother had complained. Mary had gone then to Brantford, and hadn't seen her father again. She'd heard a couple years ago that he had died, but how—or even whether that was true or another of her mother's frequent confabulations—she didn't know. But it had made her sad, just the same.

And now the excitement she'd felt all the way south on the Grand Trunk had dissipated, or at least had metamorphosed into homesickness, an emotion that she'd never considered a possibility. Here it was, though, and it couldn't be denied. Buffalo was big—she hadn't yet taken its measure and yet could sense its enormity—and exciting in a way, but it was noisy and stank of wet barnyard and the tartness of rotting garbage. No, she told herself, shaking her head. *It's far too early to lose faith. In only one day, I've found a place to live and a situation, even if the work is harder than I imagined. Now that's progress, Mary!*

Thus cheered—if only a little—she retrieved a pitcher of water from the pump behind the Revere House and returned to her room to make herself presentable. She changed into her other dress, a pretty blue frock, which she topped with a dark—deep purple, almost black—basquine, a fashionable little jacket that the ladies' magazines all agreed was very much in style. She tied a length of ribbon around her throat for a little color and set out to explore her new city as the sun came up.

Mary was almost to the staircase when the cramps began, nearly doubling her over. *The water?* she wondered. *Or last night's free meal at the restaurant?* She had certainly eaten far too much last evening, but it was the first bite she'd had since her departure from Brantford. She trotted down the hall to the conveniences but found the door locked, and from within heard the sound of someone clearly having an even worse time than she. This didn't make her cramps any better, so clutching her roiling stomach she ran down the stairs and tried the ground-floor toilet.

Thank goodness, Mary thought when she found the door unlocked. She darted into the compartment, and on closing the door was plunged into near pitch darkness. Quickly hoisting up the hoops of her skirt, she squatted deeply onto what seemed to be a strangely tiny, rough seat. *Uh-oh*, she thought, realizing that she had crouched not over the toilet but over the janitor's mop bucket. She made a hasty effort to stand and reposition herself.

Too late. Mary let go into the bucket with a thick rush and gurgle, which she prayed no one else could hear. She struggled again to get up, only to be struck by a fresh wave of cramping that she feared might overfill the little bucket. At last she gave up and sat weakly in her own stink, her eyes slowly adjusting to the thin sliver of light crawling under the door.

When at last the spasms eased, Mary fumbled around in the gloom until she found the water jug. She filled it with water from a small hand pump next to the actual toilet, splashed herself clean, and stood to drip dry. Then she dumped the contents of the bucket into the toilet and washed everything down with more water from the pump.

This ordeal caused her almost to weep, but she rallied and eased the door open a crack, mortified lest anyone should be waiting outside for a turn in the john. Grateful to find no one there, Mary slipped down the hallway and trotted out the front door.

RUNNING CROOKEDLY IN FRONT of the Revere House was a plank sidewalk built a good foot above Erie Street. And well that it was, because Erie Street was six inches deep in mud and horse shit. Mary turned right first, not knowing which way was better for exploration. She crossed the reeking canal, where below her a few boats were languidly being tugged along by teams of scrawny horses, their ribs visible through their patchy hair. One of the canal boatmen hallooed up at her, clearly trying to peek up her skirts. She hurried over the canal and came to Canal Street.

Crossing Canal Street, Mary quickly began to suspect that she may have ventured in the wrong direction. The next block seemed particularly tumbledown and had a disreputable air about it. A few men and an equal number of gaudily dressed women were lounging about on the corner, chatting in low voices. They looked over at her with what might have been amusement. Mary smiled and waved at them, which caused the group to burst into raucous laughter, cackling like a group of startled magpies. She picked up her pace and hustled past the little group.

As she approached Peacock Street, a sailor nursing an obvious hangover was leaning heavily on not one but two gaudy women, one under each burly arm. In the near distance Mary could hear the blare of ships' horns, and gathered then that she had turned toward the lakefront, which several gentlemen on the train had counseled her earnestly not to do. Just past the nearing intersection, she spotted another group of sailors, who spied her and commenced hooting and whistling.

She couldn't very well turn on her heel; she had been told by her mother that men were like dogs and could sense fear. Instead, she made a quick left turn down Peacock Street.

This was like passing through the gates of Hell. Peacock Street was a crowded narrow lane of what looked to be only a single block, each side lined with wooden buildings sporting tall false fronts, resembling more a Western mining camp than an Eastern port. It was clear even to a country girl that Mary had wandered into the heart of a vice district—and sure enough the first three buildings on Peacock were low-end saloons. Not much was going on in them this early, but a quick glance inside the first one revealed a few worn-out barflies slumped over the bar. Mary set her face forward and hurried down the street, looking to make the block back to the Revere House.

After the trio of saloons, Mary passed the first of a long line of what could only be bordellos. In front of each were two or three women, promenading to and fro, careful not to cross the imaginary line between each establishment. Mary dared to look sidelong at one of the brothels. In its front window sat a prostitute, dressed only in a petticoat, which, on cue, she hiked up above her waist to show off her wares. Horrified, Mary hustled farther into the depths of Peacock Street. About halfway down the block she was stopped by a woman in a velvet dress whose neckline was so deeply cleft that Mary could see the top curves of both areolas.

"Well, good morning, dearie," the lady said. "Looking for a little fun with a girl? Or to learn something that'll save your marriage?"

"I'm unmarried at present," Mary said without thinking. "So . . . a good day to you, madam," she stammered, sidestepping. The busty lady stepped with her.

"I'm not the *madam*," the lady said with a wink. "But if you want to meet her, I can arrange it. A pretty young thing like you would be a real prize on this block."

"Oh my, no, I'd prefer not—I mean I'd prefer to return to my lodgings at the Revere House," Mary babbled.

"Is *that* where you're staying, beautiful?" the prostitute asked, running a gloved finger under Mary's chin. "Perhaps you'll be more comfortable if I visit you there? They know me at the desk."

"No, that won't be necessary."

"You look to me like you could use a little fun in your life, dear. Fifty cents for a half an hour, and I promise to make you come twice. What do you say?"

Mary hadn't any idea what to say, perplexed by what "coming twice" might mean. "Really, I must be going," she countered with as much firmness as she could muster. "I insist."

"You *insist*, do you?" the woman said, her eyes narrowing. "I don't think that's very polite."

"Ma'am, I don't mean to be rude. I simply want to be on my way."

"Honey, I get paid for my time, and you've taken up quite a bit of it. You owe me something."

Mary thought of her two pounds and change in her reticule. "I-I don't have any money," she said. "On my person, I mean to say. I'm sorry."

The woman squinted at her. "No money on your *person*, you say? Now that seems a little hard to believe."

"It's the truth," Mary insisted, her voice shaking.

As she made to walk off, the prostitute blocked her again.

"Not so fast," she said. "If you don't have any money, then you have to give me a kiss."

"A *kiss*?"

"You heard me. A kiss, or I'll call the porter. He'll see if you *really* don't have any money on your *person*."

Mary leaned forward and kissed the lady on the cheek. "There," she said, wanting to wipe off her lips.

"On the mouth. A good one, beautiful."

She saw that the woman was serious, so she leaned forward again and ventured a quick kiss on the lady's mouth, which smelled of stale tobacco. The prostitute reached up and grabbed the back of Mary's head, forcing her tongue between the young lady's teeth. The tongue tasted of tobacco, too.

"Now that wasn't so bad, was it?" the woman said, letting go at last.

Mary wanted desperately to spit, but wisely decided that would only further inflame things. "Now may I *please* be on my way?" she said instead, as calmly as she could manage.

The prostitute stepped aside with a rustle of skirts. "Be my guest."

Mary hustled down Peacock Street in a cold sweat, feeling the woman's eyes on her back. When she was almost to the cross street, she heard the prostitute yelling after her.

"She's a good kisser, boys!"

Mary took a left on Evans Street and then another on Canal, and returned to the Revere House, winded and still tasting the whore's kiss.

The Anatomical Board

Since not everyone who dropped dead in Buffalo was fortunate enough to wind up in a cozy grave in serene Forest Lawn, there to remain unmolested until the crack of doom, someone had to look after the ones who were less so. And in a city where thousands of people came and went—by canal boat, steamer, rail, or foot—a not insubstantial number each year would give up the ghost far from home, friends, or family: assuming, that is, they had any one of them. Transients, though, were relatively few by comparison with the hordes of penniless locals, who died in droves in alleyways and boarding houses. If they hadn't been able to afford food while alive, they would certainly not qualify for a plot in the rich loam of Forest Lawn.

Someone, therefore, had to decide what to do with the unwanted, unknown, and indigent dead. In Erie County, that duty fell to five men—the Anatomical Board.

The Anatomical Board directed corpses either to the potter's field or to the pickling vat at the Buffalo Medical School. Only the choicest paupers qualified for the pickling vat; such an august institution as the medical school was certainly not the place for the old, defective, or diseased. Those inferior specimens were duly interred in Limestone Ridge Cemetery, although it was rumored that certain members of the board happily turned a blind eye to the waiting resurrectionists.

James J. Richards, Erie County coroner, headed the board, and his judgments were nigh unchallengeable. Nipping close at his heels, though, was the ambitious and slightly unpredictable Dr. Waldo von Guyaling, chief anatomist at the Buffalo Medical School. Von Guyaling aspired to be coroner one day, if only Richards would die or retire. But Richards persisted in both good health and vigor, so von Guyaling could do little more but play the long game.

George Hadley, of Hadley's Practical Chemistry Laboratory, was next in the pecking order. He focused on causes of death, opining on whether decedents had been killed by plague, poison, or accident. When not serving on the board, his main business was creating and marketing cure-alls, nostrums, and home remedies, some of which were reputed to be more dangerous than the conditions they were claimed to treat.

The other two members of the board—John Kraft, proprietor of Kraft's Dead House, and his mortal enemy, Caleb Martin, of cross-town rival Martin's Coffin Manufactory & Warerooms—were both remarkably acrid personalities and kept things from becoming too civil. Martin—an outlander who hailed from Pennsylvania, no less—had in only a few short years in Buffalo begun to erode Kraft's long-time monopoly on the fruit of the Anatomical Board's labors.

When a family could afford private interment in Forest Lawn or one of the other decent cemeteries, the Anatomical Board gener-ally stood aside, if sometimes with envious eyes. It however remained within the coroner's purview to poach a body or two from the passing parade of these protected dead—if he felt that the deceased would be of particular value to science. This was usually a "freak" of some kind: a dwarf, someone with six fingers or toes, or one memorable time, a man with three testicles—a prize rarity. Even that lucky fellow's legion of progeny could not keep him from the pickling vat.

"Today's meeting will come to order," Coroner Richards said, although he had no gavel and nothing to pound it on. The five were standing in the holding room of Kraft's Dead House, where that week's unclaimed bodies had been sent.

"Before we begin," Caleb Martin said, "I'd like to know why the week's deceased were all brought *here*. It seems like quite a windfall for Mr. Kraft."

"All of the week's unclaimed died in West Buffalo," the coroner said. "Had they died in East Buffalo, they would have come to you. It's a simple matter of transportation cost."

"I'm sure if the dead could walk, they'd choose your fine establishment," Kraft muttered out of the side of his mouth. While by no means opulent, the Kraft coffin shop was by far the tidier of the two, with prices to match.

"Very droll," Martin said. "Then tell me—someone, anyone—just what *is* the dividing line between East and West?"

"It's like Mason and Dixon all over again," von Guyaling said to Coroner Richards, "but turned on its head."

"On its side, to be precise," said Practical Chemist Hadley.

"You take my point, Mr. Hadley, I have no doubt," von Guyaling said. He was a gruff Dutchman, who had come to the United States as a young man, though even decades later he spoke in a near-impenetrable, inexplicable accent.

"Mr. Coroner?" Martin persisted. "May we settle this, once and for all? The dividing line. I want to make sure I get my fair share of the dead."

"I'd suggest Main Street," Kraft said. "Runs north and south, pretty neatly."

Martin gave a derisive laugh. "Oh, sure. Main Street. I'm on *Michigan*. That's all of two blocks east of Main—"

"They're long blocks," said Kraft.

Martin ignored him. "—which would leave you about nine-tenths of the city to the west. I don't think so, Kraft."

"May we table this for the present?" the coroner said. "Or perhaps we could alternate between you, regardless of the location of the death."

"That will cost a fortune," said the thrifty von Guyaling.

"Only until we can determine a more permanent solution," Richards said. "People are dying all over the city, and if we have to wrangle over whose is whose, the aldermen will be apoplectic. Now may we get down to business?"

"I think I ought to get half of these bodies, pursuant to your new ruling, Coroner," Martin said.

Hadley chuckled. "Which half?"

"Rulings aren't retroactive," Kraft said, unamused. "Haven't you ever taken a civics lesson?"

"Listen here, I'll have you know I know plenty about—"

"Gentlemen, a little decorum, please," said Coroner Richards, holding up his hands. "We are, after all, in the presence of the dead."

Martin muttered something but knew better than to push the coroner too hard. There were four other coffin manufacturers in Buffalo, and any one of them could replace him. Kraft was connected, somehow, to someone up the chain.

"Did you gentlemen happen to read in the newspaper this morning that there was an attempted resurrection at Forest Lawn last night?" the coroner asked. "Foiled only by the rain."

"I did," Hadley said. As a scientist, he liked to show that he was in possession of the facts.

"The mayor is furious about it," Richards said. "His view is that this board has plenty of material to distribute, and it's not good for the city if the respectable dead are being disinterred."

"They're pulling them up like potatoes at the potter's field," Hadley said.

"You get what you pay for," the coroner said. "I was referring to the better sort."

"Well said," Kraft intoned. He was known for his just-shy-of-two-foot burials—deep enough to keep all but the most determined dogs away, but shallow enough that the resurrectionists who worked the potter's field could dig up two or three in a leisurely evening.

The coroner turned to von Guyaling. "Doctor," he said, "I trust that I may count on you to refuse any resurrected body proffered to your medical school."

Kraft and Martin both snickered.

"Why, Coroner, I confess to be a little taken aback by your question," von Guyaling said.

"I meant only—"

Von Guyaling cut him off. "May we review the causes of death for this group? I, for one, would like to finish our business as quickly as possible and then seek out fresher air. Someone in here is unusually ripe."

"That would indeed be welcome," Coroner Richards said. "Yes. I have assigned the following causes of death to this week's paupers." He riffled through a handful of papers. "It's been a light week, as you can see. Two suicides, one killed by a train, and a drowning."

"The suicides," von Guyaling said. "How did they commit the act?"

Practical Chemist Hadley cleared his throat. "One, a middle-aged female, drank carbolic acid. The other, a man of about thirty, blew out his brains."

"With a pistol, or something else?" von Guyaling asked.

"Shotgun."

"Then he is of no use to the medical school," von Guyaling said.

Richards made a notation. "Kraft, that's one for the potter's field."

"Noted," Kraft said, scribbling in a small ledger book. He knew that that one would be dug right away, head or no head—the liver, lungs, kidneys, and heart would be worth at least ten dollars to the Buffalo School of Anatomical Science, a private institution that offered discreet remedial instruction to those who were already practicing medicine, but who had never dissected anything and didn't want to let on.

"The carbolic acid incident presents a more complicated case," Hadley said. "Significant damage to the mouth and esophagus, but the rest anatomically intact."

"Middle-aged, you say?" von Guyaling asked.

"That was my judgment," Hadley replied.

"May I view the body?"

"Of course," Coroner Richards said. "Kraft?"

"She's over here," Kraft said, closing his ledger. He led the small group over to a bier along the opposite wall of the Dead House. He pulled back a canvas tarpaulin to reveal the body. Lying there was the naked body of an impossibly well-formed woman of about twenty-five, who would have remained quite beautiful even in death save for the *Y*-incision from her autopsy and the contorted facial features of an agonizing death by poison. Her legs were slightly parted.

"How old did you say?" von Guyaling asked again.

"Middle-aged," Hadley repeated.

"Do you need new glasses?" von Guyaling said with a smirk.

"I may have overestimated her age slightly," Hadley said, unapologetically ogling the naked corpse.

"Such a waste," Martin said, clucking his tongue.

"*Tragic*," Kraft echoed, the first time he'd ever agreed with anything Caleb Martin had said.

"She's *perfect*," von Guyaling said, to nods. "For the school, that is. She will be an excellent subject for examination—I would suppose she discovered herself with child and unmarried, and took her life accordingly. Therefore there may be an implanted ovum or even a fetus for study. The best of the best."

"She's yours, then, Doctor," Coroner Richards said, writing something on the woman's death certificate. The Anatomical Board then stood in silence, soberly examining the dead young woman. Finally Richards sniffed. "Best cover her up again, Kraft," he said. "Dignity, you know."

"Of course, sir," Kraft replied, and with what might have been a twinge of regret, pulled the tarpaulin slowly over the body.

Richards continued. "The others, then. The train incident was a hobo. He was attempting to board a freight and fell off. Went under the wheels."

"What is the condition of the body?" von Guyaling asked.

"Mangled."

"Pass."

"Kraft, another for Limestone Hill, then," Richards said. "One more. The drowning. Male, about thirty. Fell into the Canal while intoxicated."

"How long in the water?" asked von Guyaling.

"That was hard to determine," said Hadley. "A while. Have a look."

Kraft pulled back another tarpaulin to reveal a bearded, hirsute young man, horribly bloated and whose eyes had been eaten away by whatever creatures managed to survive in the putrid water of the Erie Canal. The stench of decay would have peeled the paint off the walls of

Kraft's Dead House, if the walls had been painted. Clearly this corpse was the source of all the bad air.

Von Guyaling buried his mouth and nose in the crook of his elbow. "*Too far gone*," he gasped out.

"Cover him up, and pronto," Coroner Richards said. "Again, one for the potter's field. Make that one at least three feet, Mr. Kraft, if you would."

"With pleasure," Kraft replied.

"That's the lot of them, Richards," Hadley said.

"Then we are done for today, gentlemen. Thank you all for coming."

"Mr. Kraft," von Guyaling said, "please ensure that the unfortunate beauty—the, er, middle-aged lady—is brought directly, while fresh."

"As you wish, Doctor," Kraft said, paying no heed to the dirty look that Martin was giving him.

SECTION TEN

BARNEY BRENNAN

Fermin and Dolan soon found that digging at Forest Lawn was a far cry from the same task at the poorhouse. This didn't mean that it wasn't hard, physical work. It was, but the biggest difference was that, in the rolling vastness of the Forest Lawn grounds, the two spent their days almost entirely unsupervised. They righted tombstones that had begun to list to one side or another, kept the Conjaquadies Creek, which bisected the great cemetery, free of snags and debris, and—their favorite—laid charges of black powder in groundhog burrows. Then from a safe distance they would wait until the unsuspecting rodent would cautiously show his twitchy face, depress the handle of the detonator, and blow the critter sky-high.

A great deal of time, though, was spent smoking, swapping lies, and—when they knew Mr. Stroup was away or otherwise occupied, say with a meeting of the board of trustees—sneaking through the opening in the board fence along Gulf Street to have a drink or two at Barney Brennan's place, a barroom on the corner of Main and Gulf, just opposite the cemetery.

Barney Brennan was a fellow Irishman, although he'd been in the country longer than Fermin and Dolan—and while he too had started out as a day laborer, he was now the proprietor of a thriving business, and proud of it. Both of these facts meant that Brennan was several rungs higher on the social order than his clientele, and he made sure that they knew it.

Brennan provided two services to the large Irish community in and around Buffalo Plains: alcohol and wakes, and often both at the same time. His saloon-cum-funeral-home was located in a modest frame building very much in keeping with the other middle-class housing just south of the cemetery. The only things that set it apart were two large plate-glass windows in front, with heavy curtains that could be drawn for privacy or concealment, and a hand-painted sign above the door that read:

BRENNAN'S SALOON & MORTUARY
Fine Liquors & Cigars
FUNERAL RECEPTIONS OUR SPECIALTY

Inside, Brennan's was crammed cheek by jowl with cheap deal tables, though sometimes these would be shoved to the perimeter of the large main room to allow space in the center for a bier holding the open coffin of the deceased. After the revelry of the wake was finished, it was a short trip down Gulf Street to the main gate of Forest Lawn.

Barney himself was a tallish man, lean and well-dressed, but with a hard and hawklike face that, even when smiling, made him look like a man capable of mayhem. Rumor had it that he had done a stretch in Auburn Prison for murder, but there wasn't any hard proof of it, and not a soul—no matter how well-lubricated—would dare ask him directly. Fermin and Dolan, who had both done time back in Ireland, though for far pettier crimes than murder, agreed that Barney had "the look"—the small tell that jailbirds are said to have that every other jailbird can recognize. It certainly might have been true. One thing that was incontrovertible was that Mr. Barney Brennan didn't put up with any shit in his establishment. Men who stirred up trouble would have their heads cracked and then be thrown unconscious out the front door by Barney himself, and not allowed back. If anything off-center went on at Brennan's place, one thing was sure: either Barney Brennan was in on it or it was immediately squelched.

Brennan kept his sharp eye on Arthur Fermin and Bobby Dolan, as he would have any new set of faces. And from the start, he didn't much like them. But he did recognize in them a certain canniness and guile that he might be able to put to use. During the long winter, Dolan and Fermin would drop by for a nip at least once a day, and sometimes more, giving the saloonkeeper ample opportunity to observe their conduct. And now in spring, after a lengthy period of evaluation, Brennan decided that he'd seen enough of the pair to broach a delicate subject.

One afternoon, he had served the pair their usual boilermakers—a big shot of Irish whiskey and a mug of beer to chase it down. As they drank, and Barney put away what passed for clean glassware, he gave them a glance. It was the first one without either suspicion or contempt, or both, and they noticed.

"Tell me again," Brennan asked, although he knew the answer. "Just what is it you boys do over across the street?"

"Labor," Fermin said.

"What's that mean?"

"We've been digging a big hole," Dolan added.

"Why?"

"It's for the bodies coming from Franklin Park Cemetery," Fermin replied.

"Ah, I know it well," said Brennan. "That's George Eberly's contract." He puffed up his chest. "I've been doing all the interments, since he's not a licensed funeral director."

"That's a nice piece of work there," Fermin said, rubbing his thumb and forefinger together.

Brennan smirked. "Paid by the state, too. But these days a fellow's got to scrape up every penny he can. If there's money to be made, a man has to make it. Hard times are coming."

"Yup," Fermin said, taking a big swig of his beer. "Though it seems we've had nothing but."

"How do you like working for Mr. Stroup?"

Fermin shrugged. "He's all right, I suppose. Kind of a martinet, you know, but comes with the territory. And he's forever bitching about how little he gets paid."

"I wouldn't have expected *that*," Brennan said. "What about you boys? Does Stroup pay you well over there?"

"A dollar a *day*," Dolan said with a note of pride. "Plus room and board."

Fermin shot his friend a sidelong glance. "Well, you can believe me—we earn every red cent of it. And not just digging the big hole. We're digging individual graves, too."

"I haven't any doubt of it, lad. It's hard work you have there."

"It's a sight better than what we had at the poorhouse," Fermin said. "That much I will say for it."

Brennan finished putting away his streaky glassware. "I'm sure it is. If you boys are ever of a mind to make some easy money, though, let me know."

Fermin set his mug down carefully on the bar. "Easy money, you say? You wouldn't be pulling our legs, now would you?"

"I'm not really in the leg-pulling business. So no."

"What do you have in mind?"

"Can you keep a secret?" Brennan asked, lowering his voice.

Fermin squinted at him. "Secrets we take to our grave, Mr. Brennan."

"One way or another," Barney chuckled. "But it's good to hear, all the same. Now mind you, you'll have to keep this close, but I may have just the thing for you two."

"We're listening," Fermin said.

Brennan leaned over the bar, his face less than a foot from theirs. "Have you ever heard of *resurrection*?"

"Like the Lord Jesus Christ?" Dolan said. "Of course. On Easter Sunday."

Fermin smiled crookedly. "I don't think he means *that* kind of resurrection."

"Smart fellow," Brennan said. "You hit the nail on the head."

Dolan looked perplexed. "I don't understand, Artie."

"What he means," Fermin said softly, tapping his finger on the bar, "is digging up dead bodies and selling them."

"You can't be serious," Dolan said. "We'd go to Hell for doing that."

"I couldn't say about that," Brennan said. "But there's good money in it, that I can tell you. The medical school is constantly short of bodies that their students can cut up for practice. You have to do that kind of thing to become a doctor these days, you know."

"Will wonders never cease?" Dolan whispered, shaking his head.

"And since we're the ones burying them, you reckon we're the best fellows to dig 'em up again," Fermin said.

"Another nail hit straight on."

"But won't someone see the open pit left behind?" Dolan asked.

"You fill it in again after, idiot," Fermin said. "No one's the wiser."

"Right," Barney said. "You do the digging at night, get the body out of the cemetery, and take it to the janitor at the medical school. You have a wagon, don't you?"

"Yeah, but getting hold of one at night may be difficult," Fermin said, draining the last of his beer. "Old Stroup's got ears like a bat, and the wagons are kept near where he sleeps."

"I might be able to talk with him," Brennan said. "Make up some excuse."

"I don't know," Fermin mused, playing with his mug. "It sounds pretty risky. I don't want to go to jail."

"And I don't want to go to Hell," Dolan chimed in.

"Same difference, if you ask me," Brennan said. He took Fermin's mug out of his hands, refilled it at the tap, and set it back in place.

Fermin stared at the foaming mug. "Mr. Brennan, I don't have the money—"

"It's on the house."

"That's mighty white of you, sir," Fermin said. "Thanking you kindly."

"Don't mention it. Now then, there's not that much risk to this resurrection business, you know, if Stroup can be persuaded to look the other way."

"Why in the world would he do that?" Dolan asked.

Brennan winked at him. "You leave that to me, lad."

Fermin took a long and thoughtful pull on his mug, and wiped away the suds with his sleeve. "I suppose it's something we might could do, for the right price."

Brennan smiled. Small-timers always wanted to know about the money first. "I'd pay you each two dollars a body, delivered."

"Two dollars per!" Dolan almost yelled. "Just for—"

"I thought you were worried about Hell," Fermin said out of the corner of his mouth.

"Hush, my boys," Brennan said. "You never know who might be listening and want to horn in on the deal."

"There has to be a catch," Fermin said. "If it sounds too good to be true . . . you know."

Barney stepped back from the bar and studied him. "You've got sand, boy," he said. "But no, there's no catch. Well, except a very small one."

"I told you," Fermin muttered under his breath.

"What's the catch?" Dolan asked.

"You say any word to anyone about this, or mention my name— even in your sleep—and I'll have your throats cut. Both of you. I suppose in truth that's more a promise than a catch."

"Goes without saying," Fermin said, unfazed. "You're the boss. But what about drinks?"

"What about them?"

"You'd think a couple of trusted lieutenants could get a free one now and again."

The saloonkeeper laughed. "One free drink, each of you, a day. And you can't carry 'em over. Now what do you say? Do we have a deal or not?"

"You bet we have a deal!" Dolan said, a bit too loud. "May I have my drink now?"

THE SMUGGLERS

After a couple of weeks, Mary Carkriff found life as a waitress was still difficult, but it did seem like she was learning to smile at her customers and hear their requests over the din of the Revere House's restaurant. The place closed at midnight—per city statute—but most of the tables were empty by ten; everyone who was looking for late-night hijinks had already left for one of Buffalo's countless speakeasies. These so-called blind pig saloons could be located by finding establishments whose windows had been painted black. Beat cops couldn't see whether the lights were still burning after midnight in such places, and all the blind pigs had to do was stop the piano at the appropriate hour. After twelve, patrons knew to come and go via the rear door.

It was quarter past ten and only two tables were still occupied. Mary was resting her tired feet in a small anteroom off the dining hall when the front door banged, and in came a group of four men. Her hopes to retire early dashed, she got up to greet them.

A good-looking tall man was leading the group. He seemed too young to be leaning so heavily on a gold-handled cane. He very pleasantly tipped his hat to her. "Good evening, Miss," he said. "Table for four, if you please."

Mary gestured to the nearly empty restaurant. "Do you favor a particular one, sir?"

"You're Canadian," a shorter fellow with almond-shaped eyes said. "How did you know?"

"I'm from Port Colborne," the man said. "I recognize the accent."

"Canadians don't have accents," a very handsome tanned fellow said, removing his hat and shaking back a headful of flowing blonde curls.

The man from Port Colborne laughed. "If they don't, how do you think I knew this young lady was Canadian?"

"Lucky guess?" the man with the golden hair said.

"Don't mind my friends," the tall man said with a smile. "How about the table in the corner? We'd like some privacy. We have business to discuss."

Mary showed the men to the table and asked if they'd like a drink before supper.

"Since you're Canadian," the man from Port Colborne said, "how about you bring us a bottle of Canadian whiskey?"

"Right away, sir," Mary said, and hurried away toward the kitchen.

"She's awful pretty," said the last man, who had been silent. He was swarthy and heavily built.

"Don't get any ideas, Kirsch," the tall man said. "She's not your type."

"What do you know about my—"

Mary returned with the whiskey and poured out four glasses. "Here you are, gentlemen."

"Thank you, Miss . . . ?" Kirsch, the swarthy man, said.

"Carkriff," Mary said. "Mary Carkriff. From Brantford, Canada West."

"Then introductions are in order, Miss Carkriff," the tall fellow said. "My name is George Eberly, and I hail from Syracuse, but now I call Buffalo home."

"Ed Durham—from Port Colborne, as you already know," the Canadian said.

"Captain John Andrews, at your service," said the man with the golden curls. "From everywhere and nowhere."

"If you don't mind my saying," Mary said, "you look just like the photos I've seen of your General Custer."

Andrews shook back his locks and smiled. "You hear *that*, boys? *General Custer.*"

The swarthy man scowled. "And I'm August Kirsch," he said. "From Black Rock."

"Who looks like General Custer's horse," Durham said, earning another scowl from Kirsch.

"A toast to the lovely Miss Carkriff, boys," George Eberly said, raising his glass.

"Why, thank you, gentlemen," she said, giving them a little curtsy. "Let me see if I have it correct. Mr. Eberly of Syracuse-now-Buffalo, Mr. Durham from Port Colborne, Captain Andrews from everywhere and nowhere, and Mr. Kirsch from Black Rock."

The men applauded. "Well done, Miss Carkriff," Eberly said. "Andrews, I believe you've mystified the young lady with your origins."

"I'm master of a clipper ship," Captain Andrews explained. "My home is wherever my ship happens to be."

"Well said," Kirsch added, taking a big swallow of his whiskey.

Mary took their supper orders and then trotted back to the kitchen.

"Good night, she *is* pretty," Durham said.

"You stay away from her, Ed," Andrews said. "Yours truly, General Custer, gets first dibs."

Eberly rolled his eyes. "Can we get to business? What's coming in this week?"

"Opium," said Kirsch. "Small shipment—a few chests by rowboat."

"Durham?"

Ed Durham took a sip of his liquor. "I'll be back in a week or two with another batch of this." He held up his glass.

"Good," Eberly said. "We need to stock up so that we can sell at a premium when the holidays come around." He turned to the ship's master. "How about you, Captain?"

"My cargo is being unloaded tomorrow," Captain Andrews said. "I have in my hold four barrels of Spanish silver from Macau. I'll have a couple trusted men unload those last."

"How did you get your hands on silver?" Kirsch asked. "The Chinese don't like to let any of that go."

"Let's say I called in a little loan," Captain Andrews replied.

"You ought to get a bellyful of opium next time," Eberly said. "Demand can't keep up with whatever Kirsch can row across from Fort Erie."

Andrews nodded. "I'll do my best."

Durham suddenly sat back hard in his chair. "George, I don't mean to be impertinent, but I have to ask. What's the point of all this happy talk about goods coming in, when it seems you haven't been moving the goods we've already brought in? You haven't paid us out in more than a month."

"Thank God *someone* brought it up," Kirsch added.

Eberly sighed. "I knew you boys would be breaking my balls about that." He swirled the liquor in his glass, watching the little vortex. "We've had a bit of a setback recently."

"I don't like the sound of this 'we' stuff," Durham said.

"That's because it's the sound of not getting paid," said Captain Andrews.

"Here it comes," Kirsch said.

Eberly held out his hands. "Now listen, boys. It's not the end of the world . . . but in the past month, two of our shipments north have been confiscated."

"And that's *our* problem *how*?" said Kirsch.

"Gus, you know we all win or lose together," Eberly said.

"Then we all deserve to know how such a thing could happen," Captain Andrews said.

"Just how much do you *want* to know, John? I seem to recall that none of you—not one—wanted to know the details of how I get our goods to Niagara Falls."

Kirsch leaned forward. "Nor do we now, George. It's safer that way for everyone. But *two* shipments gone in a month? That may not be the end of the world, but it's close."

Eberly hesitated, then carefully set down his knife and fork. "As you wish. Suffice it to say that four wagons a month—very nondescript ones, too—skirt around the big Forest Lawn Cemetery, along Delaware Street, to points north. No one, but no one, is normally patrolling that road. But then all of a sudden, two full shipments are intercepted and seized by the police."

"Have you talked with Chief Sloan about this?" Durham said, red-faced. "It's an outrage."

"I thought perhaps the first time was a fluke, but after the second one I did speak to him, and in no uncertain tones," Eberly said. "He told me that he had a rogue cop who did his job."

Andrews hissed through his teeth. "And *that's* what we get for all the money we pay him and his men?"

"John, the chief of police can't very well instruct his men not to seize contraband," Eberly said. "Even he can go only so far. The cop in question was tipped off, and Sloan is hardly to blame for that."

The men grumbled a bit before Captain Andrews spoke up again.

"Now, George, you know as well as I do what 'tipped off' means. It means only one thing: you've got—"

"Oh, believe me, I know. A *rat*. And I had one of our men in North Buffalo give a very nice reward to the cop who got the tip. I found out right away who the rat was."

Kirsch frowned. "I hope you took good care of the fucker."

George returned a flat smile. "You know me better than that. Let's just say that it's amazing how many people these days are willing to risk life and limb going over the Falls in a barrel."

Captain Andrews sat back and clapped. "Now that is almost worth losing half a month's income for," he said. "I trust the man was alive at the time?"

"He was at the crest of the Falls, to judge by his screaming," Eberly said. "After that, I couldn't say."

"Well," Durham said, "then that is that. So when can you resume shipments?"

"Now, Ed, not so fast. Don't think for a second that only one cop up that way is wise to our shipments now. No matter what Sloan and I do, it's worth a lot of money to any one of them to intercept our wagons. So I can't use that route again—it's too risky."

"As I said, I don't need or want to know more than I have to," Kirsch said. "But you did say that you go *around* Forest Lawn."

"That I did."

"So why not go *through* Forest Lawn?"

"Simple. Everyone who goes in has to have a ticket, unless it's for an interment. A wagon showing up at the gatehouse with crates of liquor under a tarpaulin isn't getting through."

Durham tapped on the table. "George, if anyone can figure out a way, it's you. And I'm sure I speak for the group when I say that I have complete faith in you. Having said that—"

"Here comes the 'but,'" George said.

"I'm afraid so. I am honor bound to observe that I can't keep risking my ship—and my neck—for no return. Not for long."

"And I like to think of myself as a patient man," Andrews added. "But I have shares to pay out on every voyage soon after I reach port. This time, I can raid some of my Spanish silver to pay them, but what do I tell my sailors next time? I'll have a mutiny on my hands."

"John," George said, "I will personally front you the money if that ever happens."

"What about the two of *us*?" Kirsch said, gesturing between him and Durham.

"I can't pay *everyone*," Eberly said. "Andrews here is going to be strung up if his men don't get paid. You fellows can last a few more weeks."

"Now how about that, Gus?" Durham said. "We're second-class smugglers now."

"Come on, Ed. Be reasonable. I'm going to fix things, now that I understand the problem."

"With respect, George, I'm not sure you do," Captain Andrews said.

"Excuse me? Not sure I do what?"

Andrews took a deep drink of whiskey. "Understand the problem."

"What's that supposed to mean?"

Captain Andrews smiled. "Your real problem is not a rat turned daredevil. It's not the cops. And it certainly isn't us for, um, busting your balls. Your problem is *you*."

"John, this is rather strong talk—"

"No, no, just listen for a change, George. I've seen this problem before. I've *had* this problem before. You're behaving like a ship's master who's trying to do everything himself. Navigate, set sails, direct the crew. You can't tend everything you've got on the boil, and figure out new routes, and God knows what else. That's when slip-ups happen, and costly ones at that. What you *really* need is another one of you to look after things. A first mate."

"Hear, hear," Ed Durham said.

George fiddled with his silverware for a moment. "I will agree that's an excellent suggestion. But finding that kind of man takes time."

"How much time?" Kirsch asked.

"A month?"

The men were still grousing when Mary arrived with a tray heaving with food. She set it down carefully on an adjacent table and then began placing dishes in front of the four men.

"Thank you," Eberly said when she had finished. "You're very good at this."

"Why, thank you, sir. I still have a lot to learn, though. I only recently arrived in Buffalo."

"My dear, you are possessed of a remarkable memory," Captain Andrews said. "Not only did you recall our names, you remembered precisely what each of us ordered, without writing anything down."

Mary blushed and gave a little curtsy. "That's very kind—"

"*General Custer,*" Kirsch said, making Mary blush a deeper shade of red. She smiled, placed the rest of the dishes, and with another curtsy, left the men to dine.

"All right, George," Durham said, "enough stalling. Let's hear your plan for getting this first mate Andrews is talking about. How will another month change anything?"

"I've been thinking about asking our go-between in Buffalo Plains to work more closely with me," George lied, out of options.

"And who might that be?" Kirsch asked.

"I thought you didn't want details."

"A first mate is not the same as which roads you take or when. We have a right to know who's holding the noose around our necks."

Eberly shrugged. "All right, then. I'm thinking about Barney Brennan."

Andrews looked puzzled, and Kirsch and Durham laughed. "You want to bet our lives on *Barney Brennan*?" Kirsch said. "Oh, for Chrissake, what an idea. He's a *murderer*. He's done at least two stretches in Auburn."

"So what?" Eberly shot back. "That's why he's so connected. Convicts stick together if there's a buck to be made."

Durham shook his head. "It's not my place to question your judgment, George . . ."

"But?"

"But if Brennan flies into one of his famous rages and kills someone, we've all got a problem. He's dangerous enough as a distributor, but that's a risk I can accept. He'd be a *disaster* as your right-hand man."

"I'm open to suggestions, then, if you think it's so easy."

"There's no need to get in a snit, George," Andrews said. "We're trying to help."

"Right," Durham said. "Let's think it through. What kind of man would fill the bill?" He counted on his fingers. "Smart. Gets shit done . . ."

"Can hide in plain sight," Kirsch added. "Not some jailbird that everyone knows."

"Maybe even someone a little green," Durham agreed, "who isn't yet smart enough to cheat us."

"Ideally someone not from Buffalo," Andrews said. "Everyone knows everyone here."

"Can we not try to solve this tonight?" Eberly said, exasperated. "I've heard you all loud and clear. Trust me, I'll find someone quickly. Just give me a couple of weeks."

"I do believe George wants us to lay off helping him for a while," Kirsch said. "And I wouldn't mind enjoying my meal, either. This whole topic is giving me dyspepsia."

"Fine," Ed Durham said. "But, George—with all due respect—please understand that something has to change, and soon. Regardless of how fond of you we all are, business is business."

Eberly inclined his head. "You may count on me, gentlemen."

"I admire your confidence, my friend," Kirsch said.

George smiled—not at Kirsch's compliment, but because he had come up with an idea that could solve his problem.

THE MEN STAYED UNTIL closing, and then left to continue their conversations elsewhere. Mary stretched and walked stiff-legged over to their table to begin clearing away the remains. Next to Mr. Eberly's plate was what looked like a banknote. Her heart leapt. A gratuity!

It was indeed a folded banknote—one whole dollar, too, not fractional currency!—and she was about to slip it into her reticule when a little piece of paper worked out of it and fell to the floor. Mary picked it up. On it was written:

> *If you please, Miss Carkriff: Call for me tomorrow, Genesee House, at ten o'clock in the forenoon. You'll be very well rewarded for your trouble.*
>
> *G. Eberly.*

Outside in the humid night, the men stood chatting on the plank walkway along Erie Street.

"Anyone up for another drink?" Eberly asked.

"Always," Durham replied.

"There's a new place a couple blocks from here," Kirsch said. "It's a little rough around the edges, but with four of us, we'll be fine."

"I think I might call it a night," Captain Andrews said.

"*What?*" Durham said, agog. "Andrews, you're usually the last man standing. What gives?"

Andrews did a little shuffle on the plankway. "I thought I might see if our waitress would like to take a little evening stroll with her General Custer."

Durham and Kirsch moaned. "One compliment, and his head is turned," Durham said. "Well, be that way then."

Andrews turned and was about to go back into the Revere House when Eberly caught hold of his friend's elbow and pulled him firmly aside.

"Is something wrong?" Captain Andrews said.

"John, how about you come along with us?"

"You know I'd love to, but I think I have a good excuse."

"No you don't."

"I'm sorry?"

"Stay away from that girl—the waitress," George said.

Andrews took a half step back, puzzled. "I don't understand. Why should you care?"

"Because I have something in mind for her."

Captain Andrews laughed lightly. "It's good to be king, isn't it,

George?" he said. "But that's fine. There are plenty of other women in Buffalo."

"Not like that one."

"Don't rub it in," Andrews said, shaking back his golden locks.

SECTION TWELVE

Delicate Matters

It was still rather early on a Tuesday morning when Barney Brennan strolled over to Forest Lawn and rapped on the doorjamb of George Stroup's outer office.

"Yes?" came Stroup's voice. "My secretary's away at present. Please come in."

Brennan walked through the outer office and into Mr. Stroup's inner sanctum, where he found the superintendent sitting at an impossibly tidy desk.

"Mr. Brennan!" he said. "This is quite a surprise."

"I trust not an unwelcome one."

"Indeed not. How may I help you? Do you wish to arrange another batch of interments for the remains Eberly has been shipping to you?"

Brennan shook his head. "No," he said. "I mean to say, that's not what brings me here today. I'll get another shipment from Eberly soon, but today I have something else on my mind."

"I'm all ears," Stroup said, interlacing his fingers and sitting back in his chair.

"Would you mind if I closed the door?"

"Be my guest."

Brennan closed Stroup's office door and took a seat in a chair in front of the man's desk.

"Unburden yourself, sir," Stroup said.

"I wanted to speak with you about a question of money."

Stroup frowned. "Money? You and I are paid directly by the State of New York for the Franklin Park work. And we are up-to-date on your own interments, are we not?"

"We are," Brennan said. "It's something else entirely. Perhaps a little delicate."

"Matters of delicacy are my specialty."

"Then, while it's none of my business," Brennan said, "I'm sure you're paid quite handsomely for your work here."

Stroup unfolded his hands and looked squarely at Barney Brennan. "*Delicate indeed*," he said softly. "Why do you ask, Mr. Brennan?"

"Only because you may not be a man who needs to make more money."

"*Money*," Stroup said in a low whisper. "*Money*. You might very well be surprised if you had an inkling of how little my position at Forest Lawn pays. Oh yes, my situation is very grand in many ways. But in terms of cash on the barrelhead, it falls far short of grandeur."

"I didn't expect that, Mr. Stroup," Brennan said. "Given all of your land acquisitions and the like."

"It's kind of you to say so. But so it is. Confidentially, of course."

"Of course. Then perhaps you would entertain an idea I have been turning over in my mind."

Stroup put his fingers together in a steeple and touched his lips. "Please, go on."

"Before I get into the specifics, I should say that we would need to involve your two gravediggers."

"Mr. Dolan and Mr. Fermin."

Brennan coughed slightly into his fist. "Yes. Have you formulated any opinion about them? I'm sure that in your line of work you have learned to determine a man's gauge rather quickly."

Stroup returned what he thought was a smile, but which looked more like a snarl. "I have an idea about the type of men they are, yes."

"Do you think they could be trusted?" Brennan said.

"Depends on what one would trust them with. Mr. Brennan, please speak plainly. I'm having a difficult time following you, to be direct about it."

"You're right. Then here it is. I propose that you and I go into the resurrection business."

"Now is that so?" Stroup said, goggling briefly and then regaining his usual calm. "Well, well, well . . . that is certainly plain enough. And more than a little *piquant*. How much might such a miraculous undertaking garner?"

"Bodies are going for twenty-five dollars or more at the medical school now. And they're desperate—they had a bit of a mishap recently."

"What kind of mishap?" Stroup asked, leaning forward.

"The less you know, the better."

"Forget I asked. This idea of yours is all well and good, but the potter's field is already farmed by Kraft and Martin."

Brennan looked for a long moment at Mr. Stroup. "Yes," he said. "But Forest Lawn isn't."

Stroup wriggled deeper into his chair. "You are a man of bold compass, sir."

"I don't need to tell a man like you, Mr. Stroup, that your corpses are the best in the city. And Fermin and Dolan bury the bodies, so—"

"They can just as easily exhume them," Stroup finished.

"Exactly. You let them use a wagon, they do the work and then take the body to the medical school. I'd propose Dolan and Fermin get two dollars each, and you and I split the rest."

"So if we sell for, say, twenty-five dollars—you and I get ten dollars and fifty cents each. Per body."

"That's right."

"And how many bodies can the medical school take?"

"Just now, as many as we can send," Brennan said. "Then at least five a month after that."

Fifty dollars and change each month was half again what Stroup was being paid. It would be like receiving a fifty percent raise without having to do any additional work.

Stroup mulled this over. "You do know there is considerable risk to us in this," he said. "What if the two of them should be arrested?"

Brennan shrugged. "The boys could be arrested, but what if they are? The cops aren't going to confiscate a body, and they're easily paid off. The medical school won't breathe a word of it because they need corpses and—I can tell you—the people at the *very top* know exactly what's filling up their pickling vat."

"But what if Dolan and Fermin should give us up?"

Brennan drew his thumb across his neck. "They won't. They may be stupid, but not *that* stupid."

"I'll take your word for it. And what would be my part in this dramatic production?"

"Mostly you have only to turn a blind eye. But also guide the diggers to the choicest corpses that will pay the best. Let them use a wagon, as I mentioned. I'll handle the rest."

"Even the—potentially *delicate* matters?" Stroup drew his finger across his throat in an imitation of Brennan.

"Delicate matters are my specialty," the saloonkeeper said with a wry smile.

Stroup smiled. "All right, then, Mr. Brennan, you have yourself a deal. When do we get started?"

"Soon as you like. Do you have a likely body?"

"We did have an interment just yesterday," Stroup said. "Perhaps a little on the elderly side, but perfectly well-formed in all the particulars."

"Let's dig him, then."

Stroup dipped a pen in his inkwell and wrote down a section number. "This is where he's located. Fermin and Dolan will know it, of course—they just buried him."

"And the tools and wagon?"

"You may tell them that they are at liberty to use both as soon as the gates close. They'll have to exit to the north, though. No one can be seen coming or going through the main gate after sundown."

Brennan stood and stuck out his hand. "Then you haven't another thing to think about," he said. "I'll take it from here."

Stroup shook the man's hand. "Thank you, Mr. Brennan. Let's hope for great things ahead."

SECTION THIRTEEN

THE FIRST STIFF

"You heard the man," Fermin said to Dolan that afternoon, after returning from their free drink at Barney Brennan's. "Tonight we dig up our first stiff." He held up the little scrap of paper with the section number written on it.

"You're *sure* you want to go through with this?" Dolan asked, still wrestling with an angel about the prospect of Hell.

"What do you think?" his friend said, making him wince. "Easy work, two dollars each. What's wrong? Are you getting cold feet?"

"No . . ." Dolan said in a long, drawn out syllable.

"*But?*"

"But I still think it's wrong. It's a sin, and there's no doubt about it."

"Tell it to the priest. I told Brennan we'd do it."

"*You* told him we'd do it. I didn't!"

"What does *that* matter? Either way, we can't go back on our word now."

Dolan looked confused. "But, Artie, I didn't give my word."

"I gave it for you. Now what's this all about, lad? Haven't I always looked out for you? Ever since we were in short pants?"

His friend looked away. "Yes, you have," he said. "I didn't mean anything—"

Fermin threw his arm around Dolan's shoulders. "Aw, it's nothing. I don't take any offense."

"*Mo chara daor*," Dolan said, biting his lip to keep it from quivering.

ABOUT MIDNIGHT, DOLAN AND Fermin left their dormitory, hitched up the wagon, and struck out for the sparsely occupied Section 9. Heat lightning crawled and sizzled like burning hair along the low horizon, toward the lake. It was early in the season for a thunderstorm, but not *too* early, and both of them hoped to get their business done before they got a good drenching.

The new burial was at the far northern boundary of the old Granger holdings, so Dolan and Fermin could stay out of sight in the deep darkness in what remained of the great orchard. So long as no one was watching the main routes through Forest Lawn—and there was no reason anyone would be—they would be able to work undetected. Except for the muggy night air and swarms of mosquitoes that bred in the marshy ground near the creek, it promised to be the easiest two dollars either of them had ever made.

When they reached Section 9, Fermin reined in the horse and tied him to a tree. They took shovels, a pry bar, and a pair of unlit lanterns from the bed of the wagon, and after a short crunch up the gravel path, out of the darkness rose the fresh mound of dirt they had heaped up two days before.

"Quiet as you can, now," Fermin whispered, kneeling down beside the grave. "And let's try to get by on one lantern. You never know if a copper will happen by."

He took out his match safe from his vest pocket, flared off a lucifer on the blade of his shovel, and lit the candle behind the lantern's glass.

"Should be enough," he said, and Dolan nodded, his face burnished in the lantern's glow.

They began to work, moving aside the hummock of freshly turned earth. It was easy duty, compared to opening a new grave. They kept at it steadily for a half hour before they had to take a rest.

Dolan wiped his forehead with a muddy forearm. "We'd better hurry," he said. "I keep thinking that someone's watching us."

"No one's watching us, you idiot. It's after midnight in a graveyard, and the man who runs the place is in on it. We're more than halfway there, so bear up."

"I am bearing up."

"Then quit your whinging."

"I'm not whinging. And I don't like it when you call me names."

They resumed digging, and in another forty minutes, only their two heads were visible above the edge of the hole. Dolan was about to call for another break when his shovel thudded against something that sounded hollow.

"Pay dirt," Fermin whispered. He reached up, grabbed the candle lantern, and held it out between them. With his other hand he brushed the remaining dirt off of the lid of the coffin.

"Are you sure we have to open it?" Dolan asked. "Can't we just take the whole thing?"

"You really are a pain in my arse sometimes. We can't very well hoist a coffin out of this hole, just the two of us. Now get that lid off and let's finish our business. You see the thumbscrews?"

"I do," Dolan said. Eight little cross-shaped objects protruded from points around the outer perimeter of the coffin lid, weakly reflecting the lantern light.

"Unscrew them, then!"

Dolan dutifully unscrewed them one by one and handed them to his partner, who pocketed them. When they had all been removed, Fermin fitted the pry bar under the coffin lid.

"You're *sure*?" Dolan said again.

Fermin gave him a dirty look and leaned on the pry bar. The lid opened with a long squeal.

"For fuck's sake," Fermin said, pulling a handkerchief out of his pocket and putting it over his mouth.

"Good *God*!" Dolan said, waving his hand in front of his face.

They waited until the rising cloud of decay dissipated somewhat, and then Fermin pulled the coffin lid free. In the light of the lantern was the sunken pale face of an old man with grey hair and whiskers. The corpse was attired in a style long since out of fashion.

"Aw, sweet Mother Mary," Dolan moaned. "He looks just like my grandfather. We're going straight to Hell for this, Artie."

"Will you *stop*?" Fermin said. "I knew your grandfather, and he didn't look a thing like this geezer. Now come on and let's drag him out of the hole."

They first had to maneuver the dead man into a sitting position in the coffin, and then Dolan wrapped his arms around the corpse from behind. He wrangled the body into a near-standing pose, his face pressed into the dead man's hair. Forcing down a wave of nausea, he looked imploringly at Fermin, who stuck his hands under the corpse's armpits.

With a couple of heaves they wrestled the dead fellow's torso out of the grave. Then Fermin scrambled out and took the man by the arms, while Dolan, straddling the coffin, put his shoulder under the old man's ass. Together they hoisted the body out, and the old man came to rest face down in a pile of his own earth.

The two stood there for a minute, assessing their handiwork. They caught their breath to the distant rustle of leaves and the ghostly flicker of heat lightning dancing on the horizon.

"All right," Fermin said, "enough lollygagging. Let's get him into the wagon."

THEY LOADED THE OLD man's body into the back of the wagon and covered it with a piece of sailcloth. Then they returned to the yawning grave, where they replaced the coffin lid lightly—Fermin kept the thumbscrews, which appeared to be fashioned of silver—and hastily refilled the hole. Once they had neatly heaped up the disturbed earth, there remained little if any trace of their activity. Then it was back to the wagon.

They climbed up onto the driver's bench, Fermin clucked to the horse, and off they trundled down the hill and out of the northern service gate of Forest Lawn, as far from the main gate and the guard shack as was possible. Now it would be a leisurely ride east and south to the medical school, at Main and Virginia Streets.

Fermin clapped Dolan triumphantly on the back, sending up a cloud of dust. "Didn't I tell you?" he said. "It was a cakewalk!"

Dolan managed a half-hearted smile and willed himself to keep the horse at a steady plod, so as not to attract any police attention. In half an hour the lights of the medical school came into sight. They pulled around to the rear of the red sandstone building, and Fermin set the brake. He jumped down and banged a fist on the back door. After a minute's wait, the door cracked open.

"We're here to see Mr. Ferguson, the janitor," Fermin said.

"I'm Ferguson," the man replied, opening the door wide. "You have a delivery for me, I understand?"

"Yup," Fermin said, jerking his thumb over his shoulder toward the wagon. "In the back."

"Well, go and get it before someone happens along."

Fermin returned to the wagon, and he and Dolan lugged the dead man, wrapped in the sailcloth, into the medical school.

"God, he's ripe," Ferguson said as he led them deeper into the building. "What did he die of?"

"How would I know?" Fermin said.

"It's important to know. If I take one in that's got the plague or something, I'm done for."

"Old age, I think," Fermin said. "He's a geezer."

Ferguson stopped and crossed his arms. "Don't you know that they don't want the old ones? Just how old is he?"

"Not *that* old," Fermin said, backpedaling.

Ferguson rolled his eyes. "This one time, boys," he said, wagging a finger. "But in the future, they have to be young, and you have to know what killed them."

"Fine," Fermin said gruffly. "Now can we get rid of him and get on our way?"

Ferguson opened a large metal door, and they hauled the body in. Squatting in the center of a drab tiled room was a huge wooden vat, made of giant staves and iron hoops and resembling the type used for crushing and fermenting grapes.

"Put him on that slab," Ferguson instructed, and Dolan and Fermin laid the man out on a granite plinth.

Ferguson grabbed up a large pair of shears and began cutting off the dead man's trousers, then his jacket, then the undergarments. He threw them one by one into a rag bin adjacent to the slab. Soon the dead fellow lay there, naked and unashamed, staring at the ceiling. The janitor scrutinized the body for a few moments.

"They're not going to like this one," he muttered, shaking his head. "I hope you know I'm going to get an earful. You boys better be feeling sorry for me."

"I feel sorry for his *wife*," Fermin said, pointing at the decedent's shriveled dick.

"Aw, give the codger a little dignity, will you?" Dolan said, sick and tired of the whole mess. "I'm sure it was bigger when he was alive."

"It's funny, you know, but cocks don't shrink after death," Ferguson said. "People are surprised by that. As a matter of fact, they relax and get bigger. And I've seen a *lot* of them, that I can tell you."

"I'm sure you have," Fermin muttered.

"Some real *monsters*," the janitor added, holding his hands apart.

"May we go yet?" Dolan said.

"Soon as you put him into the vat," the janitor said, motioning to the huge tub.

Dolan and Fermin picked up the dead man and carried him to the edge of the vat. Hoisting him over the rim, they slid the corpse head-first into the soup, which gurgled hungrily. Dolan emitted a strangled cry when the old man's body bobbed right back up, like a pickled egg in a jar, staring at them with unblinking condemnation.

Ferguson made a notation in a large ledger book, then opened a cashbox and counted out some bills. "Here you go," he said, thrusting them out for Fermin.

"*Ten bucks*?" Fermin said. "What's this all about? We were told that the going rate is twenty-five dollars."

Ferguson made a wry face. "For prime specimens, it is. But bodies are like produce. Old or damaged goods don't pay as much."

Fermin snorted and pocketed the notes with undisguised disgust.

"See you next time, gentlemen," Ferguson said. "If you have better material, that is. If not, I can't use you."

The two men left the janitor, who turned and began submerging the stubborn old floater with a gaff hook.

Outside, Dolan and Fermin mounted up again, and Fermin slapped the reins. The whole way back to Forest Lawn, neither of the wagon's occupants said a word.

THE SMUGGLER KING

The Genesee House was a good two decades older than the Revere, but it was situated in the best part of downtown Buffalo and, instead of presenting a rickety wooden front, rose five imposing brick stories above Main Street. It was one of the gems of downtown, for visitors and natives alike. The entire world seemed contained in one big building; a home away from home, where a man could get a shave or a shoeshine, enjoy a cigar in the spacious lobby, or—if he felt so inclined—sneak upstairs with a first-class hired girl for a little horizontal refreshment.

Two years before, after returning from the war with his leg and all illusions shattered, George Eberly had made the hotel his headquarters—the hub of a smuggling empire. During his time in the army, Eberly had noticed that the people who made the *real* money were the sutlers—concessionaires who sold weary soldiers the little luxuries of camp life: whiskey, cigars, opium, and French pornography. Even with the war finished, the appetite for each continued to grow apace.

Ever since the recent invention of photography, one of the favored—if illicit—uses of the new technology was the creation of explicit images, mostly of women in various states of undress but also with a generous portion of harder themes, from straight-up fucking to elaborate fetishes. France had quickly become the production center for such images, which were then shipped all over the world. Whiskey, of course, was everyone's favorite quaff, and a day without a decent cigar was unthinkable to most men. As for opium, the war had manufactured hundreds of thousands of walking wounded, mutilated in body or mind—or both—and opium was the only thing that gave relief.

The problem with each of these commodities, though, was taxes. The Civil War had vastly increased the size of the federal government, and the costs for veterans' support had become a very expensive political hot potato. The needed funding was provided by ever-higher import tariffs and customs duties; smuggled goods, by contrast, were free of such pesky fees. Along the Niagara Frontier, almost anyone with a rowboat became a small-time smuggler. Canadian whiskey was plentiful and cheap, and thus in high demand on the American side, and Canada was temptingly close to Buffalo—only a little over a quarter mile across the Niagara River—an easy row for an experienced boatman.

The rewards of rowboat smuggling, though, came at considerable risk. An oarsman chunking along across the swift Niagara might find himself intercepted by a customs agent, made fast to the government steam launch *Seneca*, and raided. His small cargo would be confiscated and his boat summarily scuttled in the fast-moving river. Then the smuggler would receive a free ride to the jailhouse to await trial—all for no money at all. While there were always men who would hazard the short but perilous crossing, the odds had grown longer as the federal government had grown hungrier for revenue. One by one, the small-timers either went to prison or gave up in disgust. But since people still wanted cheap liquor, a new class of smuggler had emerged—the pirate—who operated on an industrial scale. This was where fearless, tough George Eberly had found his niche.

Where the enterprising individual smuggler was usually a harmless local fellow who needed a little extra money, pirates were professionals, and dangerous ones at that. Their boats were faster than the *Seneca* and furnished with both swivel guns and men unafraid to use them against the poorly armed customs inspectors, especially when in the disputed waters between the two countries. The government's only chance against such criminals lay in the inspection process carried out at the Buffalo wharves.

The pirates had a way around that, too. Since Buffalo was the center of the milling industry, the surest way to skirt the inspectors was to conceal liquor inside huge casks marked as containing wheat or rye. Inside, contraband bottles would be packed in bran, worthless except as cheap animal feed and as padding for fragile goods, but which still possessed the distinctive smell of grain. This would throw the customs dogs off the scent. And cash had the same effect on the customs men.

But cash and fast ships were only the beginning. As with any enterprise, someone smart had to know how to run it. And in the world of Buffalo smuggling, that person was George Eberly, the biggest pirate of all—who came to be known around town as the Smuggler King.

In only a little more than two years, Eberly had built a well-run, efficient, and expansive smuggling enterprise. He had no need to stow a few pathetic gallons of bootleg whiskey or gin in the bottom of a rowboat. Instead, he brought in oceans of the juice in Ed Durham's fleet of steam launches operating out of Port Colborne, Ontario. Captain Andrews brought back Chinese opium and French photographs from every cruise. Kirsch of Black Rock was the local man who knew the hometown boys along the docks and could motivate them to load or unload anything that needed it. And Eberly kept the whole thing running like a top.

Other than the liberal bribes paid to the customs men and to the police, George's organization was as close to without overhead as was possible. He and his men bought goods cheaply near their point of manufacture, whether Canada or China, and then moved them to saloons, restaurants, and hotels for less than they could pay legitimately. And the best markups of all were to be had in Niagara Falls, long-established as a tourist and honeymoon mecca where well-heeled young couples—as well as older men with deep pockets—came to let their hair down. No one visiting Niagara Falls gave a damn about staying on a budget, either; the casino atmosphere of the place encouraged people to spend liberally in an orgy of celebration.

George Eberly was sitting in the lobby parlor of the Genesee, idly rubbing his bad leg, when Mary Carkriff walked in. She had put on her other outfit, so as not to appear quite so straitened. He rose with some effort, leaning on his cane.

"Well, hello, Miss Carkriff," he said. "I'm delighted that you accepted my invitation." He motioned for her to sit.

"Of course, sir," she said. "You will imagine that I found your message most intriguing."

"I hoped you might. You're new in the city and, in my judgment, rightly eager for opportunity."

"I am, sir. While I am very grateful for my current situation, I'm a seamstress through and through. I thought perhaps you might know of someone looking for an assistant. In due course, I'd like to have my own millinery shop."

He smiled. "That's very admirable, Miss Carkriff. I applaud your industry, and for taking forethought to your future. So many young people do not. I, for one, never did—not in any serious way."

"I find it difficult to believe that, sir," she said, glancing around the opulent parlor. "You have the air of a very successful gentleman indeed."

He tapped the heavy gold pommel of his cane gently with a forefinger. "When I came back from the war," he said, patting his leg, "I thought I'd be a cripple and dependent on alms. That notion terrified me, so I decided to find another way. And while you are most certainly not a cripple, I hope you will take no offense if I say that the millinery trade is as close to accepting alms as a paying position can come. But worse than that—it would be a waste of your very considerable abilities."

Mary looked puzzled. "My abilities?"

"Yes. The gentlemen I was dining with last evening, and I of course, could not fail to notice your easy way with people, your poise, and frankly your beauty. None of which makes any difference in the millinery trade. Such unusual qualities can be put to better use elsewhere."

"My," she said, blushing. "I don't think I'm so very special."

"I beg to differ. And that's why I asked you to meet with me today."

"I'm eager to entertain any suggestions you may have for me, sir."

"You know my name," he said. "Have you had occasion to inquire about me?"

"No, sir, I have not. I didn't think it appropriate to pry into another's affairs."

"Commendable discretion, Miss Carkriff—another of your virtues," he said. "But do feel free to ask around. You'll quickly learn that—well, there's no point in beating around the bush—my business is somewhat *unusual*."

"And what is your business, sir, if I may inquire?"

"I'm an importer," George said.

"An *importer*," Mary breathed. "*Imagine.* How very exciting!"

"It can be. Though in my particular kind of importing, the less excitement, the better."

"I suppose that can be said of so many types of work. May I inquire as to what you import? If I'm not being impertinent, that is."

"You may indeed. Mainly I import whiskey, gin, wine, opium, and French photographs."

Mary looked a bit taken aback.

"Have I shocked you?"

"Oh no," she said. "I am familiar with all of them—at arm's length, naturally. Although I will freely confess myself ignorant of the finer points of French art."

Eberly looked at her for a long moment and then laughed. "You are simply the most charming young lady I have met in a very long time."

"You are far too kind, sir."

"Now then, Miss Carkriff, I asked you to meet me today because I have a problem with my business. And I think you may be able to help me resolve it."

"You flatter me, sir."

"Not at all. You see, at present I'm trying to manage the relocation of the old Franklin Park Cemetery to Forest Lawn—a big new burying ground north of the city. It was an opportunity that presented itself suddenly, and I have only two years to accomplish the task. Given that, I have to be personally and daily involved in directing the work. And as a result, certain elements of my importing business have been neglected. Much to my detriment."

"There is only so much time in every day," Mary said. "But if I may—if you're an importer, why the departure into the cemetery business?"

He took a deep breath. "It's important for me to have a legitimate business that I can point to should the winds shift against me."

"Your importing business is somehow not legitimate?"

He leaned forward on his gold-topped cane. "Miss Carkriff, to be quite plain with you—I am a smuggler."

"A *smuggler*," she repeated softly. "My."

"Now I *have* shocked you."

Mary took a deep breath. "Not at all, sir. Even in Canada, there is considerable demand for the forbidden fruit."

He laughed. "Yes, you might say that."

"And I take it, then, that your French photographs are not, in the traditional sense, art."

He shrugged. "Now that might depend on the buyer. They are certainly more provocative than most traditional art."

"How so?"

"Typically they depict people engaged in various acts of coition."

She blushed and looked into her lap. "I have heard of such things," she said softly.

"I recognize that I may well frighten you off," George said. "But I feel that it's best to be honest, if we are going to work together. If you have any objection to the nature of my business, please say so directly. I should not like to detain you unduly if you do."

Mary looked up at him. "Sir, I don't know enough yet to make any reasonable objection. I haven't, for example, seen any of these photographs, though I will admit a degree of curiosity about them. As well as about many other details of your business. The illegitimate one, that is to say."

George studied her. "You are a most remarkable person, Miss Carkriff," he said. "Very well then—I shall continue. My problem is simple, but a simple solution eludes me. You see, two of my shipments to the north were confiscated recently while skirting around Forest Lawn. Accordingly, the gentlemen you met last evening and I have suffered a rather sizable financial loss. Thus I have a pressing need to resume my shipments, but in a way that will avoid further detection. Either a new route, or a new method entirely. Until and if I can, I am frankly dead in the water."

"This is the same Forest Lawn where your exhumations are sent?"

"The one and only. For that part of my business, I fabricate coffins, fill them with the exhumed remains, and send them to a fellow called Barney Brennan, just across from the cemetery. Brennan has a mortuary license, so he handles the interments."

Mary swallowed hard. "Mr. Eberly, I believe I understand your predicament. And while I admit that it intrigues me, I am obligated to say that I haven't any experience in business, whether in the cemetery business or . . . the *outlaw* business."

He threw his head back and laughed. "An outlaw! I never thought of myself as an *outlaw*, per se," he said. "But it does seem rather romantic."

"I meant no offense."

"None taken. Now because I believe you can be of greater use to me than you may know, let me ask you to think about my 'outlaw business' for a few days. Perhaps you can devise some novel strategy to help me get back on track."

Mary considered this for a moment. "What puzzles me, Mr. Eberly, is how I—new in the city and without any experience in business—could succeed where *you* have failed. You would know far more about alternative methods for shipping goods than I, for example. And I know nothing at all about the streets of Buffalo and the routes such shipments could take to evade detection."

"I know, it does seem odd, but it's like this. I am, shall we say, rather well known around the city. Scouting out routes in North Buffalo personally would immediately attract attention of the most undesirable kind. You, by contrast, are unknown here—and that you are a woman is an additional advantage. Women tend to go unnoticed."

"Truer words have never been spoken, sir."

"I didn't mean it the way it came out," George said hastily. "As for alternative methods of shipment—well, sometimes one can be too close to a subject to give it a fresh look. I think you can bring a novel perspective that I cannot."

She threaded her fingers together in her lap. "I understand better now. What kind of situation would you have in mind, then? A short period of discreet study on my part?"

"Quite the contrary. If you can do what I think you can, I would propose to offer you a very attractive, permanent situation—one which Captain Andrews calls a 'first mate.'"

"A nautical term from a nautical man."

"Yes, although I believe you thought he resembled General Custer."

Mary blushed. "I ought better to have kept that to myself."

"Not at all," he said. "Not only did you give him the greatest compliment he's ever received, or is likely to receive, you gave all of us something we can use to needle him for the rest of his life."

Mary brightened. "I am glad you took no umbrage, sir."

"Well, then, Miss Carkriff," George said. "Will you at least give it a try? A few days? Poke around my operations and see if you come up with anything. Study the map of Buffalo, and see if there's something I've missed. And of course, whether it works out or not—I shall pay you very well for your time."

She mulled this for a moment and then extended her hand. "I will try, sir," she said. "Though I know nothing about business, I will admit that the prospect of becoming your first mate is quite attractive."

He shook it gently. "I value your enthusiasm," he said, rising from his chair.

"Thank you for your time today. And for giving me a chance."

"Of course. And if you should decide you can't help with my business, then I promise you I'll find you the very best possible situation as a seamstress. Or anything else you favor."

"Thank you, Mr. Eberly."

"Well then," he said. "In the meantime, is there anything else I may supply you with to help you in your investigation?"

She tapped a finger on her lips. "The location of your factory, of course, and any other parts of your operation I ought to observe. An assurance that your employees will allow me to observe them. And"—she paused—"perhaps a few examples of your French photographs."

George stared at her. "Addresses, of course. My men's cooperation, absolutely. But what would a young lady want with French photographs?"

A little smile played over her pretty face. "Mr. Eberly, just because I know nothing about something doesn't mean I have no interest in it."

It was George's turn to blush.

SECTION FIFTEEN

Quality Control

Fearing more drama at Kraft's Dead House, Coroner Richards did his best to steer a week's worth of dead to Martin's Coffin Manufactory & Warerooms, and so the next meeting of the Anatomical Board was held there. Everyone expressed satisfaction with this grand compromise, but when Caleb Martin got wind that the detested John Kraft was among the satisfied, Martin concluded that he was the target of a conspiracy.

"Before we begin," Martin said, "I'd like to know why I received only two bodies this week. Surely quite a few more than that died in this great metropolis."

Coroner Richards smiled at him patiently. "Of course more than two died, Mr. Martin, but Forest Lawn has lately been scooping them all up. Mr. Stroup over there has been selling plots to anyone who can scrape together fifty dollars. You know very well that we don't get first dibs on bodies that are claimed by their families."

"Last meeting at Kraft's place, he got *four*," Martin persisted.

"Are you deaf?" John Kraft said. "The man just said that more bodies went to Forest Lawn. What do you think, I'm sneaking over here at night and poaching yours?"

"Frankly, nothing would surprise me, Kraft."

"Gentlemen, please," Richards said. "A little decorum."

"I agree," Kraft said. "Let's get to the business at hand."

"As well we should," Dr. von Guyaling said. "But before we do, I must report a most distressing turn of events. I regret to inform this august group that our medical school is running perilously low on experimental material."

"Only a few weeks ago, you had a superabundance," Richards said.

"We did, but we had a bit of an accident with the pickling vat. Very unfortunate."

"I heard about that," said Practical Chemist Hadley, who was always in possession of the facts.

"I'm sure you did," von Guyaling said.

"Whatever happened?" Martin asked.

Von Guyaling cleared his throat. "I rather think it irrelevant to our discussion."

"My building, my rules," said Caleb Martin, getting red in the face. "I think this board has a right to know what happened to all your material. Hadley knows. And I'm *sure* Kraft knows."

"Fine," von Guyaling said. "The bottom-most hoop of our vat rusted clean through. The slow action of the acid pickle over time ate it away."

"Oh no," Martin said, suppressing a smile. "Don't tell me . . ."

Dr. von Guyaling frowned. "Yes, I'm afraid that the vat gave way entirely, and caused quite a mess. We lost all of our stock after the flood."

"How many?" Coroner Richards asked.

Von Guyaling rubbed his temples with one hand. "Seven adult specimens, two children, a fetus, two livers, a head, and two pairs of lungs. As you may imagine, in this unseasonable heat wave we're having, everything spoiled long before we could repair and recharge the vat."

"Ghastly," Hadley said.

"Quite," Richards said. "Unfortunately, Dr. von Guyaling, replenishing your supply may take some time. We haven't had our usual typhoid epidemic this spring, and thus we simply don't have enough material on hand to restock you. As Mr. Martin has made clear, we have but two potential subjects for you today."

"It's certainly been *hot* enough for typhoid," Practical Chemist Hadley mused, somewhat wistfully. "One wonders if an immunity is developing."

"Be that as it may," von Guyaling said, "the work of training doctors must go on, typhoid or no typhoid. And in view of our desperate shortage, this week we had no choice but to accept a specimen from the resurrectionists."

"Good God, Doctor!" Coroner Richards said. "The mayor will have my scalp over this. After our last meeting, and in view of your surfeit of specimens, I promised him this was all over."

"Regrettably, circumstances are what they are, Mr. Coroner," von Guyaling replied flatly.

Richards groaned. "And just as the mayor tells all the papers about his new regulation on minimum burial depth. That was supposed to foil the body snatchers."

"Deep burials are sound burials," Kraft said gravely, "but they cost *far* more. If this new regulation is to be implemented, I should like to see it amended to compensate undertakers for the additional labor required."

"This is rich," Martin interjected. "Coming from old Two-Foot Kraft."

"I'll have you know my men go at least four feet deep, even at the potter's field," Kraft shot back. "I lose money on every burial, but it's the right thing to do."

Martin laughed. "That's a good one. I was there two weeks ago and saw a forearm sticking out of the dirt."

"You saw no such thing," Kraft said, even though he was well aware of this particular botched interment. Fortunately, a pack of dogs had gnawed off the telltale limb before the newspapers could arrive at Limestone Hill.

"Gentlemen, please," Richards said. "Dr. von Guyaling, however exigent your requirement, any dealings with these—excavators—must be temporary, or we'll all be hauled up on charges. Or worse, dismissed from this respected body and subjected to ridicule."

"I'm not taking the blame for something I haven't had a hand in," Hadley said.

"Have you heard of 'guilt by association'?" Martin muttered.

"And that's *precisely* why we have to keep this *very* quiet until the crisis has passed," the coroner said. "We can't breathe a word about this to any living soul."

The members of the Anatomical Board scuffed their feet on the grey stone of Martin's storage room.

Coroner Richards took a deep breath. "Doctor, can you at least tell me how many of these specimens you've had to take in?"

"Only one."

"From the potter's field?"

"No, from elsewhere."

"You can't possibly mean *Forest Lawn*," Richards said, blanching.

"Well how about that?" Kraft said. "From a six-foot hole, too. And I'm the one held up to ridicule."

"Yes, it was Forest Lawn," von Guyaling responded, ignoring him. "Barney Brennan enlisted the two gravediggers over there to help us out."

"Brennan again?" Hadley said. "I thought we were done with that reprobate. You remember what happened last time we involved him."

"Brennan may be a reprobate, but a lot of dead Irish do come through his place," Martin said with a touch of envy.

"And every one of them buried in a George Eberly coffin," John Kraft said. "If we're to be in business with Brennan again, the least we can do is stipulate he use our coffins and not Eberly's."

"You mean *your* coffins," Martin said.

Kraft gave him a dirty look. "Did I say *my* coffins? No, I did not. I distinctly recall saying *our* coffins."

Richards rolled his eyes. "Gentlemen, let me be clear—we are not 'in business' with Mr. Brennan. This is an emergency measure only."

"Hear, hear," Martin said. "If Brennan's men are digging in Forest Lawn, though, you have to know that Stroup is turning a blind eye to it. If he is, they can gopher up the whole cemetery if they choose. Then what happens to my business?"

"Always thinking of yourself," Kraft said. "You'd think you were the only businessman in Buffalo."

"Given the quality of the Forest Lawn product, it oughtn't take long to stock up," Richards said, ignoring Martin and Kraft. "I trust that the Forest Lawn specimen was up to snuff, Doctor?"

Von Guyaling looked at the floor. "In truth, it was something of a disappointment."

"Why?" Kraft asked.

"Elderly."

"How elderly?" Hadley asked.

"Very. You may take my word on it."

Richards frowned. "Then if you have to use Brennan for now, have a talk with him and make sure he gets his men in line. And in the meantime, Doctor, may I have your word that as soon as your stock is replenished, you will suspend any such further acquisitions?"

"I will endeavor not to resent that comment, Mr. Coroner," von Guyaling said, holding up a hand. "I don't like the resurrection trade any more than you do. It creates an incentive for murder."

"That it most certainly does," Richards said. "When there aren't enough bodies for the ghouls to dig up, they manufacture them. Unless an institution has excellent quality control, into the vat they go. And crimes remain unsolved."

"And that's a shame," Caleb Martin said, looking peeved. "But can we determine what I can do with my paltry two bodies?"

Richards sighed and looked at his papers. "Yes, naturally. The first is a German girl who was ground up under a trolley. Not a pretty sight."

"Desperate times, gentlemen," von Guyaling said. "I'll take the parts, notwithstanding."

"The other is a man of about fifty-five who died in flagrante delicto with his mistress," the coroner read.

There was a long silence and some clearing of throats. "Eminently usable," von Guyaling said at last. "And a worthy moral lesson for the students, too."

"Then in view of recent developments, I'd say we might as well deliver them directly to the medical school. Mr. Martin, if you would handle that, please."

Caleb Martin glared at his fellow board members. "Do you see why I might think someone's out to get me?" he fumed. "Two lousy bodies, and now I won't even get paid for a coffin or an interment. 'Just plop 'em in the tank, Caleb, and have a fine day'—is that what it's to be?"

"And who was it wanted the bodies shipped here, come what may?" Kraft gloated. "Looks like you shot yourself in the foot, Martin."

Coroner Richards held out his hands. "Now, Mr. Martin, we don't intend to short you in any way. You'll be paid at your standard rate, even though you'll deliver the bodies directly to the medical school."

"As it should be," Martin said, folding his arms across his chest. "Fair is fair."

The First Mate

After more than two hundred exhumations, the northeast corner of the Franklin Park Cemetery looked more like the surface of the moon than the site of the new city hall. Rows of craters pocked the ground, punctuated only by intervening mounds of soil. Even so, to Mary's eye it appeared that three-quarters of the old burying ground had yet to be broken by the point of a shovel.

She walked over to a spot where two men were steadily digging out a fresh crater, and watched until one of the men shouted, "Pay dirt!" at which two other men hustled over, carrying an oblong wicker casket. Mary expected to see the diggers unearth an intact coffin, but such was not at all the case. There was only what looked to be a dark outline in the soil, and shreds of dirty cloth that had probably once been a shroud. These integuments were of interest to the two diggers only as indications that they had located their quarry.

Piece by piece, they began pulling from the black earth bones—femurs, ribs, and vertebrae—and lofting them over the side of the pit into the waiting wicker casket, while the two pallbearers stood near the edge of the pit and rolled themselves a smoke. All four of them studiously ignored Mary, as if a neat young woman standing amidst their excavations was the most normal thing imaginable.

This cascade of human remains continued for perhaps half an hour. A skull, minus its lower jaw, went rattling into the wicker as well as several dozen smaller prizes. At some point in the process, however, the two men in the pit seemed to become bored with sifting soil through their fingers for the smaller bits of skeleton—presumably finger and toe bones—and waved for the two men with the wicker casket to take it away.

Mary eased over to the side of the now-empty grave. The hole emitted a sweet, almost cloying scent, tinged with a touch of burned rubber. This, she presumed, was from a century of enrichment from the slow decay of a city's worth of dead.

"Excuse me, gentlemen," she said to the two diggers, who were plainly goldbricking before breaking ground again. "Is it unusual not to find a coffin?"

The man closer to her answered. "Depends on how long ago they were buried. This is the oldest part of the cemetery, so it's only bits and pieces." He gestured to the far diagonal corner of the grounds. "It's going to be slower going over there, because those burials aren't very old at all."

"Thank you," she said, somewhat mystified by the men's lack of curiosity about her presence. "I'm here on Mr. Eberly's behalf," she offered.

"Well then, tell him we need more men," the other digger said. This Mary found surprising since the entire enterprise seemed to be operating at a very leisurely pace.

"I will do so. Thank you for your time, gentlemen."

She walked over to a large barnlike building—the coffin factory itself. She paced off its dimensions, writing them down in a little notebook she kept in her reticule, and peered through the smudged windows at ground level. Satisfied with her exterior examination, she went in. Inside, giant steam-powered saws whined their way through stacks of pine boards, making the whole building reverberate. Mary wished she could stick her fingers in her ears, but stayed the course and walked the inside perimeter of the big building, observing the process and jotting in her notebook the number of men at work and how many finished coffins were stacked in the warehouse at the rear of the works.

When she stepped outside, her ears were still ringing. She looked up at the huge coffin factory. There was something peculiar about the place, that she knew, but she wasn't able to place it until she was almost back to her room in the Revere House.

THE FOLLOWING MORNING, GEORGE awoke in a serious funk. In a little more than another week, he would again have to meet with his lieutenants, and account for his continued lack of progress. And while Miss Carkriff seemed promising, she couldn't work miracles, either. He went downstairs, had three strong cups of coffee, and was staring at the head of his cane when Mary walked into the lobby parlor of the Genesee.

"Good morning to you, sir!" she said. "Would you happen to have a few minutes for me?"

"Why, Miss Carkriff! I didn't expect to see you again so soon," he said, thankful for any distraction, and especially such an attractive one. "I have as much time as you wish. Please, sit down. May I offer you a glass of lemonade?"

She took a seat across from him and folded her hands in her lap. "No thank you, Mr. Eberly. That's very kind, though."

"So what is on your mind today?"

She shifted a little in her chair. "Sir, I do think I have an idea about how to resolve the difficulties you've been facing."

"*Already*? It's been less than a day!"

"And in my opinion, there's not a moment to waste. So yesterday, after our conference, I walked over to Franklin Park Cemetery to observe the work."

He frowned. "That's not a very pleasant sight for a lady."

"Mr. Eberly—you'll find that I'm no china doll. You asked me to help you with the business, and I can't do that unless I first see how it's being done."

"Touché. You're entitled to my thanks, not criticism. Please accept my apology."

"It's nothing. And while I may be overstepping after so short a time, I think the solution to your transportation problem is really rather simple."

"Now *that's* quite a statement."

She smiled. "Allow me to explain. As I understand it, you have twenty-four months to clear Franklin Park of approximately twelve hundred bodies. By my count, that means that every week you must send at least twelve coffins of excavated remains to Forest Lawn."

"That's right. One wagon with six coffins on it, twice a week."

"All six are evenly loaded?"

He seemed confused. "Well, yes, for stability. If the gravediggers locate only a partial set of remains, the State of New York still pays for an individual coffin. So in such cases, my men even out the weight with sandbags before they screw the coffins shut. The ground at Franklin Park, being so close to the lake, is mostly sand."

"Good. So I would presume, then, that you could stack nine coffins, if evenly loaded, on each wagon, and still have a stable load?"

He pursed his lips. "Well, yes, but my current gangs of men can only exhume and prepare twelve a week. So it's a moot point."

"I also visited your coffin factory."

"You really do take the bull by the horns, don't you?"

"It's the only way, sir. I noticed that the carpentry shop—where the coffins are made—was entirely separate both from the exhumation operation and from the dock where the wagons are loaded. That was good to see."

George shrugged. "It wasn't planned that way. It just so happens that those tasks are entirely different from one another."

"It's a good thing for us regardless. When I was inside the factory, I paced off the areas of your factory used for each task to see how much square feet each required. And then to make sure my numbers added up, I paced off the exterior of the building. And though I did it twice, each time my count was off. Each time I came up with a differential of twenty feet between the external size of the building and the space used for your contract operations."

Now it was Eberly's turn to smile. "And?"

"And I presume it is in the unaccounted space that you store your goods. The *outlaw* kind."

"*Brava*," he said, clapping slowly. "Not even the cops have figured that one out."

"I'm happy to hear it."

"I can't help but admire your abilities as a detective. Though I'm curious as to how this helps solve my little problem."

"Isn't it obvious?" Mary asked.

"Apparently not to me, Miss Carkriff."

"I didn't mean any offense. What I meant is that all of the pieces of the puzzle are in one place. If we just look at them as a whole, and not as pieces."

"Then let's hear how you've pieced it together, Miss Carkriff."

"As I understand it, you ship the coffins from Franklin Park Cemetery to a Mr. Brennan, whose establishment is very near Forest Lawn."

"Correct. Directly across from the cemetery, at the corner of Gulf and Main Streets."

She gave him a small smile. "And might I be correct in my surmise that Mr. Brennan is both the undertaker for the disinterred bodies and your go-between for your other goods?"

His eyes widened. "You are really *very* perceptive, Miss Carkriff. And again correct."

"Good. Now then, you told me that you can't send wagons around Forest Lawn any longer, and presumably shipping contraband through a cemetery may be considered unseemly."

"To put it mildly," he said. "Hence my problem."

"Yes, but one easily solved."

"This I have to hear."

"To my mind, the solution is simple. The night before each shipment of remains to Forest Lawn, we move three empty coffins from the carpentry shop into the back space in your factory where the contraband is stored. We put a tiny, unobtrusive mark on each of these coffins, fill them with the outlaw goods, and move them to the loading dock area, where the next morning they'll be loaded on the wagons along with the ones containing human remains. There will now be nine coffins per wagon, but they will all pass through the gate at Forest Lawn without so much as raising an eyebrow. Thus, in addition to the disinterred remains, we'll move six coffins a week of goods through Forest Lawn, and be caught up in no time."

George sat back in his chair, stunned. He then struck himself in the forehead with the heel of his hand.

"Miss Carkriff, that is simply brilliant!" he blurted. "Now that I hear it, it's so painfully obvious that I cannot believe I never saw it until now."

"That can be said of every great idea," she said with a wink.

"You really do amaze me. Though, if you will allow, there are a few elements you may not have considered."

"Please."

"First, the teamsters and the dock men are accustomed to six coffins, not nine. They'll notice such a significant change. And it's more work."

"Yes, they will. But neither of those groups of men know whether you've added more gravediggers at Franklin Park, because the tasks are kept so separate. When they ask—as they will—you tell them that the contract pays a premium if the job is finished early, just as it charges a penalty if it's late. That premium you will share with them."

He rubbed his face. "Yes, that will work. But what about this: After the additional coffins are emptied of their goods, how are they to be disposed of? Coffins are rather large items, as you know."

"That's easy," Mary said. "They will become your gift to Mr. Brennan, who will certainly be able to use them in his mortuary business."

"Brennan will like that. Last question, then: the marks on the coffins. People are always smarter and more perceptive than we think, Miss Carkriff. I would not rule out that someone will notice even the tiniest mark."

"I thought you might object to that," she said slowly. "Fortunately, I have another idea."

"Of course you do."

"Imagine if I, as your first mate, should supervise the shipments being loaded. Since I would know which are the three coffins containing the goods, I would make a mental note of their position on the wagon."

"Given your skill with taking restaurant orders without jotting them down, I believe you could accomplish that," he said. "But what about Brennan?"

She loosened the drawstring of her reticule and took out a tiny notebook and a gold mechanical pencil. On a blank page she wrote:

	D	E	F
A	1	2	3
B	4	5	6
C	7	8	9

"Let's say these represent your nine coffins," she said. "Looking at them from the rear of the wagon."

"Yes, I understand."

"Now let's say we want Mr. Brennan to know which coffins contain your goods."

"I see," George said. "Then you tell him, say, Number 2, Number 4, and Number 6."

"We could do it that way, but it could be misinterpreted too easily. He might forget whether you are counting them from the right or the left, or from top or bottom. So what I'd propose instead is this. I write this down and give it to him on my visits."

AEBDBF

"You've lost me," he said.

"It's a little code for the position of the coffins containing the goods. You used Number 2, Number 4, and Number 6 as your example. This says the same thing, but by identifying their location, not their number, according to standard mathematical practice. Row A, Column E is coffin Number 2. Just as in geometry, it's row and then column. And though the positions of the outlaw coffins will likely change with every shipment, Mr. Brennan will always be able to identify the correct ones, because coffin AD is always at the top left."

George sat back into the chair. "You are a most remarkable person, Miss Carkriff."

"And you, Mr. Eberly, are a man possessed of excellent judgment."

He laughed, feeling light for the first time in months. "Apparently so. There is only one little niggling concern I have."

"Which is?"

"You'd have to see Barney Brennan at least once a week to give him the codes. And Brennan, shall we say, does not have a reputation as a gentleman."

"One of the first things an unmarried woman has to learn is how to handle a masher."

"Without question. But I like to think of *myself* as a gentleman, and a gentleman does not send a lady into harm's way."

"Mr. Eberly, please—"

"Miss Carkriff, I like your solution to my problem. It's nothing short of elegant. But I like you, too, and I'm going to have to think carefully about how to keep you out of danger. I couldn't live with myself if something happened to you."

"Sir, I do understand, and I cannot fail to admire your good nature," Mary said. "Allow me to assure you that I can manage any difficulty I encounter."

"I'm sure you can. Still, let us both sleep on it, just to be prudent. But am I correct in that you would like to join my business as my first mate?"

"Yes, sir, I would like to entertain your proposal . . . even given all of the risks. Provided, of course, we can agree on adequate terms."

"Ah, so now we come to the crux of the matter," he said with a sparkle in his eye. "*Money.* Would you happen to have a number in mind? Say, *ten dollars a week*?" George tapped the words out on the floor with his cane and then sat back in his chair, waiting for Mary's reaction to this largesse.

Mary's eyes sparkled back at him. "Why, that's three times what I could make as a seamstress," she said softly.

"I thought it seemed very fair."

"Fair to whom?"

He flushed red. "I beg your pardon?"

"Ten dollars a week represents a fabulous sum for a seamstress," Mary said, and paused. "But for a second-in-command in a smuggling empire—"

"It's hardly an *empire*."

"I beg your pardon. I simply don't know a better word for an enterprise that spans at least three countries that I know of—the United States, Canada, and China."

George was crimson red now. "Point taken, Miss Carkriff. Perhaps you might have a better number in mind?"

She bit her lip. "I wouldn't really know offhand. Would it be five or six days a week?"

"Probably seven. In this business, we work when we have to work." He cleared his throat, which seemed to have gone very dry all at once. "But I would ensure that you would have ample time to yourself."

"I see."

"Oh, and I'd pay for your lodging at a hostelry of your choosing," he added, tugging at his collar.

"That sounds wonderful. Yet given the risks of prosecution—"

"You wouldn't likely be *prosecuted*. You're Canadian. You'd simply be deported."

She made a wry face. "Deportation and prosecution are equally shameful, I should think, sir. And I might wait for months in jail before being sent back."

He stared at her, unable to make a sound.

"I haven't given this a great deal of thought, Mr. Eberly," Mary resumed. "But in the interest of speeding the plow—even at the cost of making less than I might, given sufficient time to consider your offer—I should think that a hundred American dollars a week, in gold, would be a good place to start. And if I am able to increase your turnover without incurring more expense, I'd anticipate a share of the additional revenue."

He sat back in his overstuffed leather chair. "God bless me," he marveled, "you really are one of a kind. I thought you said you hadn't any experience in business?"

"I don't. But I *do* have common sense. Risk requires reward, sir, and more risk requires more reward."

"A hundred a week?"

Backing down now would send the wrong signal, she thought, so Mary sat up in her chair. "Yes, I think that would be sufficient. Do recall that it would be in dollars, not British pounds, which of course would represent considerably more."

He sighed. "Very well, then. If you'll take the job today, without further delay, I'll pay you a hundred dollars per week."

"And the incentive? For bringing in additional revenue."

"Good Lord," he said. "I don't know—how about . . . two percent?"

"Mr. Eberly."

"Yes?"

"Under your proposal, if I bring in more money without incurring additional expense, you would keep ninety-eight cents of every one of those incremental dollars."

"It's my company," he said weakly.

"*Empire*, sir. We need to think big, you and I."

"Then what would you propose?"

"*Twenty* percent, I should think. You remain in possession of the lion's share."

"Done!" he said, eager to close the deal before this pretty young thing thought up anything else. He thrust out his hand. "Do we have an agreement?"

She delicately put out her gloved hand and shook his. "We do, sir. Thank you."

"I'm glad that's out of the way."

"Then I am going to get right to work." She stood, but didn't turn, instead standing quietly in front of his chair.

"Very well, then," he said, puzzled. "Thank you for your time."

She remained standing, looking at him.

"Is there something else, Miss Carkriff?"

"Since this is more than a full-time situation, sir, I will have to resign forthwith from my duties as waitress at the Revere House."

"Yes, I would expect so."

She tapped her foot. "Doing so will mean that I no longer have an income, Mr. Eberly. But I will still have expenses."

He opened his eyes wide. "And?"

"And so I should think that an advance of my first week's salary would be both opportune and appropriate."

He flushed again. "Yes, yes, of course you're right." He reached into his jacket pocket and took out a leather notecase. He opened it, counted out fifty dollars, and slipped the notes across the table between their chairs.

"Half your first week's salary."

Mary gently took up the bills, folded them, and slipped them neatly into her reticule. She again tapped her foot on the parquet for a moment without looking up at him.

"Is there something else?" George asked, terrified.

"As we agreed, I should like to be paid in gold, rather than in specie. The Brantford papers had a great deal to say about the present weakness of the American currency. For today, though, banknotes will be adequate, as I recognize that you may not carry sufficient gold on your person."

George wanted to put his head down on the table. "That's fine, Miss Carkriff. Henceforth, I'll pay you out in gold coin."

"Thank you, sir. Now if you don't mind, I'll be getting to work."

"I don't mind a bit," he said, relieved.

"Thank you again for your confidence in me, Mr. Eberly."

He managed a smile. "You are more than welcome. And welcome aboard."

"Thank you, Captain!" she said, snapping him a salute. Then she turned crisply on her heel and left George Eberly staring after her.

SECTION SEVENTEEN

BEARDING THE LION

May

The middle column of the newspaper—narrow and snaking off the bottom of the front page to burrow into the interior—said it in typically understated fashion:

OUTRAGE AT FOREST LAWN!

Resurrectionists at Work.

CEMETERY UNDER ATTACK!

Christ folded the newspaper inside out, so that Georgia couldn't see the front page.

"I know what you're doing," she said over her teacup.

"I'm not doing anything."

"Whenever you don't want me to see the news, you fold it up like that and hope I'll get busy with something else."

"I wouldn't do that!"

She gestured with her fingers. "Hand it over. I won't ask you twice."

Christ reluctantly gave her the paper and watched her eyes go wide when she opened it to the front page. She read for a moment and then looked up again.

"*Now* I see why you didn't want me to see it."

"I know how upset such things make you," he said, red-faced.

"And I'm such a fragile thing that I'm not allowed to be upset?"

"No, it's not that—it's that we can't do anything about it, so why get ourselves in a lather?"

Georgia poked the table with her index finger. "Who says we can't do anything about it? I'll ride over there this very morning to beard the lion in his den!"

"What?"

"It means that I plan to give Mr. Stroup a piece of my mind. Face to face."

"I don't like Stroup any more than you do, but in fairness—what can he do? Forest Lawn is a big place, Georgia. At night he can't know everything that's happening on all those acres."

She folded the newspaper again and put it down neatly next to her plate. "Christian Schamber," she began, fixing him with a stare.

He shrunk down in his chair—as much as a fellow well over six feet could. *Here it comes*, he thought. *She's called me by my full name.*

"Just because, legally speaking, that land no longer belongs to me doesn't mean for an instant that I haven't a moral obligation to it, nor that I have given up caring about what happens on it. And I will not tolerate any desecration of the place!"

"Nor should you," he mumbled into his coffee. "How about we go and see Mr. Stroup this morning?"

"A fine idea," she said. "I'm so glad you came up with it."

STROUP WAS BUSILY MAKING entries in a huge ledger when Georgia knocked on his door. She had told Christian, much to his displeasure, to wait outside.

"Mrs. Moffatt!" he said, closing his tome. "What a pleasant surprise! Do come in." He came around the desk and arranged a chair, then immediately retreated again behind the polished slab of wood. Georgia sat and forced herself to look at him, suppressing the urge to punch him in the face.

"How may I be of service to you today, *madame?*" Stroup asked, putting on his best air of helpful concern.

"Surely you are aware of the recent depredations here in Forest Lawn."

His look of concern deepened to something near contrition. "Depreda*tion*, to be precise," he corrected her. "The so-called resurrection trade is a most regrettable business withal. Though not one confined to Forest Lawn, I should add. Why, the potter's field—"

"The potter's field notwithstanding," she interrupted, "my interest lies solely with Forest Lawn, which as you well know occupies land that was in my family for three generations."

"Yes, of course, there is a distinction there."

"Indeed there is. And as such, what happens here reflects on my family's good name, sir. So I'd like very much to know what you intend to do to stop this abominable trade."

He raised his finger. "*Exactement, madame!*" he erupted. "A *trade* is precisely what it is. And a trade that owes its existence to antiquated laws about the distribution of bodies to medical science. Personally, I believe that the legislature must act!"

"That could take years, Mr. Stroup. By that time this place will look like a prairie dog village."

"Very droll!" He forced a chuckle. "But I rather think not. This was a single, isolated occurrence."

"One becomes two, and two, four—if we don't act quickly. Can't you hire a night watchman?"

"I hardly need to remind you, *madame*, that Forest Lawn encompasses more than two hundred and fifty acres."

"Yes, but you're not burying hundreds of bodies every week, or in every section," Georgia said, finding this little man even more tedious than she'd recalled. "Post a watchman near the new interments, or have one roam between them. At most, there'll be a half dozen, and even at a snail's pace, he'd be sure to interrupt a body snatcher at work. After a few days, the bodies will no longer be useful to the medical schools."

Stroup flushed. "Yes, I suppose I *could* do *that*," he said slowly. "And a fine point it is! Sometimes the feminine mind does grasp things in its own unique way."

"Kind of you to observe."

"I will confess, however, that the cost of a night watchman is not within the cemetery's current budgetary means."

"How much would it cost?"

"I'd say a dollar a night, per man. And I'd recommend two men."

Georgia unslung her reticule and fished around inside. "Here's fifty dollars," she said, tossing some notes on the desk before him. "That will just about cover the first month. After that, let's talk again." She stood, and Stroup stood with her.

"I'm very grateful for your interest and support, Mrs. Moffatt," he said. "This can be quite a lonely job sometimes. Why, a lady such as yourself is nothing short of a ray of sunlight through the gloom."

"I'm sorry that it's so bad."

"It's not that it's bad, it's that it's better—"

"Well, good then. I thank you for your time, Mr. Stroup."

"And I thank you for yours. If I may, allow me to offer my continuing condolences on your husband's demise."

"Thank you."

"I would suppose, though, that it's been nearly two years since his unfortunate passing," Stroup said with a little bow.

"Yes, almost. As you can see, I am no longer wearing mourning. Well, this little ribbon here," she said, touching a small black cockade on the lapel of her basquine. "But that's all."

"Life does go on, does it not?"

"Whether we wish it to or not, yes it does."

"Perhaps someday you'll wed again," Stroup said, in what might have been either a question or a statement.

"I very much doubt it, Mr. Stroup."

"And yet you are so young," he mused. "And comely, if I may be so bold."

"Hmm," Georgia said.

Stroup cleared his throat. "Perhaps sometime soon, since you are such an interested party, you'd allow me to give you a personal tour of the grounds? You would see all of the improvements—changes, I should say—that have been made since our acquisition of your father's land."

"I'll think about that, sir. At present, my chief concern is seeing these desecrations come to an end."

"With your generous funding, that oughtn't to take very long," he said with a thin smile. "Perhaps once that's put to rest, you would consent to a little stroll with me?"

Georgia thought momentarily that she might be ill, but wrestled down her rising bile. "Yes," she said. "Yes, perhaps we shall do that."

He smiled again. "It's said that one can never be lonely if it is two."

I beg to differ, she thought. "That's very clever, Mr. Stroup. Where did you hear that?"

"It's original to me," he said, somewhat downcast.

"Well, then that is especially clever. See, the masculine mind can grasp a thing or two as well."

He bowed deeply. "Well said, *madame*. I'll report to you in two weeks. I believe I'll have some progress by then. And then I will most eagerly invite you on that stroll of ours."

STROUP FOUND FERMIN AND Dolan out behind the offices, smoking and pretending to hitch a wagon for some nameless chore.

"I'm glad I found you both," he said to them.

"You *are*?" Fermin replied.

"I am. Because I'm going over to see Barney Brennan now and tell him we need to let things settle a bit."

"What things?" Dolan asked.

"The *resurrection* thing," Stroup whispered. "What else?"

"Why in the world?" said Fermin. "One old man and the whole thing is blown up?"

"I know, but we're getting pressure from *Mrs. Moffatt*."

Fermin frowned. "And who might Mrs. Moffatt be, now?"

"Her family used to own the land you're standing on. Though I don't see why any of this matters to you. I'm the superintendent, and if I tell you to let things settle, I expect them to settle."

"Yes, sir," Fermin said. "Do you want us to tell Mr. Brennan for you?"

"Oh no you don't. I'll tell him personally. And mind—if you disobey my directive, you'll have to reckon with him."

"No need to get testy," Fermin muttered. "I was trying to be helpful."

IT WOULDN'T BE EASY for cash-strapped George Stroup to abstain from sifting human gold from the rich soil of Forest Lawn, but he didn't need Georgia Moffatt—who was *connected*—making any mischief with the board of trustees. He had enough difficulty with them as it was.

Mostly, though, he feared her disfavor more than the board's. After her visit, he couldn't banish the thought of her—those liquid *eyes*, and that hair!—and her deep, wild scent, an impossible mix of spring flowers and autumn leaves. He imagined a hundred scenes in which the bereft young widow would again arrive unannounced at his office, though *this* time he would be well-prepared and not let her leave so easily. He would slip a comforting arm around her and become her confidant and consoler, her indispensable man. Perhaps they would exchange a few sweet nothings in French . . . and after a little while— not so long, really—with a soft rustle of crinoline, she would pull up her skirts and invite him to enter her holy of holies.

Once, behind his desk, he became so absorbed in one of these increasingly baroque fantasies that he failed to detect a soft knock on the doorframe. Startled out of his daydream, he'd looked up to see an old woman, wearing brand-new widow's weeds, accompanied by her grown son and daughter—to judge by the resemblance. Of course he'd had to rise immediately from his chair with his usual practiced solemnity, but he had been so lost in Georgia's crinolines that he had done so while sporting a very credible erection. To make matters worse, the head of his cock—straining against the baggy fabric of his trousers—snagged the lip of the desk as he stood, and then sprang up like a marionette when it snapped free.

The old woman reflexively turned away with a gasp of horror, and her son pulled her close, shooting a disapproving look at the engorged superintendent. The daughter didn't seem to care. To his credit, Mr. Stroup recognized that plopping back down in his chair at the present moment would be tantamount to admitting his arousal, so instead he rolled through his usual series of blandishments while his dick deflated.

After that, he tried as hard to avoid thinking of Georgia Moffatt as he did the plump, juicy bodies—at twenty-five dollars per, minimum—that were busily spoiling in the summer ground, inside their ridiculous boxes. Everyone knew that all that coffin nonsense was for the family's benefit, not that of the dead; it was the thought of the earthworms noiselessly working their way through Grandmother's eye sockets that her next of kin refused to imagine, and so at great cost would inter the old lady inside wood and concrete. But eventually and at last, the patient worms would find a way in. They had nothing but time.

SECTION EIGHTEEN

A Misunderstanding

After a quiet few weeks, a grieving mother and father called on Mr. Stroup to collect the body of their young son, who had recently died unmarried but not unmourned.

"Where may I find him?" Stroup asked the gentleman, who had his arm around his wife. She was gently weeping into his chest.

"He died at the poorhouse," the father replied. "In the insane ward." This last comment caused the boy's mother's sobs to intensify.

"I am terribly sorry to hear that. My deepest condolences."

"Like so many young men, he fell in with the wrong crowd. Fast women. We did our best to get him back on the straight and narrow, but to no avail."

"I'll collect him right away," Stroup said. "Would you care to have a graveside service?"

The father shook his head sadly. "No . . . in a case like this one, it's better if we let some time pass. We'll hold a memorial service for him after a decent interval."

"Understood," Mr. Stroup said. "You may rely entirely on our discretion."

STROUP FOUND FERMIN AND Dolan lollygagging over in Section 13, leaning against a big headstone, smoking and laughing. He pulled up alongside them in his wagon.

"Don't you have anything better to do?" he said, looking down at them. "You can always keep digging out the Franklin Park pit, you know."

"Only having a little *craic*," Fermin said, stubbing out his smoke on the headstone.

"A 'crack'?"

"It's an Irish word," Dolan said. "It means a chat."

"In French the word is far more mellifluous," Stroup said. "*Bavarder*. But that is neither here nor there. While I am terribly sorry to insert myself into your crack, there *is* actual work that needs your attention."

"Yes, sir," Fermin said. "What can we do for you, Mr. Stroup?"

"We've need to go to the poorhouse to collect a body."

"Shite," Fermin said.

"There's an empty coffin in the back. Climb in and let's go."

The three men and the empty coffin rumbled northwest, making the short drive to the poorhouse under beautiful fair skies.

"Ah me, I'd almost forgot how much I hate the sight of this place," Fermin said to no one.

Mr. Stroup hopped down, and the guard at the door fetched the superintendent, who walked out to the wagon. He ignored Dolan and Fermin, perched atop the empty coffin in the back.

After a brief conversation with Stroup, the superintendent went back to his office. "He's in the basement, boys," Stroup said to the waiting Irishmen.

The three of them trooped down the wide main staircase to the basement morgue, where they found a body, wrapped up in white linen, lying on a long wooden table. The shroud was stained in a number of places with serum weeping from the body. Stroup carefully peeled back the top end of the shroud to reveal the young man's features, which were puffy and distended with large blackened pustules. Dolan and Fermin leaned over to get a gander, and both winced.

"Worse than I'd thought," Stroup said. "This one didn't go easy, I can tell you that much."

"Poor fellow," Fermin said, his ratlike face pinching up in what he thought would pass for compassion. "What was it that got him?"

Stroup looked at him queerly but then dismissed whatever thought was passing through his mind. "General paresis of the insane. Only twenty-five years old, too."

"Too young," Dolan said. "Just about my age."

"Not the way I'd like to go," Stroup said, letting the shroud drop again. "But it's all too common these days. As they say, the wages of sin."

"My mother used to tell me that before bed," Fermin said. "I remember it like it was yesterday."

"Well, that's nice," Stroup said, having passed more than enough small talk. "Now get him upstairs and into his box. Because of the nature of the death, we won't have time for a mortician. So when we get back to the cemetery—the minute I tell you he's ready—see to it that he's buried *right away*. Deep, too. This one's not coming up again, and that's a fact."

"You may rely on us, Mr. Stroup, sir."

As dusk came down and the sky deepened into purple, Fermin

crooked a finger at Dolan, who was lying in his bunk smoking a cigarette. "Outside," he said.

Dolan got up with a groan and followed his friend out of the dormitory. "What is it? I was having a little siesta."

"A *siesta*? What in shit's name is a siesta?"

"It's a word I read in the paper yesterday. It's Spanish. It means 'a rest.'"

"How about we speak English instead?"

"Fine," Dolan said sullenly. "Now what is it that you want?"

"We have a good one at last. You heard Stroup—the bloke we buried today was only twenty-five."

"He didn't look too good," Dolan said with a grimace.

"So? He was *dead*, for fuck's sake. Twenty-five? He's got to be worth thirty bucks or more."

"But Mr. Stroup said to bury him deep, and that he couldn't be coming back up."

"Oh, the hell with Stroup. He probably knows the family, and feels sorry for them. And the lad didn't die in a good way."

"What was wrong with him again?"

"Stroup said he had a stroke of paralysis. And get this—to top it off, he was insane when it hit him."

"Just like in the book of Job," Dolan said in wonderment. "All those boils, too."

"If you say so. But in any event, we've got us a good one. The medical school isn't going to mind if the fellow was crazy or not. And I think once you die, the paralysis doesn't matter."

"What about Mr. Stroup? Don't we need to get his say-so?"

"What for? He doesn't want the body coming up, and if we do it on our own, we stand to make thirty bucks, split two ways. No Brennan, no Stroup. No middlemen."

"If you say so, Artie."

"Then grab your shovel and let's get to work. Siesta's over."

CONTRARY TO MR. STROUP'S instruction to bury the body deep, Fermin—who had had a plan in the back of his mind—had told Dolan to stop digging the young fellow's grave at only about three feet. It would then be a simple matter to exhume the body, although the night air was close and humid, and the low-lying ground around nearby Swan Lake was hatching out swarms of mosquitoes.

"Jesus, I'm being eaten alive," Dolan said, swatting his neck.

"Then dig faster, boyo. The sooner we finish, the sooner we get this prime cut over to the medical school."

When their shovels scraped against wood, Fermin hopped out of the grave. "Pry it open, Bobby," he said. "Then if you hoist him up a little, I'll pull him out the rest of the way."

Dolan put the tip of his crowbar under the lid and pried up, hard. Nothing.

"It's not giving an inch. It's like it's been sealed or something."

"*Sealed*? Who seals a coffin?"

"I don't know, but it's glued up tight as a drumhead."

"Pry harder, then."

Dolan tried again, but again without any luck. "I tell you, it won't budge, Artie."

Fermin jumped down into the hole. "Get out. Let me show you how it's done."

His friend crawled out of the hole, muttering, as Fermin jammed the crowbar between the coffin and the lid. Then he jumped on it.

After a few good hops on the crowbar, the lid gave way with a screech.

"Good fucking *God*!" Fermin shouted, without caring if they were heard. "I've never smelled anything like this number here. It smells like—"

"Sweet Christ on his cross," Dolan choked out, pulling his shirt over his nose. "It smells like burning cow shit."

"Burning cow shit?"

"There's just a kind of smoky air to it."

Fermin shook his head and put his back into lifting the lid free. The corpse inside was still wrapped in its linen shroud, which was now almost saturated with blood and ooze. He bent down and got his arms around the body.

"I'm going to puke," Fermin said. "How about a little help here?"

Dolan hopped down into the grave. "Jesus, you aren't kidding. Do you think it has to do with his being insane? Some of the people at the asylum smelled pretty bad."

"Not *this* bad. And he didn't smell this way this morning."

"On second thought, it's not burning cow shit," Dolan said, sniffing. "It's more like a really bad German cheese."

"Enough already!" Fermin said. "Let's get him in the wagon and us out of this hole."

Together they wrestled the pungent, seeping corpse out of its fine coffin and chucked it into the rear of the wagon. After quickly refilling the hole, they were on their way to the medical school.

"At least he'll be their problem soon," Fermin said as they rolled slowly down Main Street. "I swear they'll smell us coming, though."

AT THE MEDICAL SCHOOL, the janitor waved his hand in front of his face. "Sorry, boys," he said, "but I'll have to get the doctor on duty for this one. There's something *not right* here."

"What do you mean, 'not right'?" Fermin asked. "He's twenty-five. He was crazy, but all that killed him was apoplexy."

"I'm not calling you a liar, but if I take him in smelling like this, and he spoils the new vat, I'll lose my job. Wait here."

The pair lolled around the basement for a few minutes until a short, slightly pudgy man in a white doctor's coat walked crisply into the room. "I'm Dr. Grove," he began. "I understand—*good night*! What in God's name did you bring us?"

"A prime specimen we buried only today," Fermin said.

"Doesn't smell like it. It smells like—"

"Burning cow shit," Dolan said proudly.

"Don't mind him," Fermin said. "Look, this lad may be a bit on the fragrant side, but he was only twenty-five when he died."

Dr. Grove yanked out a handkerchief, dabbed at his watering eyes, and then placed it under his nose. "Well, then, pull off that shroud so that I can have a look."

"You do the honors, Bobby," Fermin said to Dolan. Dolan peeled back the upper layers of the shroud to expose the ravaged face, whose pustules had collapsed into raw and seeping tissue. In a few places, white bone was already exposed.

"*Jesus Christ*!" Dr. Grove said, horrified. "Look at him, will you? He's covered with *lesions*!"

"What's that supposed to mean?" Fermin asked. "Legions of what?"

"Do you have any *earthly* idea what this man died from?" the doctor asked, going very red in the face.

"Paralysis, Mr. Stroup said. And he was insane, too."

"You two," Grove growled. "It's not *paralysis*. It's *paresis*—general paresis of the insane."

"That's it!" Fermin said, snapping his fingers. "What's the difference?"

"'General paresis of the insane' is the medical term for tertiary syphilis," the doctor said through clenched teeth. "You do know *that* word, don't you? *Syphilis*."

"Of course I know syphilis."

"We know syphilis," Dolan added.

"Well, that's what this man had—or *has*, because syphilis stays alive in this kind of weather for some time after death. You brought us a *contagion*, you idiots!"

"How was I supposed to know that?" Fermin protested. "Twenty-five years old, a prime specimen. So what if he had the clap? Big deal."

"THE CLAP AND SYPHILIS ARE TWO DIFFERENT THINGS!" Dr. Grove roared. "If one of my young medical students gets this man's blood or God knows what into a cut or something, he's got *syphilis*! A death sentence!"

"Do we have any cuts, Artie?" Dolan asked, aghast. "I certainly don't want syphilis."

"You can't get it that way, Bobby. The doctor's being a bit of a nonce about the whole thing, if you ask me."

"Get him the devil out of here, *now*," Grove said, pointing at the door. "I can't use him, I don't want him, and I'm not touching him."

"You mean to say you're not giving us a red cent for this fine specimen?" Fermin said. "After digging him up and carting him all the way over here? Twenty-five years old?"

"That's precisely what I'm saying. He's contaminated, and I don't buy contaminated bodies. *You* ought to pay *me* for exposing myself to this rotten pile of meat. And Ferguson here will have to steam clean this whole room."

"And just what are we supposed to do with him, then?"

"Rebury him. Chuck him in the Canal. I don't care—just get him the *hell* out of my building!"

"You don't have to shout," Fermin said.

"And do *not* come back unless you have a good specimen," Dr. Grove said. "I'll gladly have you banned from doing any business again if you come a third time with poor quality product. First it was that old coot, and now *this*. Where did von Guyaling find you, anyway?"

"Who's Fawn Guiling?" Dolan asked.

"Come on, Bobby," Fermin said, ignoring both of them. "I know well enough when we're not wanted. I'm sure we can find some other place that would jump at the chance to buy this one."

"Try the pesthouse," Dr. Grove said. "I don't care where you go—just *go*!"

Maiden Voyage

For her first meeting with Barney Brennan, Mary donned the plainer of her two Brantford dresses—a somewhat drab cotton and linen ensemble with a tidy vest. Presentable, but commonplace enough that it wouldn't attract undue attention on her trolley trip up Main Street.

Before she left, she dropped by the Genesee. The doorman ran up the stairs to notify Eberly, and in a few minutes the Smuggler King himself walked into the lobby parlor, a big smile on his face.

"Ahoy, First Mate," he said. "Ready for your maiden voyage?"

"Ready as I'll ever be, Captain."

"Sit with me for a few minutes, would you? I'd like to go over some specifics."

George walked Mary through the potential terms of a deal with Brennan, and with Forest Lawn, to move the goods through the cemetery.

"I already know all too well how facile you are with numbers," George said. "So while this is my idea of a very favorable arrangement—for us—I will leave it up to you to give more ground if necessary. Sometimes the best deals aren't the most profitable ones."

"Why not?"

He shrugged. "The best deal is the one no one thinks about again once it's done. By contrast, if I know I've paid too much, I feel taken advantage of. And then it's all I can think about. Now if I pay too *little*, the person on the other side feels the same way. It's best if both feel good enough about the money to forget about it."

"That makes sense. I confess I never thought about it that way."

"Oh, believe me, I didn't either when I was getting started. I soon found out that what I thought were my best deals were the ones that caused the greatest resentments later. So use your judgment. If they'll take a hundred dollars per coffin-full of goods as their toll, believe me—we will be in clover. And we can afford to give up more, should you think it advisable."

"Thank you. I'll do my best."

"I know you will. And if anything seems out of the ordinary, leave immediately. I don't want you coming to any harm."

"George," she said, cocking her head. "Remember, I'm not a china doll. Don't worry. I'll be fine."

"Yes, I know," he said slowly, feeling strangely like he wanted to kiss her goodbye. He refrained, and off she went to the street railway station near the Genesee, taking a northbound trolley for Buffalo Plains. The car was nearly empty, and the horses had an easy pull to the corner of Main and Gulf Streets, at the far southeastern corner of sprawling Forest Lawn.

As she knew, Barney Brennan's place was conveniently located on the opposite side of Gulf Street from the streetcar stop, an easy walk for mourners attending one of Brennan's many wakes. She crossed Gulf and stood in front of the building that had loomed so large in her imagination.

The reality was considerably less impressive. The saloon-cum-mortuary looked more like an old farmhouse than a saloon, and it had been, once, long before Forest Lawn had begun its campaign of land acquisitions. The cemetery hadn't tried to buy Barney out, either; he was on the wrong side of the street to allow for easy expansion of the burying ground.

Despite the building's unprepossessing appearance, Mary was still a trifle nervous when she pulled open the front door. She hadn't any idea what to expect—a knot of toughs lounging at a battered bar, perhaps. And so she was taken by surprise to find that the main room was larger than she'd expected, and brighter too, with well-kept board floors, looking for all purposes like a dance hall. To complete the impression, every table had been pushed against the walls, and the chairs stacked atop them.

What made it look like no other dance hall, though, was the impossible-to-overlook presence of a coffin, sitting on a wooden bier in the very center of the expanse. At the foot of the box was a small daguerreotype of a man wearing a Civil War uniform.

"Madam?" came a lilting voice from the back of the room, and the man behind it emerged from some shadowy place in the rear. He was tall and lean, and appeared to be tough and wiry, with a long scar that crossed over the left eye socket and continued almost to the corner of his mouth. On his head was a battered Eton cap, but the remainder of his clothing was immaculate and appeared expensive.

"I'm here to see Mr. Brennan."

"The wake doesn't begin until five o'clock." The man eyed her appreciatively.

"I'm not here for the wake. I'm here on a business matter."

"A business matter, you say? What's a pretty lass like you have to do with *business*?"

"I can discuss that only with Mr. Brennan. Please tell him that Miss Carkriff is here for him. I'm Mr. Eberly's first mate."

"Mr. Eberly's *first mate*, is it?" the man said with a slightly contemptuous sneer.

Mary had expected this. "That's what I said, yes. I'm here on Mr. Eberly's behalf to discuss a potential business arrangement with Mr. Brennan. And I am authorized to speak only to him."

In the blink of an eye, the man's expression changed from contempt to bonhomie, and he whipped his Eton cap off with the speed of a striking cobra, revealing a tousled mass of russet hair. "Now why didn't you say so, Miss . . . ?"

"Carkriff."

"Miss Carkriff. I'm Barney Brennan. It's a pleasure to meet you."

She didn't return the compliment. "Thank you. My mission today is to discuss with you the terms for a particular kind of shipping arrangement."

"Yes, yes," he said. He wanted to pay her another compliment, but chose to hold his tongue. "Why don't we take this matter up in my office? You never know who might come in. Even in the morning, the gravediggers from across the street sometimes like to wet their whistle."

Mary followed him into a small back room that seemed to serve as Brennan's office. Shit was piled everywhere—empty bottles, what looked like old clothing or rags, and stacks of paper.

"My apologies," he said. "I need to tidy up a bit."

"I've seen worse. Not *much* worse, but worse."

He looked at her closely, wondering how to respond, when she laughed. He laughed along.

"You got me where I live on that one, Miss Carkriff."

"I'm happy to see that you have a sense of humor, sir."

His eyes narrowed. "Now, don't you believe everything you hear about me! And please, call me Barney."

"I didn't mean any unkindness. And I think Mr. Brennan is more appropriate for a business conversation."

"As you prefer," he said, seeming miffed. "Now then. You wished to discuss terms?"

"Mr. Eberly would like to resume shipping goods to you twice every week."

"That is good to hear. Then he's figured out how I'm supposed to get them north?"

"Yes. The goods will be carefully packed inside empty coffins, and sent to you along with the ones containing the bodies from Franklin Park."

Brennan sat back in his chair and exhaled. "That's *damn* clever. Oh, pardon me, Miss."

"Quite all right. I'll come by every Tuesday and give you a small slip of paper that will have on it a code to denote the positions of the coffins on the week's wagons." She took her tiny notebook from her reticule, tore out a page, and handed it to him. He looked at it, puzzled.

In less than a minute, though, Mary had explained her system, and Brennan again expressed his admiration for Mr. Eberly's cleverness.

"Perfect!" he said, holding up the little page. "My compliments to Mr. Eberly for this."

"I'll pass that along. What other questions may I answer?"

He leaned forward with a sly grin. "I would expect we'd need to agree on compensation. Is that something I ought to take up with Mr. Eberly, or with his *first mate*?"

Mary had been stewing about this the whole way north on the trolley. As first mate, she was making a hundred dollars a week, for seven days' work—and yet George was willing to pay this ruffian a hundred dollars *per coffin*? Three hundred a week *per wagon*? She thought back to what George had said, and was beginning to feel somewhat taken advantage of.

"Of course. There will be three coffins of goods, twice per week. Mr. Eberly is willing to pay you twenty-five dollars per coffin."

Barney's left eye—the one with the scar—seemed to twitch just slightly. "*Twenty-five*, you say?"

"Yes, twenty-five. All you have to do is get them through the front gate at Forest Lawn and then on their way, as usual."

He cleared his throat. "Has Mr. Eberly fallen on hard times?"

"He most certainly has *not*. Why do you ask?"

"I guess I've always known George—Mr. Eberly—to be quite generous. Twenty-five dollars per coffin seems rather low—but perhaps he's smarting after those shipments of his got pinched. You know as well as I do that those goods were worth ten thousand, at least."

She had not known that, but now she made up her mind that this scruffy Irishman—who reminded her more than a little of her father—should get one hundred fifty dollars a week, and not a penny more, if she was to receive only one hundred.

"I don't know about any of that," she said crisply, standing. "But that's what we're willing to offer. Take it or leave it, Mr. Brennan."

"'*Take it or leave it*,'" he said, almost in a whisper. "My, my— Mr. Eberly has obviously hired a *very* hard first mate." He gave her a crooked smile. "But easy come, easy go," he said with a shrug. "If that's what it has to be, then I'll take it."

"I am happy to hear it, Mr. Brennan," she said, sticking out her hand.

He rose slowly from his chair, squinting slightly as he took her hand. "Then it would seem we have a deal," he said softly, and then his face cleared again. "When may I expect the first shipment?"

"Tomorrow. And then again on Friday. Coffins will be in the same positions for a week, and then change."

"I'll be ready."

"It's been a pleasure," Mary lied. "Allow me to bid you a good day, sir."

"And to you as well," he said with a deep bow. "Back to the Genesee now, I presume?"

She gestured in the direction of Forest Lawn. "I thought I might first pay a visit to the cemetery. It looks so green and pleasant, and I am as yet unaccustomed to the noise and bustle of the city."

Brennan bit his lower lip. "I wouldn't recommend that, Miss Carkriff."

"Whyever not?"

"They require entry tickets now. There have been too many picnickers and casual strollers. And they've become quite strict about it."

"How inconvenient. Though I seem to recall that very near the trolley station there was a spot in the fence where a board was missing."

"I think that would be very unwise."

She put her hands on her hips. "*Unwise?* The very worst they can do is to ask me to leave."

"That depends on which *they* you mean."

"I beg your pardon?"

"I mean only that—well, the cemetery is very big, and you never know who might be wandering around. Unsavory types, if you take my meaning."

"You're very kind to look after my safety, sir. But I can handle myself well enough."

"Of course you can," he said with a thin smile. "I meant no harm by it. I bid you a pleasant day, Miss Carkriff. Please do give my best regards to Mr. Eberly—and my compliments on acquiring such a . . . *commanding* first mate."

He bowed again, and Mary walked out and turned left onto Gulf Street. Her first assignment was complete, and it had been far easier than either waitress work or sewing. The air hinted at the muggy breathlessness of summer, and despite Brennan's strange comment she wanted badly to duck under Forest Lawn's cool, green shade before returning to the Genesee and gritty downtown.

Brennan is probably just like George and every other man, she decided as she approached the trolley stop. *Overzealous in looking out for women, and with good intent, but still treating me like a child. It's broad daylight, and Buffalo will smell like manure and coal smoke. What could be the harm in a half hour spent among the trees?*

She veered away from the trolley stop and crossed Gulf Street. The board fence around the great cemetery could have used a fresh coat of whitewash, and a few of the boards were as warped as barrel staves. Mary walked away from Main until she came to the missing board. She slipped through the gap, went down a shallow gully, and stepped onto the grounds of Forest Lawn.

There weren't any graves in this area, though a few larger monuments had staked claims on the rolling landscape. From her makeshift gate, the grounds sloped gently downward and then upward again, rippling toward a meandering creek in the near distance. Ahead, just below the crest of the next hill and under a large tree, sat a single wooden bench. Next to it was a sign that read:

SECTION 18

With her handkerchief, she brushed away a thin coating of yellow pollen from the bench, sat down lightly in the dappled shade, and took in the view. Ahead were several pockets of what looked like old woodland separated by neatly trimmed greens, where a few headstones had sprouted irregularly. From this vantage point, she had a very pleasant view of the creek, the line of crooked oaks along its channel, and a little footbridge crossing it. On the other side of the creek stood a large granite mausoleum, all by itself in the center of a tidy lawn. She inhaled deeply.

Here, in the patchy shade, the air was far fresher than along Gulf Street, and Mary thought about smelly, bustling downtown Buffalo and the horrid precincts of the canal district. And to her surprise, it was in this spot that the final remnant of her homesickness for green Brantford burned away. Here, she realized, she could always find that which she had been missing—tranquility, solitude, and the ever-present reminder that human life was fleeting and that it was well to make the most of each precious day.

Forest Lawn felt like home.

She lingered drowsily on her bench for an hour or a little more, enjoying every cleansing breath and the light breeze washing over her skin. She might have stayed longer, even, but she knew that George would be expecting her report, and probably anxious for her return. With one final look down her hill to the creek, the bridge, and the stately mausoleum just beyond, Mary turned and retraced her steps to the opening in the board fence. She squeezed through, unseen, and walked along Gulf Street to the trolley stop. Luck was with her; a downtown car was approaching from the far northern reaches of Buffalo Plains, rumbling and rattling behind two careworn horses.

When she walked into the Genesee, she found George pacing in the lobby parlor, swinging his stick with such energy that she thought it might fly entirely out of his grip.

"My God!" he blurted. "Where have you been? You ought to have returned more than an hour ago."

"Do calm down. I didn't know I was on such a short leash."

"It's not a *leash*," he said, reddening. "It's that you're new at this business, and Barney Brennan is a—well, he's a shady character."

"We can agree on that. I disliked him rather intensely."

"Most do. But like him or not, he's the man to see in that part of the city. How did it go?"

"So it seems. In any case, I'm pleased to report that we have a deal, and that our shipments will resume tomorrow. They'll go every Wednesday and Friday."

"Well done!" he said, his mood lifting somewhat. "Were you able to hold him to a hundred a coffin, or did you have to go higher?"

She smiled slightly. "He agreed to twenty-five a coffin."

"What?"

"I told him twenty-five a coffin. Take it or leave it."

"'*Take it or leave it*'? You *said* that to him? In those words?"

"Indeed I did."

"Sit down, please, Mary," he said, sagging into an overstuffed chair.

"Is something wrong, George? I saved us at least seventy-five dollars a coffin. That's four hundred fifty dollars *a week*. My entire salary is only a hundred a week."

"Is *that* what this is about?" he said, exasperated. "You squeezed Brennan because you feel underpaid?"

"Not exactly, but—"

"All you had to do, Mary, was tell me if you felt underpaid. You and I agreed on your salary, and I'd hoped we could both forget about it after that."

"I *had* forgotten about it, until—"

"If you think Barney is getting more than he deserves, and you less, it's only because I have lots of experience paying the likes of him, and none paying for a first mate."

"I see," she said, looking down.

"Mary, that was most unwise. Barney knows how much those goods are worth, and twenty-five dollars is—well, it's tantamount to an insult."

She bristled. "He certainly didn't seem to take it that way. He wants to deal with us, and it doesn't pay to throw money around like it's so much scrip."

"Oh, Mary," George said, "what did I tell you about good deals? That they have to be good for both parties?"

"He *agreed*, George. If it wasn't good for him, he could have objected."

"I admire your pluck. Truly I do. But in this case, pluck can't make up for inexperience. We are going to have to find a way to pay him more, or it's going to come back on us."

"Let's see how the first month goes," she said, now a bit concerned. "Then I'll renegotiate with him. Just—please—don't go to him and countermand what I've done. I'll have no authority with anyone then."

He shook his head. "I would never do that to you. Yet in this case, please believe me: in a month we need to find a way to give Brennan a very nice bonus. We'll figure something out. Trust me—there's a *reason* he was willing to take so little. He has *something* up his sleeve. We just don't know what it is."

"I understand, George. I'm sorry if I did anything wrong. I was only trying to be firm."

"No, no, it's not *wrong*. Just perhaps a bit *too* firm for the likes of Barney Brennan. A fellow like him has a thin skin and a long memory."

"Yes, I understand."

"Then enough about that. Do tell me, now, what was it that took you so long to return? Did you do a little shopping, perhaps, along Main Street?"

"Oh no. It was such a lovely morning, and after I had concluded our terms with Mr. Brennan, I walked across the street and passed a pleasant hour in Forest Lawn."

"Alone?"

"Of course."

"Are you *serious*?"

"Why, yes I am."

"That place is not suitable for an unescorted young lady!" George nearly shouted, attracting some attention from the desk clerk and a couple of guests. He lowered his voice. "They've been having a series of grave robberies there, and the people who do that sort of thing don't want to be discovered."

"George, I really must say—you're treating me like a child. I respect your objection to the twenty-five dollars, but no one is out robbing graves in broad daylight. Furthermore, I didn't see a soul the entire time I sat there."

"Then you were lucky. But I do not want you going over there again. That's an *order*, First Mate."

Mary was growing angry, but she reminded herself that George only meant well, and that as a man he was thus far unused to having a woman in his employ—and one with her own mind. It would probably be best to train him up slowly, she thought.

"George, of course I will comply with your wishes. Although I will register a note of protest in doing so."

"Protest if you like," he said, "but it's my job now to take care of you. That's what a . . . a captain does, or is supposed to do. I could never live with myself if something happened to you and I had not done all I could to prevent it."

She found herself unexpectedly touched by his kindness. "That's really very thoughtful. I value your concern for my well-being."

And what George realized at that moment was that Mary's well-being had become the thing that mattered most to him. How that had happened, he couldn't fathom—but it had, all the same.

SECTION TWENTY

The Devil's Bargain

"Afternoon, Mr. Stroup," Barney Brennan said to the superintendent, who remained seated behind his glossy desk as the saloonkeeper walked in. Stroup was idly gazing out the floor-to-ceiling windows, which gave a panoramic view over the big new lake the cemetery had created by diverting a portion of the Conjaquadies Creek into an abandoned quarry. His mind had been drifting to Georgia Granger Moffatt again.

"I'm sorry to disturb you, sir," Brennan went on, "but I hoped you might have a moment to spare."

"Normally I would have a *very* compressed schedule, Mr. Brennan," Stroup said, swiveling around quickly and gesturing toward the chair in front of his desk. "Fortunately, today is a relative oasis of calm. How may I be of service?"

"It's about this resurrection business," Brennan said, sitting on the edge of the chair.

"Mr. Brennan," Stroup said indignantly, "as I have explained already, Mrs. Moffatt importuned me as only a woman can do. I hadn't any choice but to call a temporary halt. I don't like it any more than—"

"It's not about that. It's—well, we have another wee problem. A different one."

"What wee problem is that?"

"Last night, the boys dug one you'd told them to leave alone. Thought they'd make a buck without us in the middle."

"Which one?"

"It was a syphilitic."

Stroup smacked his forehead with his palm. "Those idiots! That one was *contagious*, for God's sake."

"Yeah. And the medical school gave them an earful about it, and then let me have it, too."

"Please tell me that they disposed of that pestilent thing," Stroup said, putting his head into his hands.

"They told me they dumped it into the Buffalo River."

"Good. No one will notice one more body bobbing along in that cesspool."

"At least they did that right," Brennan said. "But all the same, this second misstep does put our new enterprise on, shall we say, slightly shaky ground. So it's probably well that Mrs. Moffatt has called a halt."

"Ah, *c'est dommage*," Stroup sighed.

"Huh?"

Stroup smiled. "Merely an old French expression, meaning 'that's a shame.'"

"You speak French?"

"I have recently been taking evening instruction in the finer points of the language from Monsieur Neuville, whose école is on Main Street."

"Is he Canadian?" Brennan asked, intrigued.

Stroup looked indignant. "My heavens no. He's an honest-to-God Frenchman. I attended his class just last night."

"Well, how about that."

"Mr. Brennan, we can perhaps talk about the French language

another time. What are we going to do to repair relations with the medical school? When Mrs. Moffatt settles down, that is?"

"Fact is, sir, we probably only have one more chance with them. If Fermin and Dolan fuck it up again—pardon my French— we're done."

"And to think this was supposed to be easy money," Stroup whined. "So easy, I thought, that I advanced Monsieur Neuville for a year's worth of lessons. He granted me a ten percent discount in return, but it still represented a tidy sum, I can tell you."

"I'm sorry to hear that. As I say, though, we probably have one more try, so let's not give up just yet. We'll just have to wait for a *really* good one. If we can deliver a prime specimen, I think all will be well again."

"Then we will have to wait for the fat pitch."

"Mrs. Moffatt?" Brennan said, astonished. "She's not fat at all. She's *gorgeous*."

"*Pitch*," Stroup said, trying hard not to think of Georgia's crinolines again. "With a *p*. It's a baseball term."

"*You're* a baseball fan?"

"After a fashion."

They looked awkwardly at each other.

"I just hope Mrs. Moffatt doesn't get wind of the syphilitic," Stroup said at last, looking worried.

"Believe you me, no one's breathing a word about that one. The very fact that big bag of pus was allowed inside the door of the medical school would have heads rolling."

"That's reassuring."

"It is. But in the meantime, I *do* have another way we can both make some pocket money."

"Music to my ears," the superintendent said, holding them out with his forefingers. "What do you have in mind?"

"It's not my idea exactly—it's George Eberly's," Brennan said.

"*Mon dieu*," Stroup moaned. "That man is *terrifying*."

Brennan shook his head. "Not just now he isn't. He's in *way* over his head with the Franklin Park job. He needs us."

"How so?"

"You may have heard that a couple of his Niagara Falls shipments got pinched recently, somewhere along Delaware, and so he can't send his wagons around Forest Lawn anymore. His new . . . man came to see me today, and Eberly's idea is to ship goods directly through the cemetery. With the Franklin Park interments."

Stroup squinted. "Now is that so?"

"Is what so?"

The superintendent leaned back in his chair and put his fingers together in a steeple. "That the great and mighty Smuggler King wants to send his contraband through *my* humble cemetery."

"That's pretty much it, yes."

"He is a clever old fox, that Ébérlé."

"You mean Eberly?"

"Isn't that what I just said?"

Not really, Brennan thought, but why antagonize the man. "He is indeed."

"Well then? What's in it for me?"

"Easy money. As you know, at present Eberly's wagons are loaded with six coffins each, twice a week. If you will allow it, the wagons will carry nine coffins each. Six will be interred as usual, and three—containing the goods—will remain on the wagon and continue north."

"A very creative solution, I must say," Stroup admitted somewhat grudgingly, sitting forward. "*Très malin.*"

Brennan ignored the offhand French, unwilling to give Stroup additional satisfaction. "Eberly's man said that he is willing to pay you twenty dollars for the safe passage of each wagon."

Stroup reeled back in his chair again, setting it creaking. "Oh, he's *willing*, is he?"

"Yes, sir. Of course, you don't have to *do* anything for the money, just let the wagons pass—and I'll take care of the rest. It would be forty dollars extra a week to you."

"I see." Stroup thought for a moment. "Then let me tell *you* what *I'm* willing to do, Mr. Brennan."

"Yes?"

"You may tell foxy Mister George"—he pronounced it "zhorzh"—"Ébérlé this: that *I* am willing to *accept* his offer of twenty dollars per wagon. *C'est tout!*" He brushed his hands together as if dusting off flour.

This confused Brennan slightly, but he set it aside. "I'll pass that along, sir."

"Please do!" Stroup cried, roosting again behind his papers with an air of satisfaction. "Will that be all, Mr. Brennan? I really ought to attend to other—"

"There is one other, er, potential opportunity I wish to discuss with you, Mr. Stroup. Actually a much bigger one than the toll on the coffins."

"Yes?"

"I think we both know that George Eberly's shipments are worth far more than he's willing to pay either of us for keeping them moving along."

"My point exactly," Stroup said.

"Yet we both take on quite a bit of risk."

"*Sans doute*! We shoulder the risk, and Ébérlé reaps the reward!"

"Yes. So what I propose is that from each of these shipments we set aside a few things—a couple bottles of liquor here, or a little something else there. Not so much as to attract attention, of course, just something I can sell directly on our behalf. You and I will split the take."

"The *take*," Stroup said. "Yes, I like the sound of that. The *take*."

Brennan spread out his fingers on the desktop. "It's called skimming."

"I should say it is!"

"Er, yes. Then I would need only two things from you, Mr. Stroup."

"Name them, my good man."

"First and foremost, *absolute* secrecy. If, God forbid, George Eberly gets so much as an inkling that we are skimming from him—and I mean even the whiff of an inkling—we'll both end up on the bottom of Lake Erie. That is to say—dead."

"My cemetery is full of dead men, Mr. Brennan," Stroup said, waving his hand around. "Death doesn't frighten me. What frightens me is not squeezing everything I can out of life, or missing an opportunity when it comes drifting by."

Brennan suppressed a smirk. "I don't think most men are afraid of *death*—it's the *dying* part that scares them. And you may rely upon me in this: George Eberly would make that very, *very* unpleasant. He's done it many times, when he's had a reason. Or thought he did."

"You may count on my discretion, Mr. Stroup. Now what is the second thing you request?"

"Your men Fermin and Dolan—who will be interring the real coffins anyway—would open the ones with the goods, remove the items I direct them to, and then conceal the skim until I can move it along. Now I can't very well hide such things at my place, but Eberly never comes to Forest Lawn. So the other thing I need is a place to stash the goods—someplace on your property."

Stroup looked at Brennan for a few blinks of the eye.

"Quite so," the superintendent said at last. "An *oubliette*."

Brennan couldn't let this one go, since his life was on the line. "A what?"

"An *oubliette*," Stroup repeated. "A place where things are forgotten."

"I suppose you might call it that."

Stroup gave him a thin smile. "You may rest easy, Mr. Brennan. I know just the place."

SECTION TWENTY-ONE

CARPE DIEM

June 10

Mary thought that a good first mate ought always to be on time, so on a warm Monday morning in early June, she arrived at the Genesee even earlier than usual. George was not in the lobby, so the doorman escorted her to the Smuggler King's office, on the second floor overlooking Main Street.

"Mary!" George said when she rapped on his door. "Punctual as always."

"I want you to know that you may depend on me."

"I haven't any doubt of it. And tomorrow's another meeting with Brennan. Is everything in readiness?"

"Yes, all is well, though it'll soon be a month since we struck our deal with him, and you had said you'd like to give him a bonus. To make up for my stinginess."

"I've been meaning to talk with you about that. Please, make yourself comfortable."

She made to sit in front of his desk, but he stood and gestured toward a table in the corner of his office. "Why don't we sit at the table?" he said. "So much less *formal.*"

They sat and looked at each other, uncertain how to begin.

"You know—"

"You know—"

They had begun talking at the same time.

"Ha ha," Mary said. "I've been your first mate only for a little while, and already we're like an old married couple."

"That is funny!"

"Yes, it is. Why don't you go first, then?"

"Very well," he said, smiling. "I've been thinking I may have been a little too hard on you. About the deal with Brennan. You're right—he's no shrinking violet. If he hadn't wanted to take the deal, he would have said something."

"Perhaps so, but I do think I let my own feelings intrude. I am usually better at containing them."

"As am I. But in any case—as I've said before, if I was a bit harsh, it's only because I wish to keep you from coming to any harm. And I have thought of little else since."

"I implore you not to worry so, George. There can be no doubt that a woman is more vulnerable in some ways than a man, but I am more resourceful than you may think."

"You are indeed, but you have put your finger directly on the problem. You are a *woman*. I'm a man, and still I go armed."

"Oh, I haven't any need for weapons," she said, as brightly as she could manage. "George, I will be as careful as I can. May we set this topic aside?"

He shook his head. "I am afraid we cannot, Mary. Because after much thought, I keep returning to the same conclusion: in your current role, I am unable to protect you adequately."

Now she could no longer appear cheerful, and she looked down at the tabletop.

"But, George, I love my work," she said, without looking up.

"And I love . . . the work you do."

"Then let me do it."

"Believe me, Mary, I only want what's best for you."

"You keep saying that," she snapped, looking up and glaring at him. "And all because God made me a woman. I can't very well change who I am, sir."

He sat back in his chair, seeming stunned. "As usual, you provide the solution," he said softly.

"Excuse me?"

"You said that you can't change who you are. But you see, that's the solution!" He thumped his cane on the floor triumphantly.

She looked back at him flatly. "What I meant is that unless I become a man, it seems you refuse to believe I can be safe. And that, George, is impossible."

"Oh, but that's where you're not *quite* right," he said with a big smile. "While *you* cannot transform yourself into something else—something that no one, but *no one*, not even Barney Brennan—would dare to harm . . . *I* can."

Mary looked at him, mystified.

George laughed. "I ought to have broached this the first day you walked in here," he said. "Oh, I did, but in a different way. The answer is that we must marry."

"*What?*"

"It's wonderfully simple, Mary. If you became my wife, not a soul in Buffalo would dare touch a hair on your head. Everyone knows the penalty for crossing me."

Her eyebrows arched up. "This is most unexpected."

"Perhaps, but we are already a formidable team. Just imagine what we could accomplish as man and wife!"

Mary squirmed in her chair. "George, I will admit that it's a very interesting proposition—but we must be clear. Do you have in mind a business arrangement or a marital one? If the former, we may discuss it further, as I can indeed see its merits. But if the latter, I must observe that we've only just met. I don't know you, and you don't know me. Not in any profound way, that is to say."

"How much do we need to know? I know you're a very lovely and *very* intelligent young lady from Canada, who wants to make something of herself, and presumably make an advantageous match one day. And you know that I'm a smuggler with a bad leg."

"Then you are suggesting marriage, in the fullest sense of the word, and not merely a liaison of convenience?"

"That's right."

"George—"

"How old are you, Mary, if I may inquire?"

"Twenty-four and a half."

"And I'm just shy of thirty. Our ages, therefore, should not present an impediment to wedlock."

"I hardly think that it's our ages that are at issue!"

"Then what is?"

"I didn't come to Buffalo looking for a husband. In the fullness of time, naturally I would like to wed. But I certainly did not expect to do so within a month of my arrival."

"You may therefore congratulate yourself on your efficiency. Nor, incidentally, did I think I would *ever* find a woman I wished to become my wife."

"But, George . . . marriage is supposed to be based upon love. We don't . . . we don't *love* each other."

"Who says?"

"Well . . . I honestly don't know. But I find it rather difficult to believe—"

"Then please believe *me*. Because the truth is—and I felt it from that first evening at the Revere House, but have been deathly afraid to utter it until this moment—that I find myself quite fatally smitten with you. I love you, Mary, and that's all there is to it. I don't know for certain *why* I feel this way, but I *am* certain that I do. And I believe that you can and *will* come to love me."

Mary sat back heavily in her chair. "George, I don't know what to say. I confess that I find myself completely at a loss."

"If I may ask: Have you ever—even for a moment—thought of me in the way I have been thinking of you?"

"I can't deny that I find you a most presentable gentleman," she stammered, blushing deeply.

"*Presentable.*"

"More than presentable. Very attractive. Intelligent. Fearless. And it's evident that you respect me as a person."

"I do, Mary. Very much so. I could never believe I would have trusted anyone with what I've trusted you with. And so quickly."

She smiled. "Nor would I ever have thought I would so readily embrace the life of . . . an *outlaw*."

"Ha, yes, there's that outlaw thing again. Mary, hear me out: I know it's a great deal to take in. You needn't say anything now, but do understand that I am making you a full, free, and heartfelt proposal of marriage."

"And if I should refuse?"

He winced. "I would be terribly wounded. But I have been wounded before, if never so deeply."

"I was thinking of my situation here. As your first mate."

"We'd have to go back to the proverbial drawing board, and think of some other way to guarantee your safety."

"You would not dismiss me, then?"

"Of course not. Though I hope you don't think that this is all a ruse to—become intimate with you."

"If it is, it's a devilishly clever one."

He suppressed a grin. "Then let me state my entire case as plainly as I may. Mary, I have loved you from the moment I first laid eyes upon you. I've tried to deny it, naturally—I am by nature a careful man, and not one normally given to impulse. But I cannot—I will not—deny it any longer. And furthermore—not only would marrying you bring me great joy, but it would offer the additional benefit of protecting you from coming to any harm. Frankly, the whole idea satisfies both my head and my heart. So, Miss Mary Carkriff, I am asking you to become Mrs. George Eberly. I would go down on one knee, if I could, but I fear I might not be able to get up again."

Mary closed her eyes for a long moment, thinking of Brantford, which seemed suddenly so far away, like a place from another person's life. First, after so little time in her new city, she had been offered a king's ransom for what seemed like very simple work—and now, almost immediately on its heels, a chance to marry the king himself.

She opened her eyes again and looked at handsome, worldly George Eberly, very much in the prime of life, war-wounded but brimming with strength and confidence.

"You're really in earnest about this?" she whispered, looking into his eyes.

He reached across the table and gently took her hand in both of his. "Mary, I have never been more earnest in all my life. Will you marry me?"

She looked down again, studying the table.

"It would seem that with you, George, I have done a better job of concealing my feelings than I did with Mr. Brennan," she said at last, looking up at him. "Because, since the moment we met at the Revere House, I've dreamed of little else than becoming your wife."

He raised her hand to his lips and kissed it softly. "Mary, you are a most remarkable woman. And you are going to be an even more remarkable wife."

UNLIKE HIS BRIDE-TO-BE, GEORGE Eberly didn't mind wasting money, but both shared a hatred of wasting time once a decision was made—so only two days later, George and Mary were united in a simple but elegant Anglican ceremony, as she had requested. It had all come together so quickly that there was no prospect of any of their relatives coming to Buffalo in time for the ceremony. George made sure that the church was filled to the rafters, though, for what he told Mary was to be their "outlaw wedding." Gus Kirsch and his local boys were there, as was Ed Durham, who made a special trip over from Port Colborne for the big event. Captain John "General Custer" Andrews insisted on claiming the bride's first dance. Even Barney Brennan stopped in to wish the couple well, and then left again directly. And so Mary's fairy-tale day was complete.

Except for one thing—the consummation. After the wedding guests had departed into the warm June night, Mary and George walked hand in hand up to the penthouse suite—the entire top floor of the Genesee—which George called home. It was an opulent space, and in addition to the Genesee's already fine furnishings, George had hung the walls with old masters and outfitted the place in the latest style. For the first time in their short association, it became clear to Mary that her new husband possessed both money and excellent taste. And he'd been a perfect gentleman, too, insisting on carrying her across the threshold and setting her down gently inside their suite—bad leg notwithstanding.

"Welcome to your new home, Mrs. Eberly—though I apologize for the long climb. The hotel management informs me that in another year or so, they plan to install a very new thing called an elevator. It's a tiny room that carries people up and down in tall buildings."

"That will be amazing," Mary said, "but I don't mind the staircase." She glanced around at the splendor of the penthouse. "Any number of stairs would be worth this. Is this all *real*?"

"It's all real. And it's all *yours*."

"*Ours*."

They sat down together on a velvet-covered loveseat, unsure of what to say to each other now that they were man and wife.

"So when do we get down to business?" Mary blurted out after an uncomfortable minute of nervous silence.

"Good heavens. I thought we might benefit from a few days off."

"I didn't mean *that* business. I meant—you know, the other kind." She tilted her head toward the bedchamber.

George cleared his throat nervously. "My, you can be direct."

"We're *married* now, George. Surely you will want to engage in coition."

"Well, um, of course, but I thought you might prefer to take things more slowly."

"Why? I've been jumping feetfirst into all sorts of things lately."

"That you have."

"If I am afraid of anything, husband," she said, "it's that I will disappoint you. As I have alluded, I have no experience in this department."

"I can't imagine that."

"You can't imagine that I have no experience?"

He blushed. "No, not *that*. I can't imagine that you could ever disappoint me. In anything."

"Then perhaps I may do my duty by you now?"

"Yes," he said, "though you needn't feel like it's a duty. Let's think of it as something you and I do only with each other."

"That's a much better way to put it, George."

He stood and held out his hand. "May I?"

She took his hand. "You may," she said, rising.

George led her into the bedchamber, which was furnished fashionably and with a large canopy bed.

"I'll need a moment to disrobe," Mary said. She stepped behind a chinoiserie dressing screen, dropped her hoop skirt, and began shedding underlayers. Eberly shook his head, stripped down, and climbed under the sheets. In another minute or two, Mary stepped out from behind the screen.

"My God!" he exclaimed.

"Is something wrong?"

"*Wrong*? Are you serious? You're a *goddess*!"

She looked down at herself. "Do you really think so, or are you merely paying me a compliment?"

"Get in here with me and you'll soon find out."

Mary slid under the covers, and George took her hand.

"My," she said. "It's really true, after all."

"What is?"

"That it *changes*, and so impressively."

He laughed. "And you may take *that* as a compliment, dear. And I promise to explain everything as—"

"No need," she said brightly. "I know all about it."

He frowned. "But you said just now you hadn't any experience."

"Not the direct kind, no. But on one of my recent visits to your outlaw warehouse, I passed a *very* interesting hour looking through a large crate of your French photographs."

"My word," he said, under his breath. "Dare I ask what you thought of them?"

"They struck me as depicting a uniquely pleasurable activity, in all its variations. Indeed at what I took to be the conclusion of each act, the participants wore expressions of bliss so intense as to appear almost painful. I found that most unexpected, and frankly more than a little enticing. So I for one am eager to see what the fuss is all about."

"Mary," he said, stroking her cheek, "if you didn't exist, I would have to invent you."

As the days and weeks went by, both George and Mary were taken repeatedly by surprise. Not about how well they worked together—that had been obvious from the start—nor by any quarrels or sullen compromises said to be inevitable after two single people exchange rings for the first time. What surprised—shocked—them both was how compatible they seemed to be. It was almost as though love had always existed between them, and had only needed to be acknowledged to blossom.

They were also surprised at how quickly they fell into a rather placid domestic routine: breakfast together, discussions of work throughout the day, and then supper out at one of Buffalo's fine restaurants. Then they would return to their suite at the Genesee, make love, and fall asleep in each other's arms. "The pirate and his lady," George joked, and Mary would laugh. They quickly found these little rituals both comfortable and comforting—familiar, daily pleasures.

Yet any good marriage is also a conspiracy, with individual benefits accruing to each participant. For Mary's part, it was the first taste of a life that most young women could only fantasize about—the finest of everything, a handsome and tender husband, and a soon-to-be central position in Buffalo social circles. And George knew that—if everything collapsed around him—as his wife, Mary could never testify against him in any court.

SECTION TWENTY-TWO

ℭIPHERS

July

Around lunchtime on a blazing hot Monday, about a month after their wedding, George returned to the Genesee from Franklin Park and, in their suite, found Mary curled up on the settee in the library, concentrating furiously on a small book.

"May I ask what you are studying so intently, my dear?" he asked, sitting down next to her. "Not more French photographs, I trust?"

She looked up, her eyes somewhere else. "No," she said. "Not that I would mind another session with them. This one is a fascinating book I found on your shelves."

"Which one?"

Mary held it up, turning the spine toward him. In neat gold letters along the top was written:

Secret Writing
F. Kasiski

"Ah yes," George said. "I was given that in the war. Before I was wounded, my commanding officer took a notion that I might make a good spy, and to do that I'd have to learn a few codes. Kasiski's book was, at the time, the very latest word in cryptography. Perhaps it remains so."

"I've never been exposed to anything like it. It's captivating."

"Perhaps you could write me steamy love letters in code," George said with a wink. "Though if you did, I'd get nothing done. I'd spend my whole day deciphering."

"I could," she murmured, still someplace far away.

"Mary?"

"Yes, husband?"

"Would you prefer your privacy?"

She set the book down neatly on a little table near the settee. "Oh no, dear, I am sorry. I have been thinking that there must be a way to use some of these ciphers in our business."

"You've already created one—your method of identifying coffins containing our goods. That was quite novel."

"Yes, and I'm pleased it has been working out so well. Still, I keep thinking that perhaps we could use codes and ciphers to communicate with, say, men like Mr. Durham. Telegraph to him in code, telling him what goods are in greatest demand. That sort of thing."

"That would help in one important way," George said. "Sometimes, Durham will bring in a big shipload of whiskey, when I already have as much whiskey on hand as I can move. So naturally the surplus has to be discounted or stored—which not only presents a risk of discovery but also means that Durham doesn't get paid until it moves."

"Precisely. But now imagine if you could telegraph to him, 'No more whiskey—bring gin,' or the like—"

He held up a hand. "Oh believe me, I see where you are headed with this, and as usual, you're brilliant. Part of the reason I have only *one* Durham bringing goods from Canada is that I know I can trust him. If we are to grow this business, however, into the empire you think it can be—I will need *five* Ed Durhams, and I can never trust five men as much as I can one. With coded communication, though—"

"You could send instructions to our fleet of Durhams without the slightest fear of interception. Or rather, if they should be intercepted, no one could read them."

He shook his head slowly. "This is *inspired*, my dear. Truly inspired. What should we do?"

"I can think of a few things. If you can start asking about for another Ed Durham—we have to think big but start small—perhaps you can find the first captain of our expanded fleet. Unless, of course, you already have someone in mind."

"I know a few, but I will inquire more diligently now."

"And while you're doing that, I plan to study this book and determine what kind of cipher, or ciphers, we might employ. It may take some time, though. I can learn some of the simpler ciphers quickly, but that would be only to train the mind. A simple cipher may not be sufficiently strong for our purposes."

"We have all the time in the world, dear."

"And yet not a moment to spare." She picked up the book again. "So if you'll excuse me, husband . . ."

He laughed and jumped up as quickly as his walking stick would allow. "Aye-aye, First Mate. Whatever would I do without you?"

She looked up at him and blew him a kiss. "I frankly don't know, but you're never going to find out."

SECTION TWENTY-THREE

The Mausoleum

August 13
Tuesday

Her meeting with Brennan was much later than usual that day. Mary and George had taken the entire morning and the early part of the afternoon to shop for a pleasure boat they could sail on the lake. Yet the lateness of the hour was not enough to deter her from what had become a habit—though not one she had divulged to George, who would disapprove. After Mary left Brennan's place, around five o'clock, she squeezed through the gap in the Gulf Street fence. She then walked up and over the long hill to her favorite bench, with its broad view of the Conjaquadies Creek winding its way through the green heart of Forest Lawn. Dusk was still two hours away, and she had plenty of time to enjoy the slanting sunlight of the late afternoon and the rush of the creek below.

Mary smiled up into the August sun. She closed her eyes, wondering, or marveling, at how far she'd come from Brantford, and in so little time. Tonight, she and George would celebrate their two-month wedding anniversary—technically a day late, but on Mondays the better restaurants in Buffalo were closed, and they had decided to postpone until they could celebrate in proper style.

Mary opened her eyes again, leaned her parasol against the bench, and squinted through the treetops at the azure sky. Was it luck, fate, or God that had put such good fortune in her way? Her mother would have said God, her father luck, and George most certainly would say fate. Mary wasn't sure, but it didn't matter much—she was grateful to whatever power had turned its sunny face toward her.

She tilted her head back farther, watching the maple leaves high above her shivering in the summer breeze. It was peaceful here— the right kind of place for a cemetery. It had nothing in common with those stark hilltop burying grounds dotted here and there along every rural road, nor with a scruffy city cemetery like Franklin Park, with its tilted headstones turned black with lichen, soot, and ash. No, Forest Lawn was as serene as its name. Mary felt lucky to be alive, when so many who were spending eternity in this kind place could never feel its caressing breezes on their skin or be refreshed in its rustling shade.

Sleep was stealing over her when she heard distant voices down the hill and to her right. Probably some family coming to lay a wreath on the grave of a loved one, she thought, imagining that they might be sharing quiet memories together as they walked.

Then she heard sharp cursing, which startled her out of her doze. Who would be swearing up a blue streak in a place of such deep reverence? She looked down the hill and now could see that the voices belonged to two men struggling up the path, carrying between them a pine coffin. The thing was plainly heavy, and the men had to set it down on the path every few yards to catch their breath and wipe their foreheads with a sleeve. Mary found it strange that only two men would be carrying a laden coffin by hand, and especially through an area of the cemetery whose ground had barely been disturbed.

When the men drew near enough that it seemed they might be able to spy her above them, Mary ducked behind the large tree next to her bench. She watched as the pair passed by beneath her, crossed the little bridge to the far side of the creek, and half dragged the coffin—while cursing even more lustily—up four steps and onto the portico of the big mausoleum. She peered at them through the gaps in the picket line of trees. The two men set the coffin down, opened the mausoleum's bronze doors, and shoved the wooden box over the threshold. The doors closed behind them.

How very, very strange, Mary thought. There was something about these men that felt *wrong* to her, somehow, though she couldn't place what that might be. Her curiosity aroused, she carefully eased down the hill and toward the Conjaquadies, staying low and darting behind the mossy trunks of the ancient trees. As she approached the creek, the ground dipped sharply. She picked her way carefully down the bank and crouched next to the support pilings of the footbridge. From this vantage point, she could look up and through the bright spaces between the planks. Orange sunlight filtered down on her while the creek tumbled by just below, sparkling.

She had waited there for perhaps ten minutes when she heard the creak of the mausoleum's doors. Seconds later, two sets of heavy boots thudded across the bridge above her. The men were talking about something, but she couldn't make out what they were saying, though their words sounded intense and urgent, even alarmed, as though an argument might be brewing. Mary shrank close to her piling and soon the footsteps moved off the way they had come—along the gravel pathway next to the creek, leading toward Main Street.

As soon as their footfalls were safely distant, Mary scrambled out from under the bridge. She crept up the bank and watched the long shadows of the men retreating, this time carrying their coffin lightly between them.

MARY STARTED UPHILL AGAIN, for some reason finding herself terrified to look over her shoulder at the strange mausoleum, and with an odd prickling feeling that someone or something was watching her. Mary did work up the courage to turn, once, but saw no one. She crossed the gravel path at a nervous trot and scampered back to her bench, where she found her parasol leaning, just as she had left it. She collapsed on the seat, trembling.

Mary took a moment to catch her breath. She tried to collect her thoughts, too, puzzling out what the men's strange errand might mean. Her first thought was that she had witnessed a grave robbery— as George had warned her—but the men's burden had been *lighter* when they left the mausoleum, so that didn't make any sense. No body snatcher would *deposit* a corpse in a mausoleum and then hustle away empty-handed. And in broad daylight?

She would have to ask George, even though she knew he'd be angry. But now, she thought, it's well past time I ought to be starting back downtown. In the next heartbeat, though, Mary was seized with a queer notion, and took from her reticule her little notebook. She thought for a minute or two, and then with her gold pencil hurriedly jotted a note to remind herself of the details of what she had just seen. Then she replaced the notebook and her pencil in the reticule and drew the strings tight. She didn't want to stay here anymore, not for another second, even for the sake of this cherished view, which suddenly seemed sinister and threatening. Something very ugly was going on, and she wanted only to hasten back to Gulf Street, the trolley, and George.

It was then that she heard footsteps coming up the hill toward her, from her right.

SECTION TWENTY-FOUR

Lost and Found

That Evening

George had begun to worry around six o'clock. At six thirty, he left their suite, stationed himself in the lobby parlor of the Genesee, and waited. As the minutes crept by, and seven o'clock came and went, he began to be buffeted by rogue waves of apprehension and fear. Every time the big front doors of the hotel would swing open, he'd clench the pommel of his walking stick, heart in his throat, full of hope that Mary would walk in with a lovely smile and some gentle excuse on her lips. And yet every time those hopes were dashed.

When the tolling of the lobby clock marked another half hour gone by, George determined that he'd already wasted far too much time. He hurried as best he could to police headquarters, at Main and Terrace, where he found Police Chief William Sloan completing the next week's duty rosters.

"Bill," George said, "Mary's missing. I need your help."

"Slow down, George. Catch your breath. What's happened?"

George told Sloan that Mary had taken the Main Street trolley to see Barney Brennan—about what, the chief knew better than to ask—but hadn't returned home.

"She's probably doing some shopping," Sloan said. "I wouldn't worry—"

"It's our two-month anniversary," George said, exasperated. "We were going to have a nice dinner together. She wouldn't be out shopping."

"Then I'll send a few men up to Buffalo Plains right away. She may . . ."

"She may what?"

"Well, I don't quite know what I was going to say. But I'm sure there's a logical explanation. Why don't you go back to the Genesee, and I'll check in with you in—let's say an hour. It's getting dark fast, so I don't want to waste daylight."

"I'll be in the lobby parlor."

At the Genesee, though, the Smuggler King found himself unable to sit and do nothing for another hour, so he had his coachman take him north to see Barney Brennan. At the saloon, George busted in on a wake just getting underway, and found Brennan in his back office, drinking a large glass of whiskey.

"Have you seen Mary?" Eberly blurted.

Brennan looked up from his clutter. "George," he said, surprised. "Yes, your wife was here around five, I think it was. Only for a few minutes, as usual, and then she left."

"Are you sure?"

"Of course I'm sure. Same as the usual routine. Now, it may have been four thirty and not five, but she was most definitely here." He reached into his vest pocket and held up a little piece of paper. "See? The code for the next shipments."

George pressed his fingers against his temples, hard. "My God, Barney, she's gone missing. She didn't come home!"

"She didn't?"

"I think I ought to know!"

"Now, George," Brennan said, holding out his hands, "try to be calm."

"Why does everyone say that? How could anyone be *calm* in this kind of situation?"

"I'm sure there's a simple explanation. Perhaps she went to take supper with her family."

"Her family's in Canada!" George said.

"Have you told the cops?"

"I had to. I don't have men available to mount a search."

"Well, I have a couple. When she left here, she couldn't have gone far. Either back down Main or—well, I can't imagine where else."

"Do you think she might have gone over *there*?" George said, pointing in the direction of Gulf Street.

"Into the cemetery?"

"Yes, into the cemetery."

"I very much doubt it. At that hour of the day? No."

George let out a guttural growl of frustration. "You know, I told her more than once not to go over there. There's a goddamn open quarry over there!"

"Oh, that's a lake now."

"And that makes it better somehow?"

Barney cleared his throat. "I didn't mean . . . in any case, why would Mrs. Eberly sneak into a cemetery?"

"She did it once before. She's from the country, and she likes the trees, I guess."

Outside Brennan's office, the music and hollering of the wake crowd was intensifying.

"Look, George, I can't leave to look over there right now," Brennan said, nodding toward the noise. "But like I said, I have a couple of men who can walk the streets and ask a few questions."

"Thanks, Barney. And if you hear anything—I mean *anything*—I want you to come and find me personally. Wake or no wake."

Brennan stood slowly. "I swear to you I will, George. In the meantime, do your best not to imagine things."

"Famous last words," George muttered under his breath, and left Brennan's place.

9:00 p.m.

BY THE TIME DARK came down for good, the cops had done what they could. Not that it had been that hard to trace Mary's steps, at least to Brennan's. As the cops worked their way up Main Street, they spoke to at least a dozen people—relaxing on their porch steps in the late afternoon heat—who remembered seeing the pretty young thing riding in the northbound trolley, and then stepping down at Gulf and Main. But the trail went cold at the corner, after Mary had gone in to see Barney Brennan. There was one exception: an old woman who lived on Brennan's side of Gulf, just across from the cemetery. The woman swore that, around five o'clock, she had seen a young lady matching Mary's description slip through the gap in the Forest Lawn fence and disappear under the trees.

By the time the cops had finished talking with the old lady, a thick and moonless night had swallowed up Buffalo Plains, and a search in Forest Lawn proper would be impossible in the dark. The lead patrolman called the news into Chief Sloan at headquarters, who then walked over to the Genesee to break the bad news to

George: that he had no choice but to suspend the search until the following morning.

As Sloan had dreaded, George flew off the handle. But as much as the chief wanted to find Mrs. Eberly—he knew that doing so would put him in her husband's good graces for good and ever, and pay out handsomely, too—there was no prospect of sending men to comb endless acres of woodland, graveyard, and abandoned pit quarries with nothing but candles to guide them.

"We'll start again at the crack of dawn, George," Sloan said. "I promise you."

"I'll be at the Forest Lawn gate then."

Sloan put a big hand on George's shoulder. "No, my friend," he said. "You stay here, and let me do my job. It'll be easier to keep you informed if you're not moving around."

George blinked and looked away. After Sloan had gone, George limped slowly up the staircase to the penthouse suite. When he opened the door, he felt for a moment that Mary would be waiting for him on the settee, maybe reading her silly codebook, and that this whole thing would be a terrible misunderstanding, a mistake, and all would be well. Then he would take her up in his arms, and kiss her, and firmly but gently upbraid her for worrying him so.

It was all a fantasy. The suite was dark and empty.

The Next Morning

AT ABOUT SEVEN O'CLOCK, a young Buffalo patrolman got up the nerve to interrupt Police Detective John Simmons's breakfast at the Revere House to tell him that a call had come in. Two men, taking a shortcut through the Forest Lawn grounds, had stumbled over a woman's body.

No identification had yet been made, and Simmons was unaware of Mary Eberly's disappearance, so he took his time about getting to the cemetery. He finished his meal, took a shit in the Revere House's water closet—so much better than the filthy latrine at police headquarters—and arrived at Forest Lawn almost an hour later. Several cops were standing around the main gate, waiting to escort the detective to the scene.

When Simmons walked up, a crowd of at least thirty gawkers had gathered around the body, being held mostly at bay by several more harried policeman.

"Does anyone know who she is?" Simmons asked one of the cops, a sergeant who seemed to have taken something like charge of the situation.

"Nope," he said. "No one's ever seen her before."

Simmons nodded and knelt next to the body, which was lying a foot or two away from the area's lone bench.

The young woman was neatly laid out on her back, as if sleeping, on a spongy patch of moss. Her skirts were carefully pulled down to conceal her ankles, and her basquine tidily arranged and unwrinkled. The ribbon that secured her pretty straw hat was still tied in a neat bow under her chin. A parasol lay next to the body, and a reticule remained slung around her neck on its long cord. Simmons loosened its drawstring, and in it found a porte-monnaie containing a few dollars, a return trolley ticket, a small notebook, and a little gold pencil. He leafed through the notebook but found only random scribblings, most likely made by the deceased to round off the point of her pencil.

Unless she had been carrying more money than remained in the porte-monnaie, the woman had not, apparently, been robbed. As Simmons turned the body this way and that, he found no obvious sign of violence—no blood, no strangulation bruises, nothing. She may just as well have lain down on the ground next to her bench and died peacefully. Just to the right of the body was scattered a thin layer of fine sand, which seemed out of place on the carpet of moss, but Simmons didn't attach any particular significance to that.

When he turned her over onto her stomach, he noticed that the back of her skirt was stained with grass and dirt, as though she might have been dragged along the ground. But just as likely—more, even, given the lack of visible injury—the stains could be attributed to the final paroxysms of death. To his mind, the circumstances were pointing more and more to a stroke of apoplexy. It didn't happen often to such a young person, but it did happen. And it would explain a great deal.

"Who was it found the body?" Simmons asked the cop.

"Two gravediggers. One of them ran out and found me, and I called it in."

"Where are these men? I'd like to hear their story."

The policeman shrugged again. "Don't know."

Simmons glared at the man. "Well, why don't you go and find them, then? And tell headquarters to send the coroner. I'll wait here."

The cop hustled off, leaving Simmons alone with the corpse. He stood, brushed off his knees, and sat down heavily on the bench, as if keeping the dead woman company. He'd seen a lot of death, but there was something about this young woman that aroused a kind of pity. He'd noticed her wedding ring—still on her finger, another strike against robbery—and thought that somewhere in Buffalo was a young husband who hadn't any idea that this day would turn out to be the worst one of his life. And he dreaded breaking that news.

Dealing with the dead was far easier than dealing with the living.

SIMMONS WAITED WITH THE dead woman for the better part of another hour, when at last the policeman came huffing up the hill with two lanky men in tow.

"I called the coroner," the cop said to Simmons, who had very nearly drifted off in the peaceful glade.

"Good. Are these the gravediggers?"

"They are."

Simmons stood and took out a small notebook and pencil. "Names?" he said to the pair, flipping it open.

"Arthur Fermin," Fermin said, taking off his hat.

"Bobby Dolan," Dolan said, removing his as well. "Robert, properly speaking."

"You're gravediggers?"

"Men-of-all-work, more like," Fermin said. "But we do dig quite a few graves."

"Quite a few indeed," Dolan added helpfully.

"And you found this young lady's body?"

"That we did, sir," Fermin said with what might have been a touch of pride.

"Do you recognize her?"

"We saw her yesterday, sitting on this bench. She seemed perfectly fine at the time, of course. Just taking in the view."

"I see. Did you speak with her?"

"No, sir," Dolan said.

"What brought you back by here again this morning?"

Fermin was about to answer, but Dolan piped up first. "We were coming to work from our lodgings, and took a shortcut through here. That's how we found her."

"You're in this part of the cemetery frequently?"

"Almost every day," said Fermin. "There's a hole in the fence just over this hill. It's easier than walking all the way down Gulf to Delaware."

"Did you touch or move the body at all?"

"No, sir," they said, almost in unison.

Simmons closed his notebook. "You know you'll have to testify at the coroner's inquest, so don't leave the city until that's done."

Fermin and Dolan nodded. "Is that all, sir?" Fermin asked.

"For now, yes. You may go."

Simmons slipped his notebook into his coat pocket and looked down at the girl, whose skin was taking on the grey blotchiness of death. Poor thing, he thought. After the coroner takes her, the worst part begins—locating her family and giving them some very bad news. But before that, he would have to notify Police Chief William Sloan, which was standard procedure in any death under suspicious circumstances.

As soon as Chief Sloan heard the news, he knew he would have to inform George Eberly. As much as Sloan hoped that the body was not that of Mary Eberly, there was only one way to know for certain—and that was to have George view the dead woman's body.

George was sitting in his usual armchair, staring at the front door of the Genesee, when Sloan walked in. Try as he might, Sloan was unable to keep a poker face.

"Bill, don't tell me . . ." George said, rising. *"Don't."*

Sloan held out his hands. "Now, George, there's no cause—"

"Why are you here, then?"

"My men found a body—but there's been no identification."

"A woman?"

"Yes. In Forest Lawn."

"Dear God," George moaned. "It's Mary. I know it is."

"Now, we *don't* know that, George. But if you'll come with me and have a look, we can put our minds at ease. The body's been taken to Kraft's Dead House."

"It's all my fault," George mumbled, leaning on his walking stick.

The pair climbed into the police carriage for the short ride to Kraft's.

INSIDE THE DEAD HOUSE, they found Detective Simmons standing next to a plain wooden bier on which was placed a long pine box covered with a shroud. There were a dozen similar biers placed around the perimeter of the interior, but only one was covered with a shroud.

George steeled himself, walked over to the shrouded box, and shook hands with Detective Simmons.

"Are you ready?" Simmons asked.

"I am."

Simmons took hold of the upper end of the shroud and gently pulled it back to reveal the face of the dead woman.

George drew in a sharp breath. "It is she," he said through

gritted teeth. "Her name is Mary Carkriff Eberly, and she is my wife of two months."

Sloan gestured to Simmons, who began to draw the shroud back over Mary's face. George reached out a hand and stopped him.

"A moment, please," he said, leaning over the makeshift coffin and kissing Mary tenderly on the forehead, and then the lips. He straightened up again with some effort, took a last long look, and then turned to Simmons. "Thank you for taking care of her," George said. "She will be interred in my family plot at Forest Lawn. I'll arrange an undertaker."

"Perhaps I can take you back to the Genesee," Sloan offered.

George shook his head. "I can't go back there just now, Bill. But thank you all the same."

SECTION TWENTY-FIVE

The Inquest

August 26
Monday

Two days after her death, Mary was interred in the Eberly family plot, in Section 11, near the main gate of Forest Lawn and well away from the scene of her death. George had expressly forbidden any mourners, well-wishers, or even flowers. He was the only one present to see his young wife lowered into the receiving earth—except of course for Arthur Fermin and Bobby Dolan, who worked the crank handle of the lowering device while George watched Mary disappear forever.

The coroner's inquest into Mary's death was called to order on August 26, in a stifling courtroom in the old city hall, which doubled as police headquarters.

"This inquest is in session," Coroner Richards intoned precisely at nine, "in the matter of the death of Mary Carkriff Eberly. I call as the first witness Police Detective John Simmons."

Simmons stepped forward from the gallery and took the witness chair in front.

"Please state your name and occupation," Richards said.

"My name is John Simmons. I am a detective with the Niagara Frontier Police Department."

"Thank you, sir. Now then—you were notified shortly after the deceased was found?"

"Yes. Patrolman Reilly used a nearby call box to report the incident. I went up to Forest Lawn straightaway."

"Please describe the scene upon your arrival, if you would."

"There was a small crowd gathered around the body. Reilly and the other patrolmen had kept them at a safe distance to avoid any tampering with the scene."

"Who found the body?"

"Two gravediggers, Arthur Fermin and Robert Dolan. They stated that they were on their way to work when they found the deceased."

"And had any witnesses seen the deceased while still in life?"

"The same two gravediggers stated that they saw the deceased sitting on a bench the day before they found the body. In addition, I spoke with one Mrs. George Cook, who lives on Gulf Street across from Forest Lawn. She told me that she had seen a woman matching the description of the deceased enter Forest Lawn on the previous day, at approximately five o'clock in the afternoon, by stepping through an area in the perimeter fence where a board was missing."

"I see. And in your investigation, did you find any corroborating evidence of such an entry?"

"I did. I found two sets of footprints, side by side, in the gully just below the missing board. One set of prints matched precisely the cloth gaiters the deceased was wearing. The other impressions were those of a man's shoes. Those I have not been able to identify."

"Thank you. Now would you please describe the appearance of the body and any particulars of its location?"

Simmons consulted his little notebook. "The deceased was lying supine, close by a small bench and under a large tree. She was wearing a light blue dress, a black basquine, and a straw hat, which was still fastened under the chin with ribbons. Her clothing was neatly arranged, and there was no apparent evidence of a struggle. The body bore no obvious signs of violence, with the possible exception of a broad reddish area on the left temple. There was foam about the mouth and nose, and some flyblow around both nostrils. The eyes were open and fixed. The body was no longer in rigor mortis, so I would estimate the time of death must have been prior to seven o'clock the previous evening."

"Did you notice anything out of the ordinary?"

"It looked as though the deceased had quite peacefully lain down for a nap," Simmons said, "or as though her body had been carefully arranged. Her skirts neatly covered the feet, her reticule was present and seemed unrifled, and a parasol was lying parallel to the body. As to the scene itself, the only thing out of the ordinary was a quantity of fine sand, like that one might find on any beachfront, which had been scattered on the moss quite near the deceased. That struck me as unusual, as there is no sand for several miles of Forest Lawn."

"And no signs of violence, you say? Other than the mark on the temple?"

"Nothing that I could detect. It was an only slightly reddened area on the temple and forehead, and didn't resemble the typical marks of a weapon or blunt instrument. I found the deceased's peaceful attitude, lack of obvious battery, and intact reticule unusual—if, that is, the death had been a violent one. Thus my suspicion is that the young woman suffered a fit of apoplexy, struck her head on the ground in falling from her bench, and died where she lay."

"So in your experience, you do not consider this death likely to be a murder?"

"That is correct. I cannot say for certain whether it was murder or not, but if it was, it was a most unusual one."

"Thank you, Detective. You are excused. The next witness is Dr. Waldo von Guyaling."

"Present," von Guyaling said, stepping forward and taking Simmons's vacant chair.

"Dr. von Guyaling," Richards said, "did you perform an autopsy on the deceased?"

"I did, yes, with yourself present."

"Can you describe the body?"

Von Guyaling withdrew a folded paper from his coat pocket, adjusted his pince-nez, and read, "The decedent is a young woman, approximately twenty-five years of age; well-nourished; light hair and skin, blue eyes; weight, approximately one hundred and twenty pounds."

"Thank you. Your autopsy findings, Doctor?"

The anatomist squinted at the page. "I will read a summary of the unremarkable findings first. Heart, liver, kidneys, pancreas—all normal. Stomach contained what appeared to be the remnants of a light luncheon of soup or stew containing potatoes. Chemical analysis of the stomach by Practical Chemist George Hadley revealed no evidence of alcohol consumption, and trace amounts of an alkaloid. I ruled that out as evidence of poison because potatoes normally contain such alkaloids. Bowels normal, showing evidence of recent evacuation."

"Thank you, Doctor. Any remarkable findings?"

"Yes," von Guyaling said, glancing down at his paper. "The deceased's right lung had a small area of scarring, possibly from an old tubercular infection. The left frontal lobe of the brain showed what appeared to be a contusion with slight bleeding, which to my mind indicated perimortem head trauma. I must note at this juncture that the skull over this area of the brain was intact and without fracture, and the scalp unbroken but reddened. As Detective Simmons testified."

"And what do you make of all that, Doctor?"

"It is difficult to say for certain," he replied. "A blow to the head is always a possibility in such a case, but a bludgeon or heavy instrument, generally speaking, would have fractured the skull or, at the very least, broken the skin. As the detective testified, this reddened area could easily have been caused by toppling from her bench onto the moss, or occasioned by a fall somewhere else on the grounds of Forest Lawn—or even days before her death. Sometimes a head wound can prove fatal many days after the injury itself."

"Thank you. No other wounds, then?"

"None."

"Any other remarkable findings?"

"Only one other," von Guyaling said, peeking over Richards's shoulder at George Eberly, who was sitting in the front row of the gallery. He took a deep breath. "The deceased was very recently pregnant. There was a fertilized ovum embedded in the lining of the uterus."

At this George looked as though he might vomit. He leaned forward sharply, as if punched in the stomach, and then straightened slowly up again, glaring at Arthur Fermin and Bobby Dolan, who looked away.

"Anything else?" Coroner Richards asked.

"No, sir," von Guyaling replied.

"Then you are excused, with our thanks. The next witness is Arthur Fermin."

"State your name and occupation," Coroner Richards said when Fermin took the witness chair.

"Arthur Fermin. I'm a man-of-all-work at Forest Lawn."

"Did you know the deceased?"

"No," Fermin said.

"You saw the deceased while she was still in life?"

"Once," Fermin said.

"Where and when was that?"

"It was the day before Bobby—Mr. Dolan—and I found the body. The lady was sitting on the bench, near where we later found her body."

"What time of day was this?"

"An hour or so before sundown, I'd say."

"What were you doing in that part of the cemetery?"

"Bobby and I were taking a shortcut to Barney Brennan's place. We had finished with work that day."

"You were walking east, then? Toward Mr. Brennan's establishment?"

"We were."

"What was the deceased doing when you saw her?"

"I don't know as she was doing anything. She was holding a parasol over her shoulder. Folded up."

"The sun wasn't shining?"

"It was, but there's a great lot of shade there. She just had it resting on her shoulder."

"Which one?"

"The right. She was holding it in her right hand."

"Did she see you, or indicate that she had seen you?"

"Didn't seem so, no."

"How far away from her were you?"

"I'd say about thirty rods. Maybe forty."

"So that would place you about a hundred and fifty or two hundred feet from the deceased?"

Fermin shrugged. "Yes, sir, I suppose that's about it. Yes."

"And even from such a distance and with the sun going down, you could make out that she was holding a parasol in her left hand, balanced on her left shoulder?"

"I have very good eyes," Fermin said. "And it was her right hand, and her right shoulder."

"Thank you for correcting me. And you had no contact, nor exchanged any words, with the deceased?"

"That's right."

"You're excused, Mr. Fermin. Next witness is Robert Dolan."

Dolan sat down in the witness chair.

"State your name and occupation."

"Robert Dolan," he said. "Like Artie, I'm a man-of-all-work at Forest Lawn."

"Where do you live?"

"We board with Thomas Sheridan on Delaware Street, near Gulf. He runs the Forest Lawn dormitory."

"Did you hear Mr. Fermin's testimony?"

"I did, sir."

"Do you differ in any material way from that testimony? Anything you'd like to add or change?"

Dolan looked up at the ceiling. "No, I wouldn't say so, sir."

"Did you also see the deceased holding her parasol as Mr. Fermin testified?"

"I did indeed, sir."

"And you were taking a shortcut to Brennan's place when you saw the deceased sitting on her bench?"

"Yes, sir."

"Why were you going there?"

Dolan smiled. "For a little nip, of course."

"Are you intemperate, Mr. Dolan?"

"Most of the time."

"You wish to testify that you are drunk most of the time?"

"No," Dolan said, eyes bugging out. "You asked if I was *intemperate*. And by the Holy Virgin, I am, most of the time."

"I think you mean 'temperate,' then."

"As you like, sir."

"Now, then, you and Mr. Fermin discovered the body of the deceased the next morning?"

"Yes, sir. And a terrible thing it was, sir."

"Around what time?"

"It must have been around seven."

"And how did you happen to be in that part of the cemetery again?"

"We were about to start work."

Arthur Fermin squirmed a bit in his seat, and tried to catch Dolan's eye but failed.

"And in which direction were you walking?"

"The opposite direction from the day before," Dolan said.

"From east to west, then?"

Dolan thought a moment. "Yes, that would be it, sir."

Richards walked over to the stenographer and huddled for a moment, whispering. Then he confronted Dolan again.

"Now you said, Mr. Dolan, that you agreed in all particulars with the testimony of Mr. Fermin."

"Yes, sir, I did. And I do."

"Then what I don't understand is that Mr. Fermin testified that the two of you were taking a shortcut to Barney Brennan's place when you saw the deceased, still alive, sitting on her bench. You'll recall that would be going from west to east."

"Yes, that's a fact," Dolan said, reddening.

"Then how is it that you were going in the opposite direction, from east to west, first thing the next morning?"

"We were going to start work. I just said that."

"I know you did. But where were you coming from?"

"Why . . . our lodgings, of course," Dolan said, his voice catching.

"But you testified that you reside with Mr. Sheridan, at the Forest Lawn dormitory, on Delaware Street. That's at the furthermost western point of the cemetery."

"So it is, sir."

"But you said just now you were walking east to west, heading to work. How could that be, if your dormitory is on the far western edge of Forest Lawn? Where were you all night, Mr. Dolan? Were you not in your dormitory?"

"Aw, come on," Fermin said, half standing. "Can't you see the man's slow-witted?"

"Please sit down, Mr. Fermin, or I'll ask the police chief to take you into custody."

Arthur sat, fiddling with his cuff.

"Please answer my question, Mr. Dolan."

"It's like Artie said," Dolan pleaded. "I guess I do get a bit muddled in the head sometimes. I suppose I got confused about the direction."

"I see," Coroner Richards said. "Then, for the sake of argument, let's say you had it backwards."

"Yes," Dolan said, brightening. "That's all it is. I was just turned around in my head."

"So if that's so, and you were going from your lodging on Delaware Street to start work, where was work beginning that day?"

"Not far from where we found her, I reckon."

"And your tools?"

"Our tools?"

"Does someone place them at your worksite?"

"No, sir."

"And when I call Mr. Stroup to testify, will he agree with you that you began your day somewhere to the east of where you found the body of the deceased?"

Dolan put his head in his hands and sniffed. "I'm . . . I don't know, sir. My head's all in a whirl now. I'm sorry, I really am. God knows I'm doing my best to remember. I just wish you'd ask Artie. His memory is better than mine, sir."

"Pending that, I'm going to excuse you for the present, Mr. Dolan. But don't go anywhere, because you may be recalled. And that goes for you as well, Mr. Fermin."

Bobby Dolan meekly rose and took his seat again next to Fermin, who was fuming.

"You *excused* him, after *that*?" George Eberly shouted from the gallery. "What are you playing at, Richards?"

Coroner Richards looked over at Chief Sloan. "Shall I continue or recess?"

"Let's keep going," Sloan replied.

"Mr. Eberly, I'll ask you to keep your silence," Richards said.

George stabbed the floor with his cane. "I will for now."

Richards cleared his throat. "Next witness is Mr. Brennan. Mr. Brennan, your full name and occupation, please."

"My name is Bernard Brennan. I keep a mortuary and public house on Gulf Street."

"Did you know the deceased?"

"No, I did not."

"Never met or seen her before while in life?"

"Never," Brennan said.

"And can you corroborate the testimony of Mr. Fermin and

Mr. Dolan, that they came to your establishment on the evening in question?"

"I can."

"Were you there the whole time they were present?"

"I was indeed."

"And what time would that have been?"

"The two gents must've got to my place a little before sundown, like they said. They stayed until about nine or ten o'clock."

"Nine? Or was it ten?"

"It was between nine and ten. Then they left."

"Did they say where they were going?"

"Yes, they said it was time they got back to their dormitory before the doors were locked."

"And your establishment is located where, once again?"

"On the south side of Gulf Street, across from the cemetery, and near the intersection with Main Street."

"On the southeasternmost corner of Forest Lawn?"

"Yes, that would be it," Brennan said.

"Are you and the two gentlemen friends or associates?"

"Who? Fermin and Dolan?"

"Yes."

Brennan smiled. "*Friends*? No. Good customers, that's all."

"You may be excused, sir," Coroner Richards said. "We have two more witnesses. Next is Mr. George Stroup. State your name and occupation, sir, if you would."

"George Washington Stroup," Stroup said, after taking his seat. "I am superintendent of Forest Lawn."

"Mr. Stroup," Richards began, "how long have you been in your current position?"

"Going on three years now."

"I understand that you negotiated the acquisition of much of the land that is today Forest Lawn."

Stroup looked obviously pleased. "I did. Yes, sir. It was *quelque chose*, I can tell you that."

Richards looked puzzled but went on. "And in that time you've had remarkably little crime in the cemetery."

"That is so. Oh, we have to contend with the occasional mischief-maker, but nothing grave. Pardoning the expression."

"Yes, naturally. Did you know the deceased?"

"Oh no," Stroup said. "Though I have known her husband, Mr. Ébérlé, for quite some time."

"Let the record show that the witness has indicated Mr. George Eberly," Richards said, pronouncing it "Ebb-er-lee." "And do I take it that Mr. Fermin and Mr. Dolan work for you?"

"Yes."

"Do you know where their work was to begin the day the body was found?"

"Not offhand," Stroup replied. "We have so much activity these days. I could check."

"Please do, sir," Coroner Richards said. "And inform myself and the chief of police."

"I will gladly do so."

"Did the deceased possess an entry ticket to Forest Lawn?"

"If she did, she didn't obtain it from me—I would have remembered—and as I understand, one wasn't found on her person."

"Now then, do young women often visit the cemetery?"

"Of course. To visit a grave, or participate in a ceremony."

"I mean alone and unescorted."

"Not typically, no."

"Why is that?"

"Forest Lawn is a large expanse of partly wooded rural countryside. Unescorted women do not tend to feel secure in their persons in such an environment."

"No, I would expect not. So why would a young woman, without a ticket, wriggle through your perimeter fence just to sit on a bench?"

Stroup shrugged. "I couldn't say."

"But in your experience, have such events transpired?"

"Well, yes. Sometimes."

"And to what end?"

"Usually to meet someone else."

"Detective Simmons testified that there were two sets of footprints in the gully by the missing board. A man's and a woman's. The woman's were identified as those of the deceased."

"So I understood, yes."

"Wouldn't that mean that the woman had been escorted by a man?"

Stroup blinked rapidly. "It might, or that she was meeting one in the cemetery."

"Why would that be? In your experience."

"In my experience, when a man and a woman enter without authorization, it's for immoral purposes. Trysting. An assignation."

George Eberly came out of his seat. "Stroup, you bastard, I'll have your *head* for that," he yelled. "How dare you suggest that my wife was in your cemetery for an immoral purpose!"

"Sit *down*, Mr. Eberly," Coroner Richards said. "Or I will have you removed. Mr. Stroup was answering my question in a general way, not with any specific reference to your deceased wife."

George slowly took his seat, his face bright red. "I won't forget this, Richards," he said, jabbing his finger at the coroner. "That goes for you, too, Stroup."

"Now, George . . ." Chief Sloan said gently.

"Don't try to mollify me, Bill," Eberly barked. "I know very well what they're getting at. Neither of them likes me, nor ever has. And now they want to smear my wife's reputation. They've not heard the last of me."

"Then Mr. Eberly," Richards said, "would it meet with your approval if I excuse Mr. Stroup for the present and allow you to testify?"

"Fine," George said, striding to the front of the room and putting his shoulder into Stroup as the other man walked back to the gallery. He sat in the witness chair, tapping his gold-headed cane between his legs. "Come on, Richards," he said. "Get on with it, so we can all put this farcical proceeding behind us."

"State your name and occupation, please," Richards said.

"George Eberly. I own a coffin manufactory."

"Yes, yes, you do. My condolences, naturally, on this very sad and unfortunate event that has befallen you."

"Save it. Ask a question, don't make a speech."

"Very well. How long were you married to Mrs. Eberly?"

"Two months."

"And how long have you known her."

"About three months, give or take."

"Love at first sight, then?"

"You might say that."

"Did you and your wife have words on the day she died, Mr. Eberly?"

"Words?"

"An argument. Any sort of disagreement."

"No, we did not. I didn't murder my wife, sir, if that's what you are suggesting."

"I am not suggesting anything, Mr. Eberly. Simply trying to ascertain the facts."

"You've heard plenty of facts already," George said. "Why are you dragging me through this ridiculous spectacle?"

"This *spectacle*, as you call it, is a legal *inquest*, sir. Now, then, I do have a question. Do you know why Mrs. Eberly should have been in Buffalo Plains on the day of her death, and why she would enter Forest Lawn without authorization, merely to sit on a bench?"

George bit his lip. "No, I do not," he said, shaking his head. "I didn't treat my wife like a child. She was free to come and go as she pleased."

"You must think it strange, though, don't you? That Mrs. Eberly would go to such lengths just to find a suitable spot to sit?"

"No, I don't find it particularly strange at all. My wife was from a rural place, and she found Buffalo to be rather close quarters by comparison. Lots of people go up to Forest Lawn for a bit of fresh air. I expect that's what she was doing."

"I see. Do you know any of those who have testified today?"

"Only Mr. Stroup," he said. "Well, and Simmons."

"How do you know Mr. Stroup?"

"I sued him last year for his failure to maintain my family's plot."

"And were you successful?"

"What does my lawsuit against that popinjay have to do with my wife's death?"

"Because I wish to establish whether you might wish to exact some retribution on Mr. Stroup."

George's knuckles went white on the pommel of his stick. "I wish you'd been half so scrupulous in questioning those two varlets," he snarled, pointing at Fermin and Dolan. "It's obvious that they're both liars, even if the one is a half-wit."

"Mr. Eberly," Coroner Richards said, "I must caution you not to interfere with the interpretation of whatever facts we may discover here."

"That's an intriguing statement, coming from the very man who let Dolan step off the stand just as he'd become hopelessly tangled in the web of lies he'd so obviously constructed with his friend. I wonder how I ought to interpret *those* facts?"

"Mr. Eberly," Richards said, almost purple with rage, "if you continue to oppose this process, I'll have you taken into custody by Chief Sloan."

"I don't give a tinker's damn what you do. Let me simply say that I don't need *you* to discover the truth about my wife's death. Or, rather, murder. I can do that very well on my own, and I pledge before God that while I live, I will see heads on pikes for it."

"*Chief Sloan*!" bellowed Coroner Richards. "Please take this man into custody for contempt of a legal proceeding."

Sloan looked back at him calmly. "No, I don't think I'll do that."

"Why not? I am the legal head of this inquest, and I demand it!"

"I don't think an arrest is warranted, Mr. Richards," Sloan said. "Mr. Eberly has lost his young wife in a most horrible way, and if he has become somewhat worked up over it, he has very good reason. Now move this along, will you?"

Coroner Richards spluttered something inaudible.

"Looks like you've been publicly castrated, Richards," Eberly said, standing. "And in that spirit, I've played along with your charade longer than I had expected I'd be able to." He leaned toward the stenographer. "Let the record reflect that George Eberly has excused himself from this and all further such proceedings."

"Noted," the stenographer said.

George limped a couple of steps toward the gallery, and then stopped and turned. "Oh, one more thing," he said to no one in particular. "You may also underscore that bit about heads on pikes. I may be, as Chief Sloan so kindly put it, 'somewhat worked up,' but I assure all of you that I am thinking quite clearly. And I will have my vengeance."

With that George Eberly walked out of the inquest, leaving most every mouth—including Coroner Richards's—hanging wide open.

PREDICTABLY, ONLY MOMENTS AFTER George had stormed out of the inquest, Coroner Richards proclaimed that he considered Mary's death a matter of mystery, but most likely the result of an accident or a sudden medical event. He would return a final verdict within a few weeks, pending any other evidence that might come to light.

Despite Simmons's dislike for Eberly—who had flouted his authority more times than he cared to recall—the detective was none too amused with the verdict, so he left the room straightaway to have a chat with Chief Sloan, who had ducked out directly after Richards's summation. As Simmons approached Sloan's office, he almost ran full tilt into Coroner Richards. Richards breezed by him without a word.

"How did he get here so fast?" Simmons said to his chief, who was just sitting down again behind his enormous desk. "Does he have a secret tunnel?"

"I suppose he wanted to see me before you could," Sloan replied with a little smile.

"Hmm," Simmons said. "Anyway, I've heard more than enough, as I'm sure you have as well. I recommend we arrest Dolan and Fermin tomorrow, if not today. After their ridiculous testimony, it shouldn't be any problem at all to get an indictment."

Sloan folded his hands on the desk. "That's not saying much. I could secure an indictment against my grandmother, if I really wanted one."

"All right, then, so much the better."

"There's only one problem with your plan," the chief replied, shaking his head.

"What's that?"

"It's not happening."

"Why not?"

"Richards told me that we can't charge them. Dolan and Fermin are mixed up in this resurrection business—with the blessing of the whole Anatomical Board, of which Richards is the chairman."

"Oh for fuck's sake," Simmons said.

"What's more, Richards and the mayor are political allies, and if we pinch either one of those rascals, the whole house of cards comes tumbling down. On our heads."

"So what's the alternative? I didn't think so at first, but after that testimony—it's clearly a murder, Chief."

"Not according to Richards, it isn't. He's going to rule it a probable stroke of apoplexy, since whatever wounds there are could have got there after the woman's death."

"Who dies of apoplexy and still is able to arrange her skirts to perfection?"

Sloan waved his hand. "I'll grant you it's improbable. But it's not *impossible*."

"So those two scoundrels go free, then?"

The chief shrugged. "For the present. But you know as well as I do that George Eberly thinks that Dolan and Fermin killed his wife. If we step back, it's almost certain that he'll take matters into his own hands."

Simmons rubbed his cheek. "When you put it that way, if I were them, I'd rather go to Auburn. It'd be safer there."

"Yes, I have a feeling that whatever we could do to them pales by comparison with what he has in store. Feel better now, Simmons?"

"Yeah, I suppose I do, Chief."

A FEW DAYS LATER, a package for George arrived at the Genesee. It contained those few effects found on Mary's person—her hat, gloves, parasol, and reticule. George had had her buried in her pretty blue dress and purple-black basquine, attired just as she had left the Genesee House, and just as she'd been found next to her bench.

As Simmons had said, the contents of the reticule seemed to be intact and untampered with—a couple of hair combs, the small sum of money, and Mary's tiny notebook and golden pencil. George debated within himself whether to keep the items or to put them into the incinerator at the hotel as too painful to have around. At last, he decided to keep them for so long as he lived—though, if he had his way, that would not be very much longer at all.

SECTION TWENTY-SIX

DESPAIR

After receiving the little package of Mary's personal effects, a week passed by, one slow beat of the mantel clock at a time, until George could no longer bear its crisp click and touched the pendulum to stop its pulse. He stayed holed up in his suite the entire time, curtains drawn tight to keep any errant ray of summer sunlight from penetrating the suffocating gloom. He didn't dare leave, lest he bump into someone—anyone—who knew him; he couldn't tolerate condolences. Nor did he answer the cards left for him by his lieutenants and friends. Instead, he sat in near-total darkness, neither eating nor drinking anything but a little water. When he could sleep, it was on the hard settle in the front parlor; he was unable to bear even the sight of their bed, let alone pass the night in it, alone.

A single terrible thought crowded out all others: Mary was *gone*, never to return. Every hope he'd had for the future had been wiped away in a moment. Worst of all, he could not deny that she had been doing his bidding when her life—and that of their *child*—was taken. She had given her life to him not once but twice, in as many months. It seemed unreal to imagine that *never again*—even those words seemed hollow and alien—would he feel the warmth of her arms around him, the brush of her hair against his cheek, or the delicacy of her kiss. She was *gone*.

He'd been lonely before, many times, but not this *kind* of lonely—a gnawing emptiness made all the deeper and harder by the knowledge that only so recently, he had possessed the very thing that was now gone forever. He knew how it felt to lose hope—the second day at Gettysburg, with ten thousand screaming rebels charging his company's position with fixed bayonets—but he had never lost his will to live, and that had saved him. Now, though, the fight had gone out of him, and for the first time in his life, George felt something far worse than hopelessness—he was now held hostage to a fatal thing called despair.

By dusk the next day, George had made up his mind. He took a late trolley up to Main and Gulf, and crossed the street to the fence around Forest Lawn, where the missing board was still missing. He wriggled through with some difficulty and stepped onto the sloping lawn, and then walked downhill to Section 18. The grass was still slick with the previous day's rain, so George carefully edged down toward Mary's bench. When he reached it, he gently ran he hand along its top rail, which only so recently her lustrous golden hair had caressed. He kicked at the fine sand scattered on the nearby moss and then, feeling strangely weak, sagged down on the bench where, he thought with a pang, not one but three lives had ended.

He slowly took in the beautiful view of the hillside, the line of trees at its bottom, and the burbling creek just beyond. So *this* was the very last thing her eyes ever saw before all was swallowed up by darkness, he thought. I can understand why this place was so special to her. If only I had taken the time to share it with her.

It was all he could do not to weep, but weeping was a waste of time, and in this as in all things, George Eberly did not like to waste time. Get on with it, one way or the other, he thought. Either get back to work, or . . .

He patted his trouser pocket and felt the weight of the derringer inside. He carried the little pistol all the time—in his line of work he had to—as a last resort against a mortal enemy. But now he had become his own mortal enemy, and rules were rules: there couldn't be one set for him and another for everyone else. And so he knew, and had known for some time, that he would have to die.

George pulled out the pistol and cocked it, determined not to think about it anymore but to act quickly and bring all this misery to a swift end, and in the same spot where Mary's precious life had been stolen. Placing the gun against his temple, pressing hard, he trained his thoughts on Mary. He was just closing his eyes when he felt Mary's little notebook fall out of his pocket and onto the bench. He set the derringer down so that he could replace the notebook. It wouldn't do for someone else to have it.

He flipped through the dog-eared pages, smiling softly at this last thing—the very last—that her tender hands had touched. A few pages had been raggedly torn out; probably ones containing the messages delivered to Brennan over the brief time Mary had served as his carrier pigeon—and, all the while, had also been carrying their child.

The little book's remaining pages contained only a few jottings, though on the final marked page—one after the stub of another that had been removed—was an inscription that had mystified him all along. On it was written:

Augustus

U W N N I B B 20

He touched the jagged edge of the preceding page, thinking.

She had seen Brennan just before going to Forest Lawn, so this was assuredly the very last thing she ever wrote—and probably written right where he sat. He traced her letters gently with his finger.

George had occasionally wondered whether perhaps the inquest had been onto something after all; that this nonsensical string of letters and numbers may have been written while Mary was suffering some brain disorder—a stroke of apoplexy, as both Detective Simmons and Coroner Richards had asserted. While George had to admit that such a thing was *possible*—she would not have willingly scribbled gibberish into her notebook—it seemed to him unlikely. A stroke of apoplexy would have rendered the inscription an unreadable scrawl. Yet these characters were neat and orderly, if perhaps somewhat hasty, and easily recognized as being in Mary's schooled and careful hand.

If this was indeed the last thing Mary ever wrote, it *must* have significance. She must have been trying to tell him *something*. But what?

He looked up from the notebook and blinked away his tears. At the bottom of the hill, the Conjaquadies Creek frothed away to his left, eager to reach Lake Erie, then Niagara Falls, Lake Ontario, and the sea. His eye followed the water's course under a footbridge that punched through the parallel ranks of black oaks that lined either side of the creek. On the far side of the creek—though visible only through a few keyholes between the oaks—was a large white mausoleum, seemingly the only monument in the area.

George eased the derringer's hammer down and replaced it and the notebook in his pocket. He felt sure that Mary had caused her notebook to leave his pocket with the pistol, and that she was trying to tell him something, before it was too late. He stood and walked slowly down the long hill to the footbridge, scrutinizing every step, hoping to find something the police had missed. Nothing jumped out at him, though. He stepped onto the bridge; midway across he looked upstream. The bright water eddied and churned toward him, coming down a staircase of rock shelves and shooting under his feet before calming again.

He crossed the bridge and passed a neat sign that read:

SECTION 20

Directly to his right was the big mausoleum. He stepped into Section 20, walked over to the structure, and looked up. Along its entablature was a single word:

MOFFATT

In the lengthening shadows of the portico were set a pair of giant bronze doors. He tried turning the big knobs, but they were both locked.

With the sunlight failing fast, George thought it advisable to get back to the trolley before dark. Whatever had killed Mary might be prowling Forest Lawn right now; and while he wasn't afraid to die—if anything, he remained eager for its solace—he had now resolved that, until he could decipher Mary's final message, death would have to wait. *I can always do away with myself another day,* he reasoned. First things first: *heads on pikes.*

He reviewed what facts he knew: Mary had been here, or nearby, and must have heard or seen something that had given her pause. He was certain that the mausoleum—or something else in the line of sight from her bench—must hold some clue. And whatever clue it held fast was contained in the cryptic message on that last page of her little notebook—he was certain of that, too.

George's next step was now clear to him.

SECTION TWENTY-SEVEN

SURVEILLANCE

"Thanks for joining me today, gentlemen," George said to his lieutenants over lunch in his suite in the Genesee. "I'm sorry I've been making myself so scarce lately."

"No apology is required, George," Ed Durham said. "I don't know what to say about poor Mary."

"No words," Kirsch said, shaking his head.

"It's heartbreaking," Captain Andrews said.

George sighed deeply. "Thanks, boys. It's like a bad dream, but with the difference that I never wake up."

They sat in silence for a long moment, and then George waved his hand. "Well, enough of that. I called you here today to tell you that, despite my recent silence, I'm not planning to step away from our business for good. But I *am* taking on another business, for a while at least. So there may be some days when I have to focus my attention on that."

"What other business?" Durham asked.

"Finding out who killed Mary. And collecting on his debt."

"That's fine," said Andrews, "so long as you let us help."

"Count me in," Durham said . "Just tell us what we can do, George."

"You fellows hear a lot of talk," George said. "The best thing you can do for me now is to keep your ears open in case anyone spills. Men who hurt women usually don't mind boasting about it."

"I'll skin the bastard alive myself, if you'll let me," Kirsch muttered. "You know I mean it."

"Oh, that I do know, Gus," George said. "But for now, there may be something else you can do."

"Name it," said Kirsch.

"Look, you know everybody in Buffalo."

"Not *everybody*," Kirsch said with a half smile. "But most everybody."

"Would you happen to know the Moffatt family?"

"The jam-factory Moffatts?"

"That's right."

"Why the sudden interest in jam? It's entirely legal," Andrews said with a chuckle.

"Well, you never do know what the legislature will outlaw next, John . . . but no, I'm not interested in jam. I want to ask them some questions about Forest Lawn, where Mary died. I understand a lot of the place used to be their family land."

"It was indeed," Kirsch said. "They still have a few prime acres— I've bought peaches from them for ten years, at least."

"Somehow you don't seem like the kind of fellow who'd like *peaches*," Durham said.

"I like peach *brandy*."

"And the penny drops," Captain Andrews said.

Kirsch ignored him. "I knew Sam Moffatt well. He died too young. Now Georgia Moffatt is the last leaf on the tree."

"Can you introduce me?" George asked.

"Easily. And when you meet her, you'll also meet Christ

Schamber. He's a big fellow, and good with his fists. He's Georgia's right-hand man."

"Can I trust him?"

"Completely. He's a solid citizen—he was in the war, like you. You'll like him. He and Georgia live at Spring Abbey, in Cold Springs. Just a little south of the cemetery."

"Perfect. If you'll ask if I can stop by the day after tomorrow, I'd appreciate it."

"Don't mention it. I'll send a messenger up to Spring Abbey this afternoon."

"How about we all come along with you?" Durham said. "There's strength in numbers."

"Ed, that's very kind, but I'd rather know you three are looking after our business—while I take care of mine."

"Fair enough," Andrews said. "But when this whole thing is over, think about coming along with me on my next voyage to Hong Kong. Get away from all this for a while."

"I might very well take you up on that, John," George said. "Well, fellows, how about we try to enjoy some of this food? I'm finding our conversation has restored a little of my appetite."

"You've been dealt a very bad hand, my friend," Kirsch said. "But if I know anything for sure—it's that whoever's to blame has got hell to pay, even if he doesn't know it yet. You'll play the last card."

"Well put, Gus," Durham said. "You took the words right out of my mouth."

"Mine as well," Captain Andrews added, stabbing a piece of steak with his knife.

SECTION TWENTY-EIGHT

Union

Two days later, George Eberly stared down a large snarling lion head mounted on the heavy timber door of Spring Abbey. He grasped the iron ring dangling from the creature's maw and let it fall with a resounding rap. A maid answered the knock and showed him into a parlor off the main foyer.

Compared to the Genesee House's up-to-date fashion, the parlor was decidedly antique. But for an old country estate, it had a kind of rustic charm about it. George remained standing, looking at the portraits of three generations of Moffatts and Grangers neatly hung from the egg-and-dart moulding around the perimeter of the room.

"Mr. Eberly?" a husky voice said from behind him.

George turned to see what he couldn't deny was the most beautiful woman he had ever laid eyes on—after his Mary, of course. She had Mary's golden hair, her bonny blue eyes . . . *Stop*, he thought.

"At your service, madam," he said, bowing slightly. "Mrs. Moffatt, I presume?"

"I am," Georgia said. "It's a pleasure to meet you, sir."

"Please accept my condolences on your husband's passing."

"You're very kind. Sam died almost two years ago now. My loss is not nearly so keen as your much more recent one. Please accept my deepest condolences."

He bowed again. "I thank you for that," he said, placing his hand over his heart.

"Please, make yourself comfortable."

George took a seat on an old Regency settee, which creaked under his weight. Georgia smiled.

"Don't worry, you're much leaner than most of my guests," she said. "And the old thing hasn't collapsed yet."

He laughed. "That's reassuring. I was beginning to wonder if I'd been overindulging. Will Mr. Schamber be able to join us as well?"

"He'll be along momentarily. He had to check on a few things at the factory. Before the harvest we have a great deal of mechanical maintenance to do."

"Naturally. I will look forward to meeting him. In the meantime, allow me to thank you for agreeing to confer with me today."

"Of course. Mr. Kirsch has been, for many years, a fast friend of my family. And he speaks very highly of you."

"I'm gratified to hear it. He certainly has the highest possible opinion of you."

"How do you know him, if I may ask?"

"Mr. Kirsch and I have some shared business interests."

"They wouldn't include peach brandy, now would they?"

"You're not one to mince words, I see, Mrs. Moffatt," he said with a little smile.

"What's the point? Mr. Kirsch is one of the few remaining fruit customers we have. Most of our sales are jam, but Gus has always liked our peaches. And I don't mind saying I've sampled his product, and—"

George was saved from dreaming up a response by the entry of a tall man with hair plastered down against his skull. He was dressed in workman's attire and had large, powerful hands, one of which he extended to George. George leaned on his stick, stood, and they shook.

"Mr. Schamber. A pleasure."

"The pleasure is mine," Christ replied.

"I understand you keep things running for Mrs. Moffatt."

"I do my best, but she always seems to stay a step or two ahead of me."

"Women do have that gift. My friend Kirsch tells me that you served in the war."

"I did. Twenty-First New York."

George inclined his head. "A fine regiment, and one which acquitted itself with great honor."

"That's kind of you to say. And you . . . you have the look of a man who's seen the elephant."

"Perhaps a little more of the animal than I bargained for," George said, patting his leg. "One-Forty-Ninth New York, from Syracuse."

Christ paled. "*My God*. You're lucky to be alive."

"A lot of good men weren't so lucky as I."

"You were at Gettysburg?"

George returned a grim smile. "All three days. My company defended Culp's Hill."

"What this gentleman here has seen cannot be described," Christ said, turning to Georgia. "The One-Forty-Ninth was at Gettysburg, on Sherman's March, at Chancellorsville . . ." He looked George in the eyes. "Allow me to say that it's my distinct honor to make your acquaintance, sir."

"And mine," Georgia said. "And I cannot fail to note, Mr. Eberly, that I think this is the first time I've seen Christ impressed."

"You're both very gracious, but of course like all of us—and I include the ladies on the home front—I did no more than my part."

"You are far too modest, sir," Georgia said. "Please know that Christ and I stand ready to assist you in any way we may."

George rapped his walking stick on the floor between his feet. "Then as I respect and value your time, I will come right to my point. From the start I have been convinced that my wife's terrible fate was no accident but rather a cold-blooded murder. And more recently I have become equally convinced that the coroner and the police want nothing more than to sweep the crime entirely under the rug."

"Typical," Christ said under his breath.

"But, Mr. Eberly," Georgia said, "why would the authorities wish to do such a thing?"

"Because, in my experience, such so-called authorities usually are engaged in some malfeasance they wish to conceal. That may be a cynical opinion, but I can assure you it is one shaped by personal experience."

"They ought to be ashamed of themselves," Georgia said.

George frowned. "Indeed, madam—but after tasting power, all too many individuals lose the ability to feel shame."

"Power dulls the conscience," Christ said.

"That it does. And worse, it tends to attract those without any conscience to begin with. Take for example the resurrections that have been going on in Forest Lawn, and tell me—what manner of unscrupulous ghoul engages in such a trade?"

"The very lowest sort," Georgia said. "In fact, I had a rather sharp talk with the superintendent on that very topic."

"Stroup?"

"Yes, Mr. Stroup. You are acquainted with him, I take it?"

"I've crossed swords with that coxcomb more than once," George said. "So yes, I know him all too well. And knowing him as I do, I predict he will do precisely nothing. In fact, I'd wager he's in on the scheme."

"You think Mr. Stroup would allow the theft of bodies from his own cemetery?"

"For the right amount of money, men will do most anything. And if I'm right, and Stroup and others in authority are complicit in the resurrections, they won't dare give up the men who are performing them at their behest—most likely, the gravediggers, Dolan and Fermin."

Christ leaned forward and clasped his hands. "On that score, Mr. Eberly, you'll be interested to know that I paid off the janitor at the medical school to tell me what he knows. He told me only days ago that those two have been bringing bodies to the school from Forest Lawn."

"Excellent reconnaissance," George said. "And furthermore, at my wife's inquest those two miscreants lied a blue streak. So in addition to their culpability for the resurrections, I'm morally certain those two are also responsible for my wife's murder. I believe that Mary witnessed *something*—perhaps some aspect of their illegal activity—and they killed her for it."

"Why, I'd like to string the scum up myself," Christ said.

George laughed. "I like you, Mr. Schamber," he said. "And believe me, I'd help you do it. But though I am a hard man, I do aspire to be a just one. So I need evidence before I take any such . . . shall we say, irreversible action."

"Based on the janitor's statements alone, we've already got them dead to rights on the body snatching," Christ said.

"Very true, sir," George said. "Yet singling out Dolan and Fermin for chastisement may allow their superiors—people like Stroup and the coroner's little cabal—to slither away. It will be much better if we can cut the head off the snake, not just the tail. And here's where our interests align."

"I like the sound of that," Christ said. "What can we do?"

"First, we need to prove that Stroup is complicit in the resurrections—and if he is, I have an idea that will put an end to them for good. The second and more difficult matter is determining who killed my wife. No one's about to confess, of course. But Mary herself left us a very intriguing clue, I believe."

"She did?" Georgia said. "Can you share it with us?"

"Of course," George said, reaching into his vest pocket and taking out Mary's notebook. He handed it over to Georgia. "I was at Forest Lawn recently, sitting on the bench . . . where my Mary died. That bench has a clear line of sight to a row of trees, the creek, and then a large mausoleum just beyond."

"I know the spot very well indeed," Georgia said. "That's the Moffatt mausoleum. My husband, and all of the other Moffatts before him, is in there."

"I thought as much," George replied, "which is what brought me here today. I think Mary witnessed something—either down the slope, near the creek, or near the mausoleum—and recognized that she was in danger. And—just in case the worst should happen—she recorded what she'd seen in her notebook."

Georgia opened the book to the final inscribed page and held it out so that she and Christ could read it:

Augustus

U W N N I B B 20

"This is your wife's hand?" Georgia said, looking up.

"It is, although it looks to me as though she might have been in some haste."

Georgia handed the notebook to Christ, who studied it closely.

"*Augustus*," he read. "As in Caesar?"

"Yes, most likely," George replied. "I don't know any other soul by that name. Of course I don't know whether Mary did. We were married for only a short time."

Christ frowned at the notebook. "The letters and numbers under 'Augustus' suggest some kind of code."

"That's my belief as well," George said. "One day I returned home to find Mary reading a cryptography manual that I'd been given during the war. She was utterly captivated by it, and spoke of it several times afterward. So I'm sure this entry is written in code. But *what* code? That book contains hundreds of them, and some are highly sophisticated."

"If she had only a short exposure to that book," Georgia said, "even as intelligent as I'm sure your wife was, it's doubtful that—especially in haste—she would have composed something complex. Do you have the book? We might look through it and try to apply a few of the simpler ones."

"Yes, it's on my shelf at the Genesee. I can have it brought to you directly."

"Wonderful. For now, may I copy out this page?"

"Of course you may. And there is one other possible clue that I can't quite make sense of. But knowing the grounds of Forest Lawn as well as you do, perhaps you may be able to."

"Please," Georgia said.

"When my wife's body was discovered—next to the bench in question—she was lying on a patch of moss . . . but the curious thing was that there was a thin layer of sand scattered on top of the moss. Like beachfront sand. I saw it myself."

Christ frowned. "That *is* strange. I can tell you without the slightest doubt that there's no sand of that kind—or any kind—anywhere in Forest Lawn. Or in Buffalo Plains, for that matter."

"That was my understanding, and Detective Simmons went so far as to agree that there's something odd about it."

"It must have been brought there from some other place," Georgia said. "But why would it be there? And seemingly freshly scattered?"

"That's the mystery."

"Maybe I'll walk over there and have a look," Georgia mused.

"The hell you will," Christ said without thinking.

"Oh, I do like you," George said with a smile. "I wish I'd been half so protective of my Mary as you are of Mrs. Moffatt."

Georgia sat back. "Surely, sir, you don't blame yourself for your wife's untimely end?"

"I'm afraid I do, madam. While it was not my hand raised against her, I'm sure that you both know *something* about the nature of my business. And from the start, I enticed Mary to assist with certain aspects of my work that, frankly, were not without physical danger. And she did so with a full heart, because she loved me—and it resulted in her death. Her life was wasted for nothing more than my own greed."

Georgia flushed red. "Oh my. While I am sorry to say it, Mr. Eberly—I must disagree with you in the most strenuous terms, sir. You could not be further from the truth. If a wife should confront danger—even unto death—what better cause is there than in service to her family? Surely when you went to war in the service of your country, you were willing to lay down your life for it?"

"Yes, of course—"

"You and Christ were both inspired by a strong devotion to the Union," she went on, "but a constitutional 'union' is, I'm sorry to say, an abstraction that means one thing to some and quite another to others, as we have so amply seen. But the marital vow is hardly abstract; it is a holy union of souls that only death can sever—and even that, only temporarily. So, Mr. Eberly, unless you should feel that all those boys who died in the late war did so in vain, you *cannot* conclude that Mary did, either. A woman will do anything for her true love, including going willingly to her death. And it was you, sir, who inspired that feeling in her heart."

George looked down at the head of his walking stick and was silent for a long moment. When he looked up, tears were standing in his eyes.

"You have brought me as close to redemption as I am likely to come, Mrs. Moffatt," he said. "Bless you, madam."

"It's obvious that you loved your wife very much, sir," Georgia said. "And that she loved you with equal force."

George looked down again and slowly shook his head. "What is strange is that I didn't know her for very long at all. We were married only two months, but from the start she was everything I'd ever dreamed of. I never really believed in such things."

"They do exist," Christ said quietly.

"The union of souls," Georgia added.

"So it is said, my friends," George replied. "And one day soon I hope hers and mine will be reunited."

The three sat quietly, listening to the soft tick of the grandfather clock.

"I do have one question, Mr. Eberly," Christ resumed. "If it's not indelicate."

"Speak freely, sir."

"The two gravediggers were not acquainted with—had never met—your wife?"

"They testified to that effect, and in that I have no reason to doubt them."

"Then . . . as you know, the grave desecration business often leads to murder. And if they didn't know Mrs. Eberly, why wouldn't they have attempted to . . ."

"Dispose of her body at the medical school?"

"Yes, sir," Christ said, swallowing hard. "I know from the janitor that no such attempt was made."

"That is a very good question," George said, "and one I can't adequately answer, although I have considered it. All I can imagine is that the murder wasn't premeditated, and thus they had no easy way to transport her body to the school."

"If they had, that certainly would have been all the proof we needed," Christ said.

"Fate's hand was against us on that," George said. "Though if the two of you can decipher Mary's notation, it may shift back in our favor. Until we do, I have to accept that they may have gotten away with murder. Which brings me to my plan for stopping the resurrections, at least."

"I paid Mr. Stroup to set a guard, but still they go on."

"Because he's *involved*," George said. "In any case, we'll soon find out for sure."

"How?"

"Leave the details to me, if you would. In such a case, the less you know, the better. Suffice it to say that if we can catch those gravediggers in the act of grave robbery, at least we will have solved one of our two problems. And perhaps both of them."

"I'm sure we could compel the janitor to testify to what he told me," Christ said.

George shook his head. "That would only put him in the rifle sights. No, he's done well enough by us already. He's scouted out the enemy and pointed us in their direction. We can take it from here."

"Understood and agreed, Mr. Eberly. How can we help?"

"I'll have my man bring you the codebook later today, and if you can work on making sense of Mary's final message, that will be more than enough. And if we're right about Stroup being involved with the resurrections, we'll be finding out very soon."

SECTION TWENTY-NINE

UNREQUITED

"That poor, poor man," Georgia said to Christ, after George had gone.

"He's taken a hard blow."

"And after only two months of marriage."

Christ mulled this over. "As terrible as that is . . . he knew his love for her was returned, if only for a very short time. It would be even worse if Mr. Eberly had loved her so deeply and . . . she hadn't known, or hadn't felt the same."

"That's a very interesting point. Do you know *The Sorrows of Young Werther*?"

"I don't think so."

"It's an old novel by Goethe."

"Oh, you mean *Die leiden des jungen Werthers*?"

"Showoff."

"I can't help that my family spoke German at home. My mother loved that novel."

"Then you know it?"

Christ wanted to say, *I've lived it*, but thought better of it. "Oh yes, I know it well. I read it as a boy."

"Then you know that unrequited love can have fatal

consequences," she said. "You don't think that Mr. Eberly would do himself harm, do you?"

"I hope not. But you never know what will drive a man over the brink."

"It frightens me, Christ."

"What does?"

"Death."

He thought a moment. "In the war, I was frightened half out of my wits most of the time."

"What frightened you the most?"

The thought of never seeing you again, he thought. Instead, he shrugged. "Wondering if the next bullet had my name on it, I suppose."

Georgia looked at him, her eyes welling. "But—what do you think happens the second after we die? Do we just wake up again, but in Heaven or Hell?"

"Who knows? We might not wake up at all."

Her eyes went wide. "Don't you find that even more frightening? Not even knowing you're dead. It would be like falling asleep at night but never waking up."

"All the more reason to make the most of life while we can."

"People say that," Georgia said. "But how is it done?"

He pondered for a moment, looking off into the distance. "I suppose I think about Mr. Eberly, and the terrible pain he feels. He's as tough as they come, but no one seeks out pain. Yet, do I think that he would trade away the two months of joy he had in his marriage, just to be rid of the pain he feels now? I do *not*. So to answer your question, to make the most of life is not to play safe with it. Charge into battle, even if you must die. Love with all your heart, even if you may lose the thing you love."

Georgia studied Christ's hard face. "You know, Mr. Schamber, you really can be quite poetic."

He blushed under his suntan. "Pain makes people into poets, Georgia."

"You know, I think that's why my father sold our land. He didn't want it to be lost to progress. He wanted it to stay the same forever, and he reckoned that the only land that can do that is a cemetery. And because he tried to play it safe, we lost it anyway."

"With no disrespect intended, I think he couldn't envision a future for it, so he thought only of the past. And a cemetery is a place for the past."

"Christ, let's promise each other we'll never become like that. I want to live in the present, or in the future. Not the past."

"I'm willing to try." *My once and forever love*, he wanted to add, but could not work up the nerve.

"Good. Then let's resolve to do one thing each day that we've dreamed of doing but have never done."

He smiled at her. "I like that idea. Do you have something in mind to set the ball rolling?"

"I'll need to think a minute. Do you?"

Christ had made up his mind at last. "I do."

"Well, go on."

He took a deep breath. "May I take your hand in mine?"

She looked at him strangely. "Well, of course you may. But what does that have to do—"

Christ reached over and gently took Georgia's hand in both of his. He closed his eyes and clasped her hand as if it were a tiny captive bird—gently, that he might not harm it, but firmly enough that it couldn't fly away. He heard her say, *"Oh my!"* softly, as if in prayer.

He held her hand for almost a minute, saying nothing. Nor did

Georgia so much as wiggle a finger, and after a few seconds she closed her eyes, too—whether to explore her own thoughts or to give him privacy in his, she wasn't sure.

Christ opened his eyes and his hands at the same time, but Georgia left her hand lying in his cupped palms. They locked eyes for only a second, but it was enough. Christ had found his old battle courage again—the steel that had saved his life over and again in that horrible war—and so he slowly raised her hand to his lips and kissed it tenderly. Then he set it down again with a shy smile.

Georgia's heart was thumping hard, one thought pulsing through her mind—*How could I have missed this? How?*

"Christ," she said, almost under her breath, "is that truly what you've been dreaming of?"

He looked down for a heartbeat, and then into her eyes again. "Georgia, I've dreamed of that for as long as I can remember."

"I don't know what to say."

"You don't need to say anything."

She wiped her eyes with the back of her hand. "May I tell you what I'd like to do, then? But have never done?"

"Of course! What do you have in mind?"

"I'd like for us to take a walk in Forest Lawn."

"Now wait a second—that's something we've done many times before. You're supposed to choose something you've never done."

"Yes, we *have* walked there many times. But never hand in hand."

DISCRETION

Stroup shrank into his chair when George Eberly's boots thudded across the board floor of the superintendent's office and stopped in front of his desk.

"I trust you're not here for any trouble, Mr. Eberly," Stroup said in a quavering voice, looking at the tall man's big fist gripping the golden head of his cane. "I repaired the fence around your plot when your wife—God rest her soul—was interred. Thus I had very much hoped that our former difficulties were at an end."

"I couldn't help but notice that you repaired it. Though I would have preferred that it be accomplished without a lawsuit and the death of my wife."

"As I told you before, it took time. Surely you understand that the demands on our maintenance men are numerous."

"Oh, that I do, believe me. Notwithstanding all that, it's done, and that's what matters. And in any case, that's not why I came to see you today."

"It's not?"

"No, it's not. May I sit?"

"Of course. I'm sorry—you startled me somewhat."

George smiled. "There's nothing at all to be alarmed about, I assure you. Quite the contrary. I'm here today to buy a burial plot."

Stroup looked puzzled. "I'm not sure I understand, Mr. Eberly. Your family plot is quite large and, er, very nearly unoccupied."

"This one is not intended for a near relative. A cousin of mine in Syracuse has—had—a daughter who got herself into some trouble. So my cousin sent her here to stay at Mrs. Dixon's Home. I'm sure you take my meaning, sir."

"Mrs. Dixon has done much good for wayward girls," Stroup said evenly.

"She has, and I've long been among her patrons—hence my cousin's selection of Mrs. Dixon's establishment. Sadly, though, just this morning the misguided young waif died unexpectedly, and of course I have need to see her interred quickly and with dignity. Tomorrow, if possible."

"Yes, naturally, sir. We are at your service." Stroup opened a desk drawer and, with a flourish, took out a blank form. He dipped his pen and poised it over the paper. "Name?"

"Rosella Leonard."

"Age?"

"Twenty-five, I believe."

"Such a tragedy," Stroup said, looking up. "Cause of death?"

"Dysentery."

"Yet another case," the superintendent murmured. "How far along was she?"

"About six months."

"Does her bastard remain in utero, or will we be needing a second coffin?"

"Yes, mother and child remain together in death. There is no greater tragedy."

"So very, *very* sad," Stroup intoned. "No matter how long one does this kind of work, one never grows accustomed to such things."

"Naturally not. But at the very least I want her to have a decent burial. I feel it would even out the score a little, if you know what I mean."

"Oh, I do indeed," Stroup said, nodding. "A peaceful repose helps make up for the catastrophes of life."

"One would like to hope so."

"Would you like a graveside service?"

"Perhaps at some later date. So soon after my wife's demise, I might find it difficult ..."

Stroup placed a hand over his heart. "Of course. The wound is still fresh."

"You are very perceptive, Mr. Stroup."

"Thank you for saying so, sir. Now only a few more questions, and I can issue a burial permit. Which undertaker will you employ? Mr. Brennan, I presume?"

George leaned forward. "Now on that matter I must take you fully into my confidence. And so what I am about to tell you must go no further."

Stroup's chair squeaked. "I will take your secret to my grave, sir," he whispered, leaning over his desk until he and George were only inches apart.

"Then here is the crux of it," George whispered back. "I *would* normally use Mr. Brennan, but ... Barney *talks*."

"He does? About what?"

"Let's just say that he has difficulty keeping a secret."

A look of alarm bobbed up from beneath Stroup's solemn expression. "That—that can be a most unfortunate quality," he stuttered.

"Indeed it can be. And as my cousin has already borne more than his fair portion of shame from his daughter's blighted life, gossip would only make the burden greater."

"Just so," Stroup replied softly, squeaking back in his chair. "A single loose tongue can do untold harm."

"I *knew* you would understand. But that leaves me at loggerheads about how to find a more *trustworthy* mortician. To come right to the point, Mr. Stroup, I have been holding out hope that you might handle the task yourself."

Stroup folded his hands in front of him. "Alas, the State of New York prohibits me, as superintendent of a cemetery, from serving as a funeral director. Potential conflict of interest."

"How unfortunate," George said. "Mightn't you be able to make an exception, though? The poor child is in one of my coffins now, in my coffin factory. Really all that you'd have to do is collect the casket and see that it is decently interred."

"Well, it could put me in a difficult spot . . ."

George took up his cane and sat forward in his chair. "It has been wrong of me to put you in a difficult position, Mr. Stroup. I would never ask a man to compromise his integrity. Perhaps I ought better to ship the body to Syracuse."

"If I may say, sir," Stroup said, placing his hand on his chest, "I believe there is a higher duty at stake here than the slavish adherence to the bureaucratic whims of a distant legislature. My duty is to *remove* impediments—not to *impose* them. So as you have relied upon my discretion, I trust that I may rely on yours?"

"Why, of course you may. Utterly."

Stroup lowered his voice. "From time to time, I *do* make special exceptions. In such cases, though, I'm sure you'll understand that there are a few additional charges, simply because, well, I must ensure the notary's discretion, and that of—"

"Say no more. The less we both know about it, the better. Suffice it to say that I'll be happy to defray any additional costs associated with this special exception you are kind enough to make."

The other man drummed his fingers on his desk. "You are a most generous uncle—cousin."

"If I may echo your sentiment, a higher duty is at stake here than mere money," George said. "Now that you have put my mind at ease about the undertaking arrangements, what other questions might you have for me?"

"The most important one of all," Stroup replied. "And that is— what kind of plot you'd like to purchase."

"I've been thinking about that very thing. My cousin's daughter always liked the water. I wonder if you'd have something near one of your ponds? And discreetly away from other burials—at least for now."

Stroup brightened. "You're in luck, Mr. Eberly," he said, standing. He strode over to a large map of the cemetery tacked to his office wall. "This area has only just been opened—Section 1. And it's not called *Section 1* for no good reason, either. Section 1 offers a lovely view over one of our delightful new lakes—you might call them *ponds*, but few cemeteries can boast such expansive bodies of water, so they're lakes to us. Ha ha. And no other burials nearby, at present."

"Section 1 will do nicely, then. How much will, say, a double plot cost? Since the poor girl was with child, I'd feel rather poorly if I bought only a single plot."

"Your cousin's daughter is indeed fortunate to have such a bene-factor as yourself, sir," Stroup said. "A double plot in Section 1 will run—about five hundred dollars."

"And the collection and interment?"

"Normally those would be another twenty-five. But in an excep-tional case like this one, as I said, there are—"

"Would a thousand dollars take care of everything? The plot, the collection, your confidence—everything?"

Stroup's eyes bulged. "*A thousand dollars?*"

"Yes, a thousand. Would that do it?"

"I should think so, Mr. Eberly. Thank you very much indeed."

"The pleasure is mine, sir," George said, pulling out a thick wad of banknotes. He counted them off onto Stroup's desk as the mesmerized superintendent watched the notes shower down. "I hope you will think of this transaction as a way of putting the past behind us."

"Mr. Eberly, I confess I misjudged you somewhat, sir. For that I am deeply sorry."

"No need for any apology. You have every right to be wrong from time to time. Ha ha."

"You have a rapier wit, sir!" Stroup said, jumping up and sticking out his hand. George stood and shook it.

"Have we covered everything, then?"

"Yes, I believe so. I'll collect the deceased tomorrow morning, if that would be convenient, for interment directly after. From your coffin manufactory, you said?"

"That would be fine. I'll be there when you arrive. One final thing—after you pick up the poor thing, would you mind taking your time driving her back here? I would like to think that before being consigned to the bosom of Mother Earth, she might enjoy a stately funeral procession."

"Of course. We will treat your cousin's daughter with delicacy and, if I may say, tenderness."

"Thank you, Mr. Stroup. This is quite a weight off my mind. I can tell you I'm going to sleep much better very soon."

"I'm delighted to be of service to you, sir. It's been a pleasure. And I should say that I'm happy that bygones are bygones."

"Water under the bridge," George said. "Better days are ahead."

SECTION THIRTY-ONE

Jack-in-the-Box

The next morning, Mr. Stroup collected the coffin containing the unfortunate Eberly relative. George himself helped load the wagon.

"Now do handle her gingerly, sir, if you please," George urged. "She was such a delicate thing in life, and I wish her to be treated as such in death."

Stroup bowed. "You have a tender heart, sir. You may rest assured that she will be treated with great care. And she will enjoy a nice slow ride to her new forever home."

George stuck out his hand. "You'll be by the grave, I hope, when she's lowered down," he said, almost to himself.

"You may count on it, sir." Stroup shook George's hand and replaced his hat on his head.

Mr. Stroup did take his time driving George's dead niece, or cousin, back to Forest Lawn, but mostly because he was considering whether to inter the girl at all or take her directly to the medical school and collect the full fee for himself. He quickly dismissed the notion—in broad daylight it would be madness, and it would be far better to give up a third of the take to Dolan and Fermin and keep his name and face entirely out of it.

Still, he couldn't keep himself from chuckling over his good fortune. *This is the one we've been waiting for*, he thought. *A young girl, healthy enough, and with child still in utero? A* twofer. *Such a corpse would be any medical school's dream. And Georgia Moffatt will never be the wiser, because Eberly needs to keep this shameful chapter to himself.*

"Open a grave for this one in Section 1," Stroup called down to Fermin, who was standing by the gatehouse when Stroup rolled up. "Not too deep though—it'll be coming up tonight."

"I thought we were giving all that a rest."

"We are, but this one's impossible to pass up," Stroup said, motioning over his shoulder. "It's a young mother, still with child—worth sixty dollars, at least. And don't take a penny less. I'll drive her over to Section 1 and leave her there for you. Now chop-chop."

"This doesn't seem right," Dolan said to his friend, as Mr. Stroup clattered off. "A mother still with her baby inside her belly?"

"Dead is dead is dead," Fermin intoned. "Bobby, sometimes I swear I think you've gone completely around the bend. Stroup said sixty, so you know she's worth seventy-five. That's an extra fifteen dollars to us, boy, for the easiest work there is."

"I just don't think it's right," Dolan groused. "It's not. A mother and her wee one? Come on now, Artie. We could go to Hell for doing something like this."

"Are you back on that load of stuff and nonsense again? *Hell*?

If you don't have a few extra dollars, *life* is hell—that I can tell you. How'd you like to be back in the poorhouse?"

"I wouldn't like it a bit."

"No, you wouldn't. And that means we have to do whatever it is we can to make a buck. Don't go any softer in the head than you are already, will you?"

"I don't like it when you say things like that. Calling me a half-wit, or barmy, or around the bend. It's not nice, and I'm plenty smart enough for whatever it is I have to do to get by."

"You're right, chum," Fermin agreed, clapping his friend on the back. "I'm just pulling your leg a bit. Taking the piss out of you."

"Well, it's not very kind, if you ask me. And when people say they're joking, they're usually not."

"Just like when blokes say, 'Honestly,' is that it? You know they're being anything but honest."

"Like that, yeah."

"Look, then, forget I said anything. Let's get this one done, and we can always take a break after."

Dolan shook his head. "Fine, but I still don't think it's right, Artie."

"They're *dead*, Bobby," Fermin said. "They're not even there any-more. It's just their bodies. Their souls are in Heaven, God be praised."

"Let's just hope they're not looking down on us."

AROUND ELEVEN THAT NIGHT, the boys crept out of the dormitory to hoof it across the quiet cemetery to Section 1.

"Not so fast, gentlemen," said Stroup's voice from somewhere in the darkness. Fermin lifted his candle lantern to see the superintendent step out from under the eaves of the dormitory.

"Mr. Stroup? What are you doing out at this time of night?"

"I thought I might supervise the exhumation."

"How come?"

"I promised Eberly that his niece—or whatever she is—would be treated with care. And I keep my promises."

"I'll bet you didn't promise him you'd leave her in the dirt." Fermin snickered.

"Your attempt at humor is noted, and not appreciated."

"Sorry."

"Now let's go, and we'll see you do this right." Stroup strode off in the direction of Section 1.

Fermin looked at Dolan and shrugged. "Maybe we can get him to pick up a shovel," Fermin whispered, and Dolan laughed.

Section 1 wasn't too far from the dormitory, but having doused their lantern—it was a new-moon night and the smallest flicker might be detected—there were an unusual number of stumbles and falls and curses before the fresh mound of dirt loomed up before them. Stroup's silhouette was already standing next to it.

"Man must have eyes like a cat," Dolan said to his friend.

They had left the wagon by the gravesite earlier that day, and the horse was snoring softly in the muggy night air. Dolan relit the candle lantern. Fermin then pulled out their shovels and tossed one to Dolan, and the two began their practiced choreography of digging and piling earth so that the hole could easily be refilled. They had developed a routine now, and not a word between them was required. Both dug for a while; as the hole grew deeper they took turns, one digging while the other rested. Stroup stood nearby, keeping just beyond the arc of flying dirt.

After about three-quarters of an hour of sweaty digging, Fermin's shovel thudded on the coffin lid of mother and child. He scraped away the dirt and removed the thumbscrews, as usual. Dolan was standing next to Stroup, a few steps away from the pit, not wanting to see the sad contents of the shiny coffin—incidentally, a much better grade than usual.

Fermin was about to pry open the lid when he had a droll idea. "Bobby," he said, poking his head up above the edge of the hole, "why don't you do the honors?"

"Thank you but no thank you," Dolan replied. "I've already told you how I feel. I would have left this one alone. So you can open it. And what's more, I'm going to close my eyes when we hoist the poor girl out."

"Ah, you're such a big baby."

"I am *not* a baby," Dolan retorted. "Take it back."

"Will you two quit arguing and make up your minds?" Stroup said. "One of you, open the damn thing and let's be done with it."

"I am *not* a baby," Dolan repeated, putting his hands on his hips. "And what did we just agree about your calling me names?"

"Well, I didn't agree to lie. I wouldn't call you a big baby if you weren't one. Shite, you can't even bear to look at a dead girl? Sorry, but that makes you a baby. A *big* baby."

Dolan jumped down onto the coffin lid with a thud. "Get out," he said, jerking his thumb. "I'll show you who's a baby."

"Too late. You said you didn't want to do it, so don't. I'll do it. You go on and stand next to Mr. Stroup."

"I will *not*, Artie. You've made it a matter of pride now, and I'm not going to be denied."

"Have it your way, then," Fermin said, scrambling out of the hole. "I'm going to have a smoke."

"You do that," his friend said, looking up. "Throw down the pry bar, though, will you?"

Fermin kicked the tool into the hole, walked over near Stroup—who was fuming impatiently with all the back-and-forth—and began rolling a smoke. Down below, they could hear Dolan prying and cursing.

"What's the problem now, boyo?" Fermin said, the cigarette wagging between his lips.

"Damn lid's tight as all get-out."

"Put your back into it, then!"

"I know very well what to do," Dolan said from the pit. "Wait, I think I've got it."

Fermin sat on the dead girl's headstone—a nice granite one—and was fishing around in his pocket for his match safe when at last he heard the lid squeal as the seal gave way. Then he heard a more peculiar sound—a kind of high-pitched *whizz*, followed by a sharp metallic *click*, like the action of a switch.

"What in the dev—" he heard Dolan mutter, but in the very next heartbeat his confused voice was erased by a tremendous, earsplitting roar. Fermin was blown clean off his perch on the gravestone by the blast's concussion, and his unlit cigarette was torn from his lips. Stroup collapsed in a heap, clutching his ears and wailing like a banshee, and the horse took off running down the long hill to God knows where, dragging the clattering wagon behind. A deep, rolling boom echoed after the terrified animal.

Stunned, Fermin and Stroup were still trying to determine just what the hell had happened when a shower of earth, bits of coffin wood, and lumps of Bobby Dolan came raining down on them. "Jesus H. *Christ*!" Fermin yelled. "What in the name of God?"

When the cascade of dirt and bits of Bobby tapered off, from the grave could be seen rising an angry pillar of churning blue smoke and cinders, as from a locomotive's stack. The two survivors, caked with dirt and blood, ears ringing, crawled over to the edge of the pit—now more like a crater—and peered in. As the billowing sulfurous smoke eddied and cleared, they could make out down below the burning bottom of a coffin and a few of the larger hunks of Bobby's earthly remains.

"For the love of all that's holy," Fermin breathed. "The goddamn thing was booby-trapped."

"WHAT?" said Stroup, deafened by the explosion.

Fermin thought to call out for Bobby, as if he'd been blown temporarily into some parallel universe and would at any moment come walking up, wearing his usual dopey expression. But it was clear that most of Dolan had been scattered to the four winds.

Stroup looked over at Fermin and saw him wordlessly mouthing something like "we've got to get out of here." The thought finally occurred to the dazed superintendent that there would be no mistaking a blast like that one. He clambered unsteadily to his feet, Fermin grabbed his sleeve, and the two hustled back toward the dormitory.

THE MORNING PAPER READ:

EXPLOSION AT FOREST LAWN CATCHES RESURRECTIONIST IN THE ACT

Blown to Smithereens!

GRAVE ROBBERIES AT LAST ENDED?

Late last evening, the stillness of Forest Lawn was rent in twain by a thunderous blast, possibly set off by a grave robber thinking to employ high explosives to speed along his work of illicit excavation. For reasons unknown, the charge went off prematurely, blowing the resurrectionist to bits. This morning, Robert Dolan, a gravedigger employed by the cemetery, did not report for duty as usual, and accordingly it is thought that he was both culprit and victim in this singular event. Forest Lawn has in recent months been plagued by a series of grave robberies, which have frustrated both Superintendent Stroup and the cemetery's board of trustees. It is hoped that the guilty ghoul of Forest Lawn has now been banished for good.

"Ha ha ha," Christ exulted. "He did it!"

"Barbaric," Georgia replied, sipping her coffee.

"You didn't like them any more than I did."

"No, but 'blown to smithereens'? Really? I never thought he meant *that*."

"At least it was quick," he chuckled. "Oh, that George Eberly is a genius."

"I'm sure he is. You two."

"I know exactly how he did it, too," Christ said gleefully.

"Should I ask? I *know* you want me to ask."

"You don't have to ask."

"How'd he do it?"

He smiled. "Three-second time-delay artillery fuze, activated by the opening of the coffin lid," he said. "The fuze then detonated an entire keg of black powder, I would estimate. Based on the size of the blast."

Georgia shook her head. "I'm almost sorry I asked."

"It appears that he got only one of them, though. The stupid one."

"No matter," Georgia said, nibbling at her toast. "If those two did kill Mrs. Eberly, Mr. Fermin's as good as dead anyway. And I think I'd rather be blown to bits than face whatever else Mr. Eberly might have in store."

"That's a very fine point," he said.

"You're one of a kind, Christ," Georgia said, returning to her toast and jam. "I don't know what I'd do without you."

"Well, you're not ever going to find out," he said, looking over at her across the tiny breakfast table, so small that their knees were almost touching. His gaze lingered for a moment on her graceful, muscular neck.

Georgia looked down and straightened the lapels of her robe. "Hey!" she said. "Are you looking down my dressing gown?"

"Heavens no!" he babbled, blushing. "I wouldn't dream of it!"

"Of course you wouldn't." She scrutinized his face. "You know, Christian Schamber, I do believe you're lying."

"I am *not*! I would never lie to you."

"Then will you answer honestly, if I ask you a question? One I've been thinking about since our walk in Forest Lawn."

Christ hid behind his coffee cup. "Naturally I will," he said into the china.

She took a demure bite of toast. "Have you ever been in love?"

He set his cup gently in its saucer and looked down into his lap. "Why do you ask?"

"What does that matter? You said you'd answer my question honestly. So answer."

"Then yes, I have been. In love."

"With anyone I know?"

"That's a second question," he protested. "You're allowed only one."

"I'll let *you* ask me a question, then, if you answer my second one."

"All right, then. Yes. I've been in love with someone you know."

"I see . . ." Georgia said, drawing out the syllables. "Now go ahead, ask your question."

"Have *you* ever been in love?"

"Of course," she said.

"I meant other than with Mr. Sam."

She smiled sadly and shook her head. "No, I wasn't in love with Sam. Sam was a good man, but we were never in love."

Christ's heart was beating out of his chest. He and Georgia looked at each other for a long moment.

"Ever since I was a boy—" he began.

"Shhh," she said, and leaned over the little table to kiss him gently on the lips.

SECTION THIRTY-TWO

Loud and Clear

Stroup's ears were still ringing, and his hearing still muddy, when Forest Lawn's eight-man board of trustees convened two days after the explosion. Yet it was important that he betray no sign of hearing loss, since he had had no business being within a country mile of an exploding grave, and ought by right to have been sound asleep in his bed when the blast occurred.

"Gentlemen!" he roared when the trustees had taken their seats. "First let me say that the recent explosion was most unfortunate!"

"Why are you shouting, Stroup?" asked Mr. Langford, a very wealthy maker of harnesses.

"Why am I what?"

"Shouting, for God's sake! You're *shouting* at us, man!"

"I beg your pardon," Stroup said, cocking his head like a robin after an earthworm. "A touch of hay fever, perhaps! And I'm distressed by the injustice done to one of our revered dead."

"*Injustice* is putting it mildly," said Reverend Doctor Seth McDermott, the head man of the large Presbyterian church downtown. "One might better say 'desecration.'"

"Oh yes," Stroup agreed, "it *was* quite a detonation."

"*Desecration*, I said," Reverend McDermott repeated.

Stroup let it go. The pastor sounded as though he were speaking to him from forty fathoms under.

Thomas Kilmartin, a prominent lawyer, piped up. "Perhaps you can tell us what steps you think advisable—to prevent another such atrocity?"

Thankfully, Kilmartin was blessed with a piercing nasal voice, and Stroup heard him perfectly.

"I very much doubt lightning will strike twice in the same place," Stroup said. "To coin a phrase."

Reverend McDermott scowled. "That's not much of a *plan*," the man of the cloth said. "Seems more like blind faith."

Several of the trustees looked over at the Reverend queerly.

"We are more than two hundred and fifty acres of forest and greensward," said Stroup, moving on. "It would be impossible to patrol every portion of it. Yet thanks to a recent donation by a well-wishing local family, I will soon hire two guards to keep an eye on new graves."

"Well, that's certainly a step in the right direction," said Robert McAndrews, a very successful grain dealer, "but I hope it's not too little, too late. I've already heard from one very distressed visitor, who reported that he found an index finger lying atop his mother's grave."

"A finger, you say?" Stroup asked.

"Yes, a finger. An index finger. Presumably that of the resurrectionist."

"Surely, sir, you will recognize that in a blast of that magnitude, a few miscellaneous oddments may have escaped detection. I did have my man comb the area as thoroughly as he could." Stroup tried to clear his ears by making a sharp clicking with his jaw, which made him look like a cormorant swallowing an especially large fish.

"I think it's fair to say, Mr. Stroup, that the sense of this board is that we cannot tolerate any additional . . . shall we say, *events* of this type," said the chairman, John Rumsford. "It's injurious to the cemetery, but worse, it's injurious to the personal reputations of those of us who serve on this board."

"Hear, hear," Kilmartin said.

Because he couldn't hear Rumsford at all, Stroup cracked a broad smile of assent, but then erased it just as quickly when frowns appeared. He took a stab at a likely response. "I fully agree with you, Mr. Chairman. Allow me to assure all of you that these recent anomalies have been nothing more than a few unfortunate contretemps."

"I hope that is so, Mr. Stroup," Rumsford said. "You do recognize that this board does not receive any monetary compensation for its services, so anything deleterious to our persons would be viewed as most unwelcome."

"*Blah, blah, blah*" was all Stroup heard, and for the first time since the blast, he felt a sense of profound gratitude that his hearing was shot.

"It seems almost unnecessary to add, gentlemen," Stroup said, "that the likely perpetrator of the recent outrages seems to have been hoist with his own petard. I rather doubt we will be troubled again."

Rumsford rapped on the table and focused his keen blue eyes on the superintendent. "Let us hope that you are right about that, Mr. Stroup. A bolt from the blue, as it were. Yet even so, as chairman I cannot fail to underscore that we as a board can tolerate no further embarrassments at Forest Lawn. Am I getting through to you on this, sir?"

Very little of what the august chairman had uttered had penetrated the cotton wool feeling in the superintendent's ears, but there could be no doubting the man's intensity.

"Loud and clear," Stroup replied.

SECTION THIRTY-THREE

The Fall Guy

After Bobby Dolan had been vaporized, Stroup and Fermin had staggered back to headquarters without being spotted. Everyone within five miles of Forest Lawn had heard the roar and beheld the roiling column of smoke and fire barreling skyward above the dark treetops, as though Vesuvius itself had erupted in the heart of Buffalo Plains. Two dozen of the most stalwart residents had gone running toward the blast, which left Stroup and Fermin the entire western half of the cemetery to make good their escape.

The newspaper had gotten everything right, for a change—not only the account of the detonation but also the very likely prospect that the booby-trapped coffin had, in one fell swoop, put an end to the resurrection trade in Forest Lawn. No one would bother to rig one of the cheap boxes of the potter's field crowd, and—equally important—no one, especially Arthur Fermin, was going to risk life and limb to disinter and open up a high-class coffin ever again. As such, the moneyed dead were now officially priced out of the market. Twenty-five bucks would still buy a serviceable pauper, but the tariff would have to be a hundred or more to induce even the most daring or desperate resurrectionist to turn a spade in Forest Lawn.

For a few days, Fermin lamented the loss of his lifelong friend Bobby Dolan. Loyalty, however, is only for the living, and as soon as word of Dolan's death got around, thoughtful minds began churning about how to make hay out of it. When questioned about his former bosom friend, Fermin naturally answered that there was always something that "seemed a little off" about Dolan, but that he'd never quite been able to put his finger on what it was. Now he knew.

Coroner Richards, Dr. von Guyaling, and Chief Sloan—as the figureheads for the Anatomical Board, which was up to its ears in the grave robberies, and Buffalo officialdom as a whole—also found opportunity in Dolan's disaster. It had been painfully clear to most everyone during the inquest that Fermin and Dolan had lied, and preposterously, about their whereabouts at the time of Mary Eberly's death, and were very likely the guilty parties. But Richards and von Guyaling had known—as Sloan had made clear to Simmons—that indicting either or both of the Irishmen for murder would result in the very embarrassing revelation that the two gravediggers had also been supplying the medical school with material for dissection, and right under the noses of the cops and the mayor.

Thus Dolan's sudden and dramatic demise was like manna dropped from Heaven. Richards could now appease the vindictive George Eberly by declaring his wife's death a possible murder, pin it on Dolan—Fermin would play ball and highlight the discrepancies between his testimony and his former friend's—and everyone's problems would go away. Sloan, Richards, and von Guyaling didn't discuss it; they didn't need to enter into any type of conspiracy, since the benefits to each of them were so obvious that they all acted in perfect, wordless alignment. And so, three days after the rigged coffin had blown Bobby Dolan sky-high, in Richards's final verdict the unfortunate Irishman was named posthumously as the probable murderer of Mary Carkriff Eberly. And that closed the file to everyone's satisfaction.

Except, of course, to that of the wrathful George Eberly, who wasn't anywhere near done getting even.

SECTION THIRTY-FOUR

A DIFFERENT LANGUAGE

Now that their long-simmering romance had reached a rolling boil, everything changed for Christ and Georgia. There was no prospect of keeping secrets within Spring Abbey, so at Georgia's invitation, Christ moved out of the caretaker's house behind Spring Abbey and took up residence in the bedchamber next to hers. The two rooms shared a communicating door, which they kept open except when necessary to maintain a degree of propriety—when breakfast was served, for example. And they also agreed to maintain a discreet distance from each other when George Eberly came to visit. It wouldn't do to perform a courtship dance in front of such a recent widower, and especially one who had taken his young wife's death so hard.

He arranged to see them four days after the big blast. Eberly arrived at the appointed hour and took his usual seat in Georgia's parlor, while Christ and Georgia sat on their usual settee, trying to keep from touching, even by accident.

Christ was bubbling over with excitement. "Commendable work, sir!" he said, almost giddy. "I told Georgia that—given the size of the explosion—a time-delay fuze must have ignited a whole keg of gunpowder."

George chuckled. "You know your munitions well, my friend,"

he said. "But since I had to give the coffin enough weight to make it believable, it was in fact two half barrels."

"My *God*," Christ said, awestruck.

"But you are right—I employed a standard time-delay artillery fuze. At least I learned something useful in the army."

"Talk about red-handed," Christ said.

Georgia shifted in her seat. "While I can't say I approve of exploding a man—*please* stop smiling, Christ—if both had been dispatched, justice would have been done for the crime of grave robbery, at least."

"An only partially satisfying outcome on that front, it is true," Eberly said. "Though I think we've proven beyond a reasonable doubt that Mr. Stroup was at the head of the enterprise."

"How is that, Mr. Eberly?" Georgia asked.

"A . . . contact of mine inside the Forest Lawn board has informed me that the esteemed superintendent seems rather suddenly to have been stricken nearly stone-deaf. In my experience, that suggests that he was, er, *proximate* to the charge when it went off."

"This only gets better," Christ muttered, struggling to keep a straight face. He looked sidelong at Georgia, who was scowling at him, and with considerable effort pulled himself together. "If I may say, it was a most impressive blast, sir. Rattled our windows here at Spring Abbey." Christ then put his head down, his shoulders shaking with mirth.

"I'm sorry, Georgia," he gasped between cackles. "Truly I am."

George's face quivered for a moment but quickly regained its composure. "That is very kind of you to say, Mr. Schamber. I myself heard the report all the way down at the Genesee. Reminded me of the Union cannonade just before Pickett's Charge."

"*My*," Georgia said, now trying not to break into a smile herself. She coughed lightly into her hand.

"In short," George resumed, clearing his throat, "my guess is that Mr. Stroup and his hooligans—er, sorry, *hooligan*—will be out of the resurrection business, effective immediately."

"And for that I am grateful, sir," Georgia said.

"Believe me, Mrs. Moffatt, the pleasure was mine."

"But of course the far graver crime remains to be solved," Georgia replied.

George nodded. "Indeed. Everyone will be keen to blame my wife's death on Dolan, but that's a matter of convenience, not evidence. As I've made clear, though, I require evidence to take action, now that Providence has seen fit to keep Fermin off the firing line."

"Mr. Eberly," Georgia said, before Christ could burst into laughter again, "I've read that the crime scene always tells us the answer, if sometimes it does so in a different language than our own. So I have been eager to ask you if there may be anything else unusual you remember from the inquest—about the crime scene, specifically."

"That's intriguing," George said. "I think I told you everything that I couldn't fathom from the testimony. There was the thin layer of sand, which remains a mystery. And of course you have Mary's coded message, and I'm hoping you will find the key to that. I don't think . . ." He snapped his fingers. "Wait! There *is* one other thing that didn't quite square in my mind."

"What would that be?" Christ asked.

"It was a comment Fermin—or was it Dolan?—made, to the effect that Mary was holding her parasol in her *right* hand, over her *right* shoulder. The coroner even tried to trip him up on his recollection, suggesting that it was in her left, but he held firm in stating that he saw it in her *right*."

"Why do you find that odd?" Christ said.

"The line of sight and the distance. To see how she held her parasol—from the path near the creek, all the way up the hill and through some trees to her bench? I was a pretty fair marksman in the army, and my eyesight is still as good as any man's. Yet I could never swear with such vehemence to a detail so small, and at such a distance—without the assistance of field glasses."

"He insisted on it, though?"

"That he did. They both did. Fermin and the vaporized genius."

"*Don't*," Georgia warned Christ.

Christ cleared his throat. "I won't."

"The sand I still cannot account for," Georgia said, "but there is something very striking to me about the parasol."

"That he claimed to see it from so great a distance?"

"No, not that. That is queer, to be sure, and seems unlikely, but it's not what I find intriguing. Remember what I said about the crime scene speaking a different language?"

"I do."

"Your wife was brought up with good home training, I have no doubt."

"She was. Although her family was not one of means, she had a fine education in Latin and Greek, music and drawing, and was exceptionally well-mannered."

"And that tells me all I need to know. You see, you gentlemen don't carry parasols as we ladies do. And even though I tried very hard to ignore all the girly things that my mother taught me, I could never forget the language of the parasol."

"The language of the parasol?" Christ said with a chuckle.

Georgia frowned at him. "It's a language of gestures, smart aleck," she said. "If you crook a finger at someone, it means 'come here.' If you salute, you are showing respect to a superior. Is that not the case?"

"Yes, it is," Christ said, chagrined.

"Well then. The parasol has its own similar vocabulary. Wait here a moment."

She got up and trotted out of the parlor and, in a minute or two, returned with a parasol.

"Now then," she began, "every young lady who is taught good manners is taught the meaning of a dozen gestures she can make—wordlessly—with her parasol. And gentlemen brought up in better homes know them, too."

"That would eliminate me," Eberly said.

"And me," Christ agreed.

"And the two Irishmen," Georgia said. "I mean no offense, Mr. Eberly, but though you would not understand the language of the parasol, your Mary would, and she would employ it without giving it a second thought. Allow me to demonstrate."

She stood, dangled her closed parasol in her left hand, and twirled it.

"That gesture means 'I am engaged,' and it will prevent an unwanted approach from a well-bred man. Now this"—she changed hands and twirled it in her right—"means 'I am married,' and no one would dare accost a married woman."

"You ladies never fail to amaze me," George said.

"Oh, believe me, sir, we ladies don't understand gentlemen any better. But we do understand another lady's parasol."

George tapped his cane on the floor. "Then does holding the parasol over her right shoulder—as Fermin insisted he saw—have a meaning?"

"Ah, you see, Mr. Eberly, I've already come to understand that when you tap your stick on the ground, you are becoming impatient."

"I'm terribly sorry," he said, blushing.

"I'm having a little fun, that's all," Georgia said. "But the way we hold or use things in our hands does reveal something about our unconscious state of mind. Even if those watching do not fully understand, they may notice. To answer your question directly, holding a parasol over the right shoulder most decidedly has a very specific meaning—and that is 'you may approach and speak with me.'"

"That would suggest that my wife could make out the two Irishmen as clearly as they could her," George said. "I simply don't understand."

"Even if she had, Mr. Eberly, the right shoulder gesture is unquestionably *not* one a married woman would make—*ever*—to a man or men not of her acquaintance. And we've established that your wife did not know either of the Irishmen."

"Agreed," he said.

"And thus she would *never* encourage such persons to approach or address her. So to my mind, there are only two possible explanations for her gesture, now that we understand the language that your wife was speaking at the crime scene. Either she was acquainted with the man or men who murdered her, or Mr. Fermin's testimony—and Mr. Dolan's corroboration of it—was so much fabrication. There is no third explanation. Your wife, brought up well in a good home, would never make such a gesture otherwise."

"Mrs. Moffatt, you are astonishing. I do wish my Mary could have met you. I think you and she would have become great friends."

"I have no doubt of it, Mr. Eberly. And I share that wish. The affection and respect in which you hold her commends Mrs. Eberly as the kind of friend any lady would desire."

George blinked and studied the gold pommel of his cane. He took a deep breath and looked up again.

"Let me say again how much I value your kindness," he said. "It has touched a deep chord."

"Of course, Mr. Eberly. I have many faults, naturally, but I could never fail to recognize when a man truly loves a woman."

Christ bit his tongue.

SECTION THIRTY-FIVE

Mary's Message

The following evening, Georgia and Christ were relaxing in Georgia's bedchamber. Christ was sitting in an armchair, reading a book and gazing idly into the cold hearth, and Georgia was bent over her writing desk, staring at a sheet of paper under the light of a student lamp. Eberly's cryptography manual was sitting beside it.

"*Damn*!" she blurted, jolting Christ out of his reverie.

"What's wrong?"

"These *characters*," she said, holding up the crumpled piece of paper on which she had been writing. "I have been wracking my brain for an hour, rearranging the letters." She thrust the paper toward him. On it she had written:

U W N N I B B 20

NUBBIN W 20

WINNBUB 20

BBINNWU 20

WUNN

and then had presumably given up in disgust.

Christ stood up, stretched, and took the crumpled paper from Georgia. "I have a feeling it has to be more complicated than scrambling letters," he said. "If Mary Eberly was studying that codebook, I feel that the answer must be in there. May I have a look?"

"Be my guest," she said, handing him the cryptography manual. "If you can make something out of it, I'll be overjoyed. I can't."

He flopped down on the floor next to Georgia's desk, opened the codebook, and flipped through the first few pages. "The simplest codes and ciphers, it says here, are substitution ciphers. Where one letter or number is substituted for another according to some formula or key."

"Yes, I know that now—but the problem is that we don't know the key."

"But I think we may," Christ said. "Since 'Augustus' is the only thing written in plain English, it seems to me that it has to be the key to the coded message below it."

"We've been over this so many times, Christ."

"I know. I'm only going over what we know—or think we know—and what we don't. So let's say we know that 'Augustus' is the key. We also know that if George Eberly doesn't know anyone by that name, probably neither did his wife."

"All right," Georgia said. "Forgive me for being so testy. Go on."

"Now we also know that the most famous Augustus of all time is—"

"Augustus Caesar."

"Right," Christ agreed. "He's even in the New Testament."

"I'm with you. But what would Augustus Caesar have to do with Mary Eberly?"

"Here's what strikes me as interesting," Christ said, going back a few pages. "It might be nothing but coincidence, but one of the simple ciphers in the first part of the book is called a 'Caesar's Cipher.' It is said to have been used by Julius Caesar. And since Augustus was a

Caesar, I tend to think that Mrs. Eberly was indicating that she had used a Caesar's Cipher."

"Very intriguing. How does a Caesar's Cipher work?"

"It's a substitution cipher, and it's quite straightforward. The letters of a message are, one by one, replaced by shifting them a certain number of places *backwards* in the alphabet. So let's say someone picks the key of five—you would shift each letter back by five places. So *A* would be written as *V*, which is five places back from *A*. *A* would be a substitution for *F*. And that's all there is to it."

"But we'd have to know the number of places," Georgia said.

"And if that's so, the name Augustus may indicate that number."

"What number would be associated with him?"

"Correct me if I'm wrong, but Augustus Caesar was the second Caesar, right after Julius."

"Yes, he was second."

Christ reached up and took Georgia's pencil from her hand. "Then that would mean that the shift would be two places. Let's see." He wrote Mary's cryptogram out on the reverse side of Georgia's crumpled notepaper.

$$UWNNIBB\ 20$$

"So if we shift each letter, and the number, back two places . . . we get—"

$$SULLGZZ\ 18$$

"—which, of course, doesn't make any more sense." He let himself fall backward onto the rug. "Damn! And I thought we might have solved it."

Mary picked up the paper and tossed it into the wastepaper basket. "I don't know about you, Christian Schamber," she said, looking at his big frame sprawled out on her bedroom floor, "but I can't do any more of this tonight."

"Neither can I," he said, his eyes closed. "And why so formal all of a sudden? Ought I to start calling you Georgia Moffatt?"

She laughed and stood up from her desk. "No, just sometimes you seem like Christian Schamber to me, the same boy I used to play hooky with when we were schoolchildren."

"Those were good times."

"They were."

"Do you think about those days much?"

"Sometimes," Georgia said. "But just now, all I can think about is crawling into bed. You?"

Christ's eyes flew open. "Me *what*?"

She looked down at him, puzzled. "I was asking if you were ready for bed."

He sat up. "You'd want me to stay? For the *night*?"

"I must be the one speaking in code," she said.

"It's just—I just normally go back to my room when we retire."

She crossed her arms in front of her. "You are, of course, free to go—if that's what you'd prefer."

"It's not that I'd *prefer* it."

"What *would* you prefer, then?" she said, less sternly. She slid into her bed and patted the coverlet next to her.

Christ looked at her and bit his lip.

"Well?"

"I'd prefer to stay."

"*Finally*," she said, holding out her hand.

SOMETIME IN THE DEEPEST part of the night, Georgia sat bolt upright in bed. Christ was snoring gently next to her. She shook his shoulder.

"What is it?" he mumbled.

"I've figured it out!" she said, jumping out of bed and going to her writing desk.

"Figured what out?"

"Mary Eberly's cipher."

Christ's eyes flew open. "You have?"

Georgia took another sheet of writing paper from the desk drawer. "I think so. Give me just a second." She dipped her pen in the inkwell and scratched on the paper for a minute. Then she sat back in her chair, disbelieving.

"It's so obvious," she said under her breath. "I can't believe we didn't see it."

"What does it say?"

"Out of respect to Mr. Eberly—since this is his wife's final message to him—I'd rather wait until we can tell him. He ought to be the first to know. Well, the second."

"I understand. We'd better get down to the Genesee House, then."

She looked at the desk clock. "It's three in the morning."

"I should think Mr. Eberly would want to know, three o'clock or not."

"You're right," she said, leaning over and kissing him.

"I'll get the carriage hitched," Christ said, jumping out of bed and grabbing his trousers from the stand.

She watched him pull his trousers over his lean, hard legs. "What's wrong?" he said.

"Nothing," she replied. "For once, nothing at all."

THE SLEEPY NIGHT MAN at the Genesee seemed more than a little annoyed when Christ and Georgia banged on the locked front doors of the hotel. He came around the desk and shuffled over to the entrance.

"Closed up for the night," he mouthed through the glass pane.

"We know," Georgia countered, "but it's essential that we see Mr. Eberly. It's urgent."

The man shook his head. "I haven't any idea who you are, and Mr. Eberly has given strict instructions not to be disturbed."

"He'll want this disturbance," Christ said. "Tell him it's Georgia Moffatt and Christian Schamber."

"I will *not*. Now go away before I summon the police."

"Summon anyone you like," said Georgia. "But if you don't tell Mr. Eberly we're here, and in the morning I have to tell him that you wouldn't let us in, believe me, you'll need more than the police."

The night man stared sullenly through the wavy glass. "All right, I'll tell him you're here," he said at last. "Stay put." He turned and disappeared up the curving staircase.

Two minutes later, the night man returned, rattled the lock, and opened the door. "Mr. Eberly will see you," he said. "He will receive you in his suite. It's the penthouse."

"Thank you," Georgia said, "and may I borrow a sheet of hotel stationery and a pencil?"

When the night man had given them to her, she and Christ sped up the stairs to the penthouse.

They pulled the bell knob beside George's suite door, breathing hard, and he immediately answered. He'd had just enough time to put on trousers, a neat shirt, and a vest.

"I do beg your pardon, madam, for receiving you in such a state of undress," he said with a bow, letting them in.

"Not a word of it," Georgia replied.

"I'd say you got dressed pretty fast, considering it's not yet four in the morning," Christ said.

George chuckled. "You're an army man. You know what it means when reveille is sounded."

"That I do."

They took a seat in George's private parlor. "Now, I'm sure you'll pardon this early intrusion," Georgia said, "when I say that we have the solution to Mrs. Eberly's cipher."

"It wasn't 'we,'" Christ said. "This was all Georgia."

"I find women are usually smarter than men, my friend. So tell me—what have you found, Mrs. Moffatt?"

"It wasn't all me, you two," she said. "Look." She smoothed out the piece of hotel stationery. "Here's what Mrs. Eberly left us." She wrote:

Augustus

U W N N I B B 20

"That's right," George said.

"In your book of codes, Christ found something called a 'Caesar's Cipher,'" Georgia said, her voice rising. "It's a simple code that is based on the substitution of one letter for another. But one needs to know the 'key'—or how many letters to shift one for another."

"Yes, I've heard of such ciphers," George said.

"Christ and I were talking about Augustus being the second

Caesar, so we thought the key, or shift, would be two letters. But it was not."

"That's too bad," George said, downcast.

"But in my sleep, it came to me—and I immediately awakened Christ."

"My dear madam," George said, cocking an eyebrow. "If I may be so bold, you ought not to have left the safety of your home on my account. The matter could have waited until Mr. Schamber had arisen in the morning."

Both Christ and Georgia flushed to the roots of their hair, and a heartbeat later, so did George.

"That's—terribly kind of you, sir," Georgia said. "To consider my welfare."

"Very kind indeed," Christ mumbled.

"Don't mention it," George said.

Georgia coughed into her glove. "In any event, Augustus Caesar was the second Caesar, to be sure, and yet with a backwards shift of two spaces, Mrs. Eberly's cryptogram was still so much gibberish."

"So you have stated," George said, trying to keep a straight face.

"But in my sleep the penny dropped. And when I woke, I remembered that 'Augustus' was the name given to him some time after he'd begun his rule as emperor."

"I do seem to remember that from my school days," George said. "But I can't recall what his original name was."

"And that's the key!" Georgia said, exulting. "His real name was *Octavian*."

"Octavian?"

"Yes. Which in Latin means 'the eighth.' And for good measure, August is—"

"The eighth month."

"Mrs. Eberly left us no doubt as to the key, then. It's not *two* spaces—it's *eight*." She poised her pencil over the leaf of hotel stationery and wrote out Mary's cipher. "Mrs. Eberly left us the sequence of 'U W N N I B B 20.' Now if we count eight places back from *U*, we have . . ."

George counted on his fingers, his lips moving silently. "*M*," he said.

"Right. And *W*?"

Christ counted this time. "*O*."

"Now two *N*s."

"*F, F*," George and Christ said in unison.

"Right. And now *I* is—"

"*A*," Christ said.

"Last, then, two *B*s."

"Those will be *T*s," George said, counting.

"Now look," said Georgia, writing.

U W N N I B B 20

M O F F A T T 20

"Good Lord," George said.

"*Moffatt*?" said Christ.

"That's right. And the number twenty is indeed simply twenty."

"How do you know that?" George asked.

"Because the bench next to which Mrs. Eberly—I'm terribly sorry—was found overlooks Section 20 in Forest Lawn," she replied. "And the only thing in Section 20 is—"

"Your family's mausoleum," George said.

"Yes. As you suspected, it must have been something about it that cost her her life."

"MAY I HAVE A look inside the mausoleum?" George asked, after they had recovered somewhat from Georgia's revelation.

"Whenever you like," she said. "I have the key, and I'm the only one who does."

"Not *quite* the only one," Christ said softly.

"What does that mean?" Georgia asked.

"Well, this past winter, I was pruning some of the trees around Mr. Sam's mausoleum, and I wanted to go in and make sure there weren't any leaks. I didn't want to walk all the way back to Spring Abbey if I didn't have to, so I walked over to Mr. Stroup's office."

"Of course," Georgia said.

George looked puzzled. "What does Stroup have to do with it?"

"Because he has a key to all of the mausoleums in Forest Lawn. He has to, in case of some emergency or if a family member happened to lose the key. He walked back to Section 20 with me and let me in. He came in and stayed while I took a quick look around, and since everything was fine, he locked up behind me."

"What's in there?"

"Just a big stone sarcophagus," Georgia said. "Otherwise the building is vacant."

George smacked his cane down with more than expected force. "Then what in *thunder* could have happened in or around a vacant mausoleum that would lead to murder?"

A flash of understanding crossed Georgia's face. "Oh, I understand now," she said in an undertone.

"What is it? What's inside?" George asked.

"It has to be seen to be believed."

"May I borrow your key, then, madam?" George asked. "I'll go over there this very morning and investigate."

"Oh no you won't," Christ said. "First of all, if those men are as dangerous as we think, they won't scruple at killing another person to keep their secret."

George gave a little bow. "You're a good man, Mr. Schamber, and I gratefully acknowledge your concern. Yet to go down fighting the men responsible for my wife's death . . . such a death would be far sweeter than one on any battlefield. Thus I simply must insist—"

"While yours is a truly noble sentiment, Mr. Eberly," Georgia said, "the secret is one that I will have to show you. You will not discover it otherwise. Mr. Stroup and I, presumably, are the only ones who know about it."

Christ smiled at her. "Then I'd suggest we'd best go under cover of darkness. He'll be asleep while we investigate."

"I will respectfully yield, then, until tonight," George said. "But if then I encounter the enemy . . . I *will* engage him. And I will give no quarter."

"And I will be by your side when you do, sir," Christ said. "To the death, if necessary."

Georgia looked steadily at the two men. "As will I," she added quietly.

SECTION THIRTY-SIX

The Oubliette

It was well after midnight when George, Christ, and Georgia slipped through the opening in the fence along Gulf Street and picked their way downhill toward Section 20. George paused momentarily by Mary's bench, brushing it gently with his fingertips, and then followed the two others down the long slope to the burbling Conjaquadies. They crossed the footbridge and quietly trotted over to the Moffatt mausoleum.

The three huddled under the portico, close to the big bronze doors, staying out of the moonlight. Georgia set down the small canvas bag she had insisted on carrying all the way from Spring Abbey. She bent over and fished a key on a ribbon out of her basquine.

"See something you like?" she asked Christ, as she straightened back up.

"I wasn't looking at anything."

They heard George chuckle in the soft darkness.

Georgia inserted the key into the lock plate on the doors of the mausoleum. It clicked a couple times, and then she pushed open one of the big doors. "Come on," she said. The two followed her in, and Christ closed the door quietly behind them.

There was just enough moonlight filtering in through four high windows, set under the roofline of the mausoleum, that they could make out the crypt containing three generations of Moffatts.

"Over here," Georgia whispered, and the three went around behind the crypt. There, she knelt down, reached into her canvas sack, and removed several candles, a coil of rope, and a match safe. She handed a candle to each of the men, lit hers with a match, and then lighted theirs with her candle's flame.

The base of the Moffatt crypt was oblong, set off behind four prominent short columns. The sides of the base were decorated with large bronze rings hanging from ornate bosses.

"Ready to see a little magic trick?" she said, handing her candle to Christ.

George and Christ nodded.

Georgia took hold of one of the big bronze rings and twisted it, hard. A fine square outline appeared in the stone, perhaps two feet across, or a little more. She then gave the ring a solid tug, and a stone panel came smoothly away from an iron frame inset into the crypt. Behind it was darkness.

"Good God," Christ said, "are their *bodies* down there?"

"Of course not," she hissed back. "They're in the crypt. This is something else entirely."

She took her candle from Christ and held it up. "They've been here, all right. We won't be needing this tonight," she said, stuffing the coil of rope back into the sack. She slid the match safe into the pocket of her basquine.

In the flickering candlelight, George and Christ could make out a knotted loop of hemp rope, which was secured to the iron frame behind the stone panel.

"Ready?" she said.

"Ready for what?" Christ said.

"Ready to go down," she said, pointing at the floor.

"Down where?"

"You'll see." She unbuttoned her waistband and let her hooped skirt fall around her ankles. George looked away.

"God's sake, Georgia!" Christ spluttered.

"'God's sake' yourself, you old prude. I've got bloomers on. Surely both of you have seen a lady in her bloomers."

"That's not the—"

She ignored him. "Mr. Eberly, you stay up here, just in case one of those men shows up."

"Nothing doing," George said. "If this is what cost my Mary her life, I'm seeing it for myself."

"Then, Christ, you have to stand guard."

"I don't want—"

"Please don't argue so with me, dear. You may come down when Mr. Eberly returns. But we cannot all be down there if someone else comes."

Christ nodded reluctantly, and Georgia blew out her candle and George's. "I'll light them again at the bottom," she said. Then she put her feet into the opening where the stone panel had been, gripped the end of the knotted rope, and wriggled backwards into the hole. When nothing but her head remained poking out of the base of the crypt, she smiled at the men's astonished expressions.

"Don't worry," she said. "I've done this before. In bloomers."

She began to lower herself and then paused. "Mr. Eberly—when you see the light from my candle, follow me down," she said, and then disappeared entirely. Christ tried to follow her with his eyes, holding his candle over the blackness under the crypt, but all he could make out was that the rope seemed to disappear down an almost vertical shaft. He and George squinted into the pitch-black for a minute or so, when they saw the faint yellow gleam of a candle.

"Your turn," Christ said. "Be careful, though. If your leg gives you any trouble, let me go instead."

George set his jaw. "My leg will be fine."

It took considerable effort for George to squeeze his broad frame into the opening, and once or twice he felt a shiver of fear at the thought of being trapped in whatever this thing was. He'd read newspaper articles about boys playing in sewer pipes who had gotten lodged and couldn't go forward or back, and so could only wait for death. He tried to banish the thought, telling himself that he had seen and survived much worse.

At last he felt his hips sliding down the shaft, and he lowered himself carefully down the rope. The shaft was indeed nearly vertical, though probably only twenty feet long, but when he finally felt something solid beneath his feet again he nearly cried out with relief. He let go of the rope and landed in a heap next to Georgia, who was squatting and holding her candle.

"Are you all right?" she said, her voice echoing dully.

"Never been better," he said, regaining his feet. "Dratted leg, that's all."

She held her candle out and lit his with it.

George looked around. In the yellow light, he could see that they were inside a small domed chamber made of what looked like amber. The floor and walls were as slick as glass, and the ceiling—which was pocked and dimpled, like the surface of the moon—was just high enough for a man to stand, if slightly stooped. The whole space was perhaps a dozen feet in diameter, no more, but seemed smaller. The heat was oppressive, and the air smelled like stale cigarette smoke. At one end of the chamber, a large piece of canvas was draped over some unknown bulk.

"Well, what do you think?" Georgia said.

"Who made this?" he asked, flabbergasted.

She shrugged. "God, I suppose. It's a salt cave. There's a big salt deposit under parts of Forest Lawn, and in ages past this little cavern must have been carved out by groundwater."

"How in the world did you know about this?"

"Quite by accident," she said. "I must have been only ten or twelve, out running around as usual, and almost fell into the opening above. And if I had, I'd have been a goner, because there's no getting out without first fixing a rope up above."

"It's very strange," he said, looking around. "I've never seen anything like it."

"There was one other one on these grounds, north of here, but that was destroyed years ago when they began quarrying up there. After the land sold and Sam died, I had the family mausoleum built over this one, because I didn't want some child to fall in. I couldn't have slept ever again if that had happened."

"You have a good heart, Mrs. Moffatt."

"Thank you, but my motive wasn't *entirely* pure. I had that removable stone panel put in up above because I thought this little cave might be useful for hiding things. I don't trust banks, for example. I thought I might keep money or gold down here."

"No one would find it. Not until the crack of doom."

"No indeed. First of all, no one goes into a mausoleum—there's nothing to steal—and then, to find *this*, under a crypt? I can only imagine that Mr. Fermin and Mr. Dolan knew about it because Mr.

Stroup told them. He probably learned of it from the men who built the crypt to my specification."

"How long could one stay down here, I wonder?" George asked.

"What do you mean?"

"The air. It's awfully close. How much air is in here?"

"It's not pleasant, but one won't suffocate so long as the door up above stays open—or even a little ajar. I've tested it. Right after the mausoleum was built, I came down here for several hours one day and observed the candle flame. When I left the upper door open, it burned steadily, and—while it did get a little stuffy—I felt perfectly fine. But when I climbed up and pulled the door shut—"

"You didn't! What if it had stuck closed?"

"Then I would have been in a very bad way, because in only a few minutes, the candle flame was almost out, and I was pretty dizzy. I climbed out and was fine again."

"Promise me you won't ever do that again, Mrs. Moffatt."

She smiled in the golden flicker of the candle. "You have a good heart, too, it seems."

George looked toward the canvas-covered heap. "Now what could be under that, I wonder?"

"It certainly wasn't here when I visited a year ago." She sniffed the air. "Nor, in case you are wondering, do I smoke tobacco."

George handed Georgia his candle, and she held them both up as he drew back the canvas. Under it were stacked at least two dozen crates of whiskey, several chests of opium, and half a dozen bolts of very fine silk cloth.

"Well, now," George said, whistling through his teeth. "It would appear that our Irishmen have been skimming from Mr. Brennan."

"Skimming?"

"Spiriting away some of my goods that pass through Barney Brennan's place," he said. "Taking a little at a time for themselves—skimming, like cream from the top of a container of milk—but not so much that anyone notices. A bottle or two of liquor at a time, or a chest of opium. I suppose they store them here until they can sell them on."

"So they are both grave robbers *and* thieves," Georgia said.

"And probably murderers. I am guessing that from her bench, Mary spied those two coming and going and thought it suspicious. It would be like her to investigate."

"So they saw her looking at them—"

"And decided that they couldn't leave a witness to their hiding spot. They knew, I'm sure, that Mary was my go-between with Barney Brennan, and that within ten minutes' walk she could tell Barney what they were up to. And believe me, he's not a man to steal from."

"I am truly very sorry, Mr. Eberly."

George sat down on the slick floor and leaned against the wall of the salt cave. "I wonder if she came down here," he said softly. "Once you get used to it, it's kind of a special place."

"It is." She tilted one of the candles, let some wax drip from the pool around its wick, then planted both candles upright in the cooling wax. They sat in silence for several minutes, the candles burning steadily.

"I'd better go back up," George said, "and let your beau have a look." He got up stiffly and walked over to the rope.

"He's not my *beau*, exactly."

George smiled at her over his shoulder, his face glowing in the candlelight.

"Call him what you wish, but I know what true love looks like," he said, and began pulling himself up the rope.

Thirty Pieces

Two Days Later

For the price of a round of drinks, in the fat part of Friday night he could have taken part in any one of fifty conversations going on in Barney Brennan's place. Instead, Christ sidled up to the one man who was quietly studying himself in the mirror over the bar—Arthur Fermin.

"Mind if I join you?" Christ asked.

Fermin spied him in the glass and then glanced over. "Do I know you?"

"Christ Schamber. We met over in Forest Lawn sometime early this year."

The other man faced forward again.

"Yeah, I remember now," Fermin said, feeling either agreeable or apathetic.

"What are you drinking?"

"Why? You buying?"

"Sure, I'll stand you one," Christ replied.

"Whiskey, then. Thanks." Fermin tossed down the rest of his drink and shoved the empty glass away.

Christ ordered two whiskeys from Barney Brennan, who examined the newcomer from behind the bar. Fermin had again lapsed into silence.

When the whiskeys were in front of them, Christ raised his glass, but Fermin still didn't respond. Christ took a sip, put his glass down, and looked over at Fermin. "Something bothering you, old fellow?"

Fermin raised his eyebrows but didn't turn to face Christ. "You're drinking with a dead man."

"That's a hell of a thing to say."

"It's a hell of a thing to be. But it's the God's truth, sure as I sit here."

"May I ask why?"

"My best chum got blown up a little while back, and I'm next," Fermin said slowly. "He was robbing a grave and the thing was rigged."

It was all Christ could do not to laugh. "I heard about that," he said instead. "Condolences."

"Thanks. He was a good lad. If a little slow."

Too slow to climb out of a grave within three seconds, Christ thought. "Well, slow or not, he went quick," he said, choking down a laugh with a swallow of whiskey.

Fermin now looked over at him. "Are you making a joke?"

"Not at all. I just mean that he didn't suffer."

"Oh. Right. No, that he didn't."

"Do the cops have any idea who rigged the thing?"

Fermin took out a pouch of tobacco and some papers, and began rolling himself a smoke. "Now you *are* joking," he said. "The cops don't care about the likes of me and him. And besides, everyone already knows who rigged it, and no one's about to touch *him*."

"They do?"

"You must not be from around here," Fermin said, planting the cigarette between his lips.

"Cold Springs."

"You know about the explosion, but not about the dead girl in Forest Lawn? George Eberly's wife?"

"I *heard* the explosion. Otherwise I don't follow the news."

"So much the better for you. Let's just say that one Mr. George Eberly, the king of all smugglers, has made up his mind that Bobby and I did his wife in. And he's told plenty of people around town—and made us marked men."

"Surely a man wouldn't—"

"George Eberly's a first-class rotter," Fermin said. "He does as he pleases. And if he wants to touch you, he'll touch you. He wanted to get us both, and he'll keep coming until he gets me, too." He made circles with his glass, watching the whiskey swirl almost over the rim.

"Can't you just explain to him that you didn't do it?"

Fermin gave a smoky laugh. "He doesn't care whether we did it or not."

"But you didn't."

"Hell no, we didn't. As usual, it's the poor mick who gets the blame. Same as back in Galway. I tell you, Eberly—"

"Now, Artie, you wouldn't be running down my friend George Eberly to this fine gentleman, would you now?" said Barney Brennan, who had been cocking an ear from halfway down the bar.

"No, sir, Mr. Brennan, I most certainly would not."

"Sounded to me like you had some very nasty things to say about him."

"I didn't mean no harm," Fermin muttered.

"And who might you be, friend?" Brennan said to Christ. "What brings you in here, chatting this fellow up when he's obviously suffered a shock?"

"Trying to cheer him up, that's all," Christ said. "Passing the time of day."

"Well, I'm thinking it might be better if you passed the time of day some other place." Barney reached into his apron and jiggled a pair of coins in his hand. He slapped them on the bar and slid them across to Christ.

"Your drinks are on the house," Brennan said with a thin smile. "So no hard feelings, but I think it's best you were on your way."

"I'm not bothering a soul here," Christ said.

Brennan leaned across the bar, his nose only two inches from Christ's. "You're bothering *me*, son," he said through gritted teeth. "Now I've asked you nicely—"

Christ's right hand shot up and went behind Brennan's head. He brought the barman's face down on the bar with a sharp crack, and Brennan's nose exploded into blood. He reeled for an instant, more surprised than stunned, and then calmly spit out part of a tooth onto the bar. Blood streaming down over his mouth, he grinned and reached for a leather-wrapped blackjack hanging on a hook behind him. Then he strode cursing around the bar and charged Christ, who stood back and braced himself for the impact.

Brennan had done as much barroom brawling as any man in Buffalo, and he hit Christ low, knocking the taller man off his feet. Quick as a cat, he knelt on Christ's chest. "Lock the door, boys!" he shouted. "I've got to give this one a lesson in manners."

He raised the club and was about to bring it down on the pinioned man's head when a memory flashed through Christ's mind: something that had saved his life in the Cornfield at Antietam. On that day he had collided—hard—with a young rebel running the opposite way through the dense cornstalks, and the two had grappled in the dirt, each trying to strangle the life out of the other. The rebel must have had the better position, because he succeeded in getting his hands around Christ's throat. Blackness had been closing in when Christ had come up with a tactic that—in anything but a life-or-death situation— he would have considered dirty. He had grabbed the boy's testicles through his hunger-slack trousers and squeezed for dear life. In agony, the boy had loosed his grip just enough to allow Christ to wriggle free and stab him to death with a sheath knife.

Christ repeated the trick with Brennan, and the man howled as one of Christ's strong workman's hands closed like a vise on his balls. Dropping the blackjack with a thump, Brennan reached down with both big mitts and slowly pried Christ's fingers open. By the time he had nearly peeled them off his nuts, though, Christ had, with his free hand, grabbed up the fallen weapon. He could have brained the writhing barkeep, but wisely reckoned that he didn't need to hang for killing the likes of Brennan. Instead he stood and stalked toward the door, raising the cosh and menacing two men blocking his exit.

"Stand aside or I'll crack your skulls," he said, hoping the men would comply before Barney's balls stopped throbbing and the man could tackle him from behind. They did, and Christ scrambled out into the night, running fast down Main Street and away from Brennan's place. When he at last slackened his pace, almost at Spring Abbey, he realized he was still clutching the blackjack. He thought to throw it away, but something stayed his hand. He stuffed it into his pocket and jogged panting through the iron gates of the Moffatt estate.

GEORGIA WAS SITTING UP in bed, a candle flickering next to her, when Christ opened the door between their bedchambers.

"Where have you been?" she said. "I expected you home hours ago."

He sat down on the edge of her bed.

"Now don't be angry. I thought I might have a talk with Arthur Fermin," Christ said.

"Are you *insane*?"

"I don't think so."

"Well, I think you are. And you didn't give me so much as a vote in the matter."

"I'm sorry, Georgia, but I wanted to do my part."

She seethed quietly for a moment. "Well, then? Did you talk with him?"

"I did. And he knows that Mr. Eberly is coming for him."

"I'm not sure whether that's a good or bad thing. He might leave town."

"He hasn't yet," Christ said.

"Did he say anything about Mrs. Eberly's death?"

"Only that neither he nor Dolan did it. But what do you expect him to say?"

"And that was it?"

Christ looked away. "Almost. But Barney Brennan was listening in, and let's say he took offense to my questioning Mr. Fermin."

"Did he accost you?"

"He tried," Christ said with a grim smile. "He very nearly bashed my head in, but I had a surprise in store. I grabbed his sack."

"His sack? Sack of what?"

"Georgia, I'm a little disappointed in you, after the other night."

"Oh Lord," she said. "Well, I'm sure that took the fight out of him."

"That it did." He reached into his pocket and pulled out Brennan's blackjack. "And I took this cosh away from him, too."

"I'm so happy you're safe," she said, relenting. She threw her arms around him. "But promise me you won't ever do something like that again."

"Don't worry. Once was plenty."

GEORGIA SENT A MESSENGER to the Genesee that Christ had news, and George showed up at Spring Abbey early the next morning. He seemed older each time they met, leaning more and more heavily on his walking stick.

"I spoke with Fermin," Christ said.

"That seems foolhardy, if you don't mind my saying."

"I don't mind at all. Georgia has already expressed a similar opinion."

"Well, then, I am in fine company. Did the man incriminate himself?"

"No, I'm sorry to say. He denies having anything to do with Mrs. Eberly's murder. But he knows you think he did."

"Good. If I can't sleep anymore, neither should he."

Georgia poked Christ. "Tell him about Mr. Brennan."

"What about Brennan?" George asked.

"He was eavesdropping on my conversation with Fermin, and accused me of—well, I'm not quite sure what he accused me of, but he most definitely wanted us to stop talking with each other. Fermin had brought you up and said you were a scoundrel—if you'll pardon me for saying."

"No pardon required! I *am* a scoundrel. What happened with Brennan?"

"He told me to get out, and I bloodied his nose."

"You did more than that," Georgia said.

"He was trying to brain me with a blackjack at the time," Christ said.

"Now is that so? He must have meant business," said George.

"Oh, he did. But I got the thing away from him and escaped with my scalp."

George mulled this over for a moment. "Do you have the weapon still?"

"I do," Christ said. "Upstairs in our—my bedchamber."

"Would you mind getting it for me?"

"Not at all."

"Mrs. Moffatt," George said when they were alone, "I wouldn't suggest that Mr. Schamber pay another visit to Barney Brennan, ever. It's a good thing he escaped with his life, but embarrassing a man in front of his plug-uglies . . . Well, you can bet Brennan won't let *that* happen a second time."

"I've already given him an earful about that," Georgia said. "But perhaps you might still mention it to Christ. He thinks I'm just a frightened *woman*. But he'll listen to you—he knows you're no coward."

"I will gladly mention it to him, madam," George said as Christ came back into the room, carrying Brennan's blackjack.

"Here you go," he said, handing it to George.

George hefted it in his hand and then squeezed the bulbous weighted end of the club. "Well, I'll be," he said, almost to himself. "I'm ashamed to admit I never thought of this. Though I should have."

"Thought of what?" Christ asked.

Eberly dangled the leather blackjack from the strap that held the narrow end closed. "This is the key to the whole thing," he said. "Thank God you seized it, or I might well have made a serious error."

"What do you mean, Mr. Eberly?" Georgia asked.

"Come with me, and I'll show you." George stood up and gestured with his head for the others to follow. He crossed the parlor, went into the main hallway, and opened the front door of Spring Abbey. "You'll understand very soon."

On the front steps, he fiddled with the drawstring that kept the blackjack's contents from falling out.

"Remember how I mentioned sand was found near my wife's body?"

"Of course," Georgia said. "It was a mystery."

George upended the blackjack over the edge of the steps, loosened the thong that held it closed, and let the contents pour out like an hourglass.

"Not anymore, it isn't."

"It's filled with sand!" Christ marveled. "Why would that be?"

"It's a trick used by men who know a thing or two about how to injure or kill someone without leaving any evidence," George replied. "As I'm sure you know, most blackjacks are filled with lead shot. Some men will use small pebbles, though, because after a fight, one can empty the weapon. You'd have pebbles on the ground, instead of lead shot. Pebbles are everywhere, and only a flat leather pouch remains in the pocket. If the cops pinch you, there's no law against carrying a leather pouch, which can be used for anything.

"But a man like Brennan, who's been to prison for murder, has learned that filling the blackjack with sand—wet sand, especially—is the best choice of all. Lead shot or pebbles have hard edges and, even through a leather covering, will leave a telltale mark on the victim's head. Not so with sand—it's almost as heavy as lead, but it conforms to the shape of the skull. It delivers an equally damaging blow, but leaves almost no mark on the skin. All of the force of the strike is transmitted to the brain."

"And how does that factor in with Mrs. Eberly's death?" Georgia asked.

"The autopsy showed only a faint red mark on her scalp—on the left—where someone right-handed would have struck her. There was bleeding on the brain under the mark, and"—George looked away—"she had foam around her mouth, which indicates a brain injury. I've seen it all too many times in the war."

"He's right," Christ said.

"So what kind of weapon, then, could deliver a lethal insult to the brain and leave almost no trace?" George held up the empty blackjack. "This kind. Criminals know it as a sand cosh."

"But why," Georgia asked, "was the sand scattered on the ground? This doesn't look like it has any holes in it. Other than at the top, of course."

George gave her a grim smile. "That's the other advantage of a sand cosh," he said. "After the deed is done, the culprit empties the weapon and makes his escape carrying only the leather cover. If he's arrested . . . well, there's no law against carrying a leather pouch. It's not a weapon without its contents."

"It does have a horrible logic to it," Georgia said.

"That it does. Frankly, I'm surprised I didn't think of it sooner."

Georgia frowned. "I do wonder where he obtained the sand, though. As you know, there's none anywhere in this part of the city."

"Oh, that I think I know—now," George replied. "I even out the weight of my coffins with sandbags—which are filled with sand from Franklin Park. That part of the city was once the foreshore of the lake. As a result, it's mostly sand."

"Of course," Christ said. "But I have to wonder . . . how could Fermin or Dolan take Barney Brennan's blackjack from behind his bar? He would certainly have noticed that it was missing."

George gave them a rueful smile. "Along with the type of weapon used to dispatch my wife, there was another thing I never considered. It may well have been Barney Brennan who wielded it."

"It makes all the sense in the world, once you say it aloud," Georgia said, "but why would Mr. Brennan hurt your wife? Surely it was Mr. Fermin and Mr. Dolan she saw near the mausoleum, since they had been stashing goods in the salt cave."

"Oh yes, I haven't any doubt she saw them—and they saw her too, all right. But where I may also have been wrong was in assuming the two of them had been skimming off of *Barney*, and wanted to prevent Mary from giving them up to him. Now I am beginning to think that Brennan may have been the betrayer all along—and skimming off of *me*, using Fermin and Dolan as his pack mules. I'd bet that when Fermin and Dolan spied her, they ran off to inform Brennan. And Brennan knew that he had to take care of it, because he knew that if she told me what she'd seen, I wouldn't fail to investigate. And if I found out that he was stealing from me, it wouldn't end well for him. So I surmise that he took his weapon and went through the fence along Gulf Street, across from his saloon—which would also explain the second set of footprints in the mud in the gully there. You see, the two people who made them weren't *together*—they were made a little time apart by Mary and Brennan."

"And it would explain your wife's gesture with her parasol," Georgia said. "Holding it to indicate that someone approaching could speak with her. As I said, she wouldn't have made such a gesture for Mr. Fermin or Mr. Dolan, whom she didn't know, but . . ."

George nodded. "She wouldn't have been particularly alarmed to see Barney Brennan, having left his place less than a half hour before. She may have thought she'd left something behind at his saloon."

Christ and Mary looked at each other, and then at George. "It's—so awful, Mr. Eberly," Georgia said. "Words fail me."

"I shall not forget your kindness, madam," he said. "And I will say that tonight may provide the first decent sleep I've had since Mary's death. I have my answer, and I know what to do next."

"What can we do to help?" Christ asked.

"For now, we have to keep a cool head and not let anything slip. Barney Brennan's a wily old criminal, and he'll know if we suspect him. Mr. Schamber, that means you *stay away*—far away from him and his saloon. That man can smell suspicion a half mile off."

"I understand, sir," Christ said. "I'll go nowhere near."

"*Finally,*" Georgia said in a stage whisper.

"I have an idea for how we finish this business," George said. "I won't take action against Brennan himself without direct evidence, any more than I would against Fermin or Dolan. So give me a day or two to think it through. Once I act, though, we will have only hours—at most—before Brennan slips through our grasp."

"We'll be waiting on your command, sir," Christ said.

"Thank you. Now I'll go and leave the two of you in peace. May I keep this?" George held up the empty blackjack.

"Wouldn't you prefer we burn that hideous thing?" Georgia asked.

"That's very thoughtful, but no. It *is* a hideous thing, but it is also the last thing that touched her in life. That makes it a sacred thing, too."

With that, George Eberly turned and walked to his carriage, which was waiting in the curving drive in front of Spring Abbey.

SECTION THIRTY-EIGHT

SKIMMING

George walked into Barney Brennan's place and rapped his cane on the floorboards. Brennan emerged from his back office.

"George," Brennan said, "now this is a surprise."

"I like a good surprise now and then."

Brennan chuckled. "Like the one that got Bobby Dolan?"

"What makes you think I had anything to do with that?"

"A little bird on my shoulder told me. It's pretty obvious that Dolan and Fermin were—well, you know."

"Believe me, Barney, I'd much rather be a peaceable man. Do my business, keep my nose out of other people's. You know me."

"I do, and never a truer word has been spoken. And you know I'm the same kind of fellow."

"It's the only reason that I do business with you. It's certainly not because of your looks."

The two men laughed. "May I offer you a drink?" the saloon-keeper asked.

"No, I can't stay very long. I have a big shipment of product coming in from up north."

Brennan grinned. "And should I expect a big shipment of coffins very soon, then?"

George looked down and tapped his cane on the floor. "Well, Barney, that's just what I came to talk with you about."

"I'm not sure I like the sound of that. You know that I've got plenty of space, and the men, to move your goods."

"I do, Barney, but here's the problem. See, your same little bird only recently told me that—in addition to whatever hand they may have had in Mary's death—your boys Dolan and Fermin may have been doing a little skimming. Well, Fermin now, since Dolan isn't with us anymore."

"George, now, Artie Fermin knows better than to pull a stunt like that."

"I would have thought he'd know better than to do a lot of things. Stealing bodies or stealing goods, Barney—it's all the same to me. A man who will filch a body will filch anything."

"Stealing from you is not just 'anything.' Anyone who does knows he'll pay a price."

George pursed his lips. "Now, I must say that I don't know if he, they, whoever, is skimming from me or from you. And I don't really care, for that matter. You're my partner, and so I had to tell you—because we have to get it stopped. Once people think they can get away with it, there's no end of it."

"You're damn right about that."

"Mind, I'm not accusing him," George said. "All I know for certain is that—somewhere between my warehouse and Niagara Falls—a couple dozen cases of whiskey, some opium, and a few bolts of fine silk have gone missing. And as all those goods came through Forest Lawn, well, the finger does rather point to Mr. Fermin. I'm sure there are plenty of spots over there where a man can hide a few choice items."

"I swear to you, George, if I find that scoundrel has taken so much as a thimbleful of anything, I'll deliver him to you personally."

George sighed heavily. "Barney, I've been at this long enough that I don't take any pleasure from dealing with petty thieves. It's tedious. And so instead I'd like to leave this matter in your very capable hands. Talk to Fermin. If he owns up to stealing my goods—and I think he will—tell him that he has until tomorrow morning to move them along to their rightful destination. If he does, he has my word of honor that bygones will be bygones. Now if he refuses, *then* I'll have no choice but to take further action."

"That's mighty white of you, George," Brennan said.

"Mary's death changed me, Barney. Even more than the war did, I think. I suppose I just don't want to hurt anyone anymore. Death only invites more death."

"I understand."

George cleared his throat. "May I count on you, then, to handle this little matter at your earliest convenience? I'd like to clear it up by tomorrow, so that my new shipment can start coming your way."

"You have my word," Brennan said. "I'll find Fermin right now and have a little chat."

George extended his hand, and they shook. "Thank you, Barney. It'll be a pleasure to put all this behind us for good. I'd like to get my life back on track."

SECTION THIRTY-NINE

Secrets

George left Brennan's place and directed his driver to take him straight to Spring Abbey. Christ and Georgia were waiting for him in the parlor as nighttime began to close in.

"Did you talk with him?" Christ said.

"I did. And I gave him a deadline of no later than tomorrow morning to fix things. He'll be making his move now."

"No time to waste, then," Georgia said.

"Are you sure about this, Mr. Schamber?" George asked.

Christ straightened up to his full height, as if at attention. "Yes, Mr. Eberly. It will be my honor to serve in your company."

"What's this 'Mr. Schamber' stuff about?" Georgia asked. "You two don't think that I'm staying here at Spring Abbey, do you?"

"Well—I assumed . . ." George began.

"You are *not* going with us," Christ said. "You stay here, where I know you're safe."

"I really do hate men sometimes," she said under her breath. "I'm coming with you, like it or not."

"You do remind me of my Mary sometimes," George said. "Such spark."

A HALF HOUR LATER, George, Christ, and Georgia again crept down the slope of Section 18 and across the footbridge to the Moffatt mausoleum. The Conjaquadies was swollen with the early autumn rains, and its churning water was making so much noise that the three of them could approach without fear of detection.

They found the big doorknob unlocked, and quietly eased into the building. They tiptoed across the dark space and huddled behind the crypt, listening.

A yellow glow was emanating from the open stone panel that concealed access to the salt cave. The hemp rope was still secured to its iron frame. Brennan's voice drifted up from down below. He was plainly having a heated discussion with someone.

"Typical dumb country mick!" Brennan shouted. "How many times have I told you to bring the stuff here in a sack, a little at a time? But no, you and your idiot friend had to lug a whole coffin-full over. Just to save yourselves some shoe leather."

"And in broad daylight, at that," Stroup's piping voice added. "Every time you came to my office to borrow the key, what did I tell you? *Wait until dark.*"

"It was *dusk*, for Chrissake!" Fermin said.

"This is what happens, Mr. Brennan, when men like *us* are too generous with men like *him*. From the start, it was my position that you ought to have taken a firmer hand."

"Oh now, that's rich," Fermin said. "While you lot sit back and collect the money, what do I get? My best friend blown to kingdom come, and Eberly still thinks that Bobby and I did his wife in. When all we did was run like good little boys and tell you that the lady spied us stowing away your stolen goods. You said you were going to talk some sense into her, that's all."

"Well, she was a pigheaded, stingy little bitch," Brennan said. "So of course she wasn't having any of it. She said she was going to march right back to Buffalo to tell her husband everything. What do you think would have become of all of us then? Over the Falls, boy. How would you like that?"

"It'd be a sight better than sleeping with one eye open after you let me and Bobby almost swing for it after that inquest. And all the while we're repeating your shit about her parasol, like a couple of parrots! Right hand, no, left hand, twirling it, waving it!—how in God's name was poor, feebleminded Bobby supposed to keep all that straight?"

"You were paid very well for telling that tale," Brennan said. "And I've had more than enough of your lip, so button it. Stroup, you and I need to hightail it out of here before someone gets any other bright ideas. Artie, I'll send over one of my other fellows with a wagon, and the two of you get all this shit out of here. He'll move it north."

"What's the all-fired rush?" Fermin said.

"Because Eberly's too smart to show all his cards. If he knows we've been skimming, then he may also know where we've been stashing the goods. If I know him, he's being a sport, and giving us a head start."

"I thought you said he doesn't suspect anything," Stroup said. "Did you let something slip?"

"Let something *slip*? What's that supposed to mean?"

"Eberly told me himself—in confidence—that you have difficulty keeping secrets."

"You gullible little asshole!" Brennan yelled. "For fuck's sake, Stroup, this place was *your* secret! And why would I spill the beans, anyway? Who was it told *you* that if Eberly ever got wind of our scheme, we'd both be dead men? I did, that's who."

Stroup let out an inarticulate moan.

"Oh, stop your whining," Brennan said. "All you have to do, as soon as Fermin here gives you the all clear, is to lock this place up and forget that it ever existed."

"You may rely upon it," Stroup said.

Up above, George looked over at Christ and Georgia. "I've heard enough," he said, pulling a large knife from his boot. With one smooth stroke, he severed the rope. It fell slackly down into the shaft.

"Give me a hand with this, would you?" he said. Christ and George put their weight behind the stone panel and shoved, hard. It slipped tightly into place behind the Moffatt crypt. George twisted the big bronze ring and shot the bolts securing it in place.

"See you on Judgment Day," George said to no one.

Without another word, the three walked out of the Moffatt mausoleum, and Georgia locked the door behind her.

SECTION FORTY

ℰXTINGUISHED

Down below, Brennan and Stroup were turning to leave when a look of alarm passed over Fermin's face. He pointed toward the opening of the shaft.

Stroup and Brennan turned in time to see the last few feet of rope slither into a pile on the floor of the salt cave. Brennan stooped, picked up an end, and examined it. Then he looked up the shaft.

He put his hands on his knees and bent over. "That sly dog," he said quietly.

"What dog? What's happened to our rope?" Stroup asked, his voice a dry squeak.

"It's been cut," Brennan said, holding up the neatly severed end.

"Cut? How?"

"By Eberly. Who else? I should have known there was more to it. God *damn*."

Fermin walked over and stared up the shaft. All was blackness.

"I don't understand," he said.

Brennan let himself slide down the cave wall into a sitting position. He put his arms around his knees. "I *knew* there was more to his visit," he said, shaking his head. "But I thought, no, I've got him fooled for once."

Fermin looked at Brennan, then up the shaft again, and then

back to Brennan. "Then how are we supposed to get out of here?" Fermin said.

Barney Brennan gave a soft, bitter laugh. "We're *not* supposed to get out of here. And unless Eberly changes his mind—which he will not—we won't be, rope or no rope. That panel opens only from the outside."

Fermin's eyes bulged in the candlelight. "What the devil are you saying? There has to be a way out!" He stared up the dark shaft, almost willing himself to levitate, then began yelling upwards at the top of his lungs. "Help! Help! We're down here!"

"Who do you think is going to hear you?" Brennan said.

"Eberly, who else? He's probably up there right now, having a laugh at our expense."

"He's having a laugh, all right, but he's not up there. He's halfway back to Buffalo by now."

"He wouldn't just leave *me* here to die!" Stroup cried. "I'm the *superintendent* of Forest Lawn Cemetery!"

"Good news, then, Stroup," Brennan said. "You'll be on duty forever."

"He can't possibly know I'm down here," Stroup persisted. He lifted his face up into the dark tunnel and cupped his hands around his mouth. "Mr. Eberly! It's George Stroup! There's been a terrible mistake!"

There was only silence from above.

Fermin paced back and forth in the tiny cavern. "If he wanted us to die down here so badly, why didn't he just chuck a stick of dynamite down the hole?"

"Because that would be quick. He wants us to know what it feels like to be buried alive. And at his hand."

"I'm not going to die like that," Fermin said. "You can, if you want to, but I'm not!"

He dragged a case of liquor under the opening of the shaft and climbed on it, jumping up and trying to claw his way up the slippery vertical walls.

Brennan watched him impassively. "It's at least twenty feet to the top, Artie."

When his fury was spent, Fermin slumped down against the wall of the salt cave, wheezing.

"Satisfied?" Brennan said.

"At least I'm doing *something*."

"You are, and that's a fact. Take a look at the candles."

The candles' flames, a good inch high only minutes before, were now half that height, and fluttering.

Stroup began to sob. "I don't deserve this," he wept. "I've been learning *French*. Making something of myself."

Brennan laughed again, a croupy, hollow laugh. "Matter of opinion," he coughed out.

"Are we really going to die like this?" Fermin asked.

The candle wicks had now almost disappeared into their tiny pools of wax, each only a little blue speck in the darkness of the salt cave. The men were breathing in great, futile gulps, six lungs straining to feed three ravenous hearts with what little remained of the oxygen.

Then the tiny flames guttered out, and darkness collapsed around them.

"It's just not *fair*," Stroup choked out, his voice cracking. "I never killed anyone."

"*Goddamn*," Fermin whispered in the thick blackness. "Damn me to Hell."

"I have a feeling you'll get your wish," Brennan gasped.

And then, except for the fading rattle of failing breath, all was quiet in the salt cave—as it had been for uncounted thousands of years, and would be again.

A Proposal

The next morning, Georgia rolled up the newspaper and dropped it next to their bed. "I don't know about you, Christ," she said, "but I keep reading the same line over and over . . ."

"Same here. And I keep thinking about Mr. Eberly, going back to the Genesee last night all by himself. While I came home with you. I almost feel a little guilty."

She leaned her head over on his big shoulder. "You're a good man," she said. "And I feel much the same way. Justice has been done, but no justice can bring his Mary back to him."

They sat in silence together, holding hands. "I wonder what's next?" Christ said.

"Next?"

"Next. For Mr. Eberly. For us."

"I don't know if Mr. Eberly will ever be the same again. I don't know if he can be."

"I wish I could snap my fingers and make it all better for him," Christ said.

She snuggled against him. "You know, at times like this you seem like the same innocent boy I used to play hooky with."

"And now you know I loved you even then."

"I suppose I loved you, too, but—it wasn't possible."

"But now we're together. At last, just Christian Schamber and Georgia Moffatt."

She sat quietly for a moment, savoring the scent of his nightshirt. "Christ," she said after a while, "may I ask you something?"

"Why, of course you may."

"You know I wouldn't do anything to dishonor my late husband's memory, don't you?"

"I know that very well. Nor would I. Mr. Sam was a good man. I liked him, and he was good to you."

"He was," Georgia mused. "And he loved me, Christ. Deeply. If there's anything I feel *really* guilty about in life, it's that he loved me so—but that I, well, I didn't have that same feeling for him."

"I'm sorry, Georgia. I truly am. That would have been hard for both of you."

She sighed. "I didn't love my husband, and I couldn't love you, so the two men in my life—both *wonderful* men—never knew what it felt to be loved back. It's *horrible*." She started to cry softly. Christ put his arm around her and drew her close.

"None of that was your fault, my dearest," he said into her hair. "You were the heir to the Granger name, and Mr. Sam was heir to the Moffatts'. You never had any choice. Nor did he, for that matter. You both did the only honorable thing."

She sniffled and looked up at him. "I know, but now I *do* have a choice. And what I'm getting at—what it's taken me all this time to ask you—is that my remaining 'Georgia Moffatt' is only keeping all that hurt alive."

"And now you've lost me," he said, kissing the top of her head. "As usual."

"What I mean to say is that being 'Georgia Moffatt' is giving neither Sam nor you the respect—the love—you deserve. Sam deserves to be free, and to be at peace forever. He oughtn't to be chained one moment more to a woman who merely *liked* him, and whose body will never join his in that mausoleum. And you oughtn't to have to look at me and see 'Mrs. Moffatt.'"

"But what is there to be done about it?"

She sat up higher in bed and looked into his eyes. "It's time for me to change my name, Christ," she said. "Long past time."

"Back to Granger?"

"No, silly. To *Schamber*."

It took a moment for this to register, and when it did, he clasped her hand.

"Are *you* proposing to *me*?"

"If that's what it's going to take, then yes. Yes I am."

"Well, this isn't the way it's supposed to go. Am I supposed to accept, or what?"

"I've made the proposal," she said. "So I suppose it's up to you to say yes or no."

Christ put his head down for a few seconds, and when he looked up again, tears were running freely down his weather-beaten cheeks. "Oh, Georgia," he said, "it's been yes since the first day I met you."

SECTION FORTY-TWO

The Phantom of Forest Lawn

As the years passed, and the wheel of the seasons slowly turned, a growing number of visitors to Forest Lawn noticed a neatly dressed gentleman, greying gently at the temples, sitting on a particular bench in Section 18, holding a gold-headed walking stick between his knees, taking in the view.

At least three days a week, he would appear when diamonds of dew still carpeted the grass, take his place, and lose himself in his thoughts. No soul dared intrude upon his reverie, so deep and profound did it appear.

He always sat on one end of the bench, as if waiting for someone.

When dusk crept across his glade, the gentleman would again vanish, disappearing as quietly as he had come. No one knew his name, only his strange behavior, and in time people began to call him the Phantom of Forest Lawn.

One year, in a shimmering August, with only the lapping wetness of the creek to keep the parched landscape alive, the fellow's bench was suddenly vacant, and so it would remain thereafter. It was a great mystery—where had he gone?

No one knew, but people said that perhaps the person he had been expecting had come to him at last.

THE END

Retrospective

This book—like all of my books—would not exist absent the assistance and support of many others. From the initial research to the printing, distribution, and marketing of the finished volume, I am fortunate to have been surrounded and supported by some of the best and nicest people I've ever chanced to meet.

At lovely Forest Lawn Cemetery in my hometown of Buffalo, New York, I owe special thanks to Jennifer Kovach, Lindsay Gregg, and Debbie Hernik—to Ms. Kovach for showing me around and for arranging access to the cemetery's fine archives, and to Ms. Hernik for helping me secure my own (eventual) permanent residence. Readers are cordially invited to visit me (at some point in the unknowable but hopefully distant future) in Section GG.

My wife's patience, thoughtful commentary, and overall enthusiasm and support for my work defy easy description. I am beyond grateful.

Ashwood Press, my publisher, has proven again and again that I made the right choice to sign with a smaller imprint over the "big guys." Thank you so very much.

My editor, Kimberly Laurel, is due tremendous credit for helping make my work the very best it can be. It's always a delight to work with her.

And to all the readers, book clubs, and reviewers as well as everyone else who inhabits an author's world—and makes it a possibility—my humble and sincere thanks.

Robert Brighton

About the Author

Robert Brighton is an authority on the Gilded Age, an inveterate explorer, and the author of the Avenging Angel Detective Agency™ Mysteries.

He began writing fiction after spending four years researching the liminal period of 1898–1905 in which his novels are set. Prior to that, he has been a bison rancher, a mule handler, and a vintage automobile restorer, and has made several other equally quixotic career choices. He has traveled to some fifty-six countries and is looking forward to adding the Faroe Islands and Patagonia to his life list.

When he's not writing, he's either spending time with his wife and their two cats or exploring some new part of the world. He has an enthusiasm for Japanese tin toys, antique weather instruments, and anything mechanical.

Find out more at:
RobertBrightonAuthor.com